Surrender
of the
Heart

Surrender
of the
Heart

Sally John

**Five Star
Unity, Maine**

Five Star Christian Fiction Series.

Published in 2000 in conjunction with Crossway Books,
a division of Good News Publishers.

The text of this edition is unabridged.

Set in 11 pt. Plantin by Elena Picard.

Printed in the United States on permanent paper.

Library of Congress Cataloging-in-Publication Data

John, Sally D., 1951–
   Surrender of the heart / Sally John.
     p. cm.
   ISBN 0-7862-2711-7 (hc : alk. paper)
   1. Women teachers — Fiction.   I. Title.
   PS3560.O323 S77 2000
   813′.54—dc21   00-034751

To Tim,
my knight

Special thanks to Diane
for sharing her insight into the
world of the vertical dance

"Whoever finds his life will lose it, and whoever loses his life for My sake will find it."—Jesus
Matthew 10:39

One

"Tony, you left your jacket on your chair." Kendall O'Reilly stood just inside the classroom door, chatting with her fifth graders as they filed out.

"Thanks, Ms. O'Reilly!" The boy flashed his disarming grin. Head and shoulders above the other youngsters, he was almost eye level with her. He turned and sauntered toward his desk. "My mom woulda really been ticked off."

Kendall stifled a groan and chose to ignore his breach of acceptable language. She knew the challenge he would offer was too much for a Friday afternoon at three o'clock. Alex, however, was a different matter.

"Alex!" she called as another boy scooted through the doorway. "Where's your library book?"

He turned back and rolled his eyes. "Aw, c'mon. It's the weekend."

She folded her arms. "I know, but you're behind schedule. Trust me on this one, Alex—if you don't turn in an outline by Tuesday, you won't catch up before I make out report cards." She raised an eyebrow. He shuffled his way back through the departing students.

Meanwhile, two girls wrapped their arms around her waist. She returned their hugs and continued with her good-byes. At the beginning of each school year she taught her students that it was tradition in Ms. O'Reilly's class not to leave without saying good-bye. For her, sending off each one with a smile was as important a priority as teaching spelling. Probably even more so. A little individual attention could even affect spelling.

And, hopefully, late book reports. The room emptied except for the somber Alex, now shoving a book into his backpack. Taking a deep breath, she walked across the room and sat down on the piano bench near his desk. "Alex?"

He looked up, his brown eyes cloudy, his nose wrinkled into a frown. "I got the book."

"This project should only take you two hours at the most."

"It's just that my dad is coming to town, and he's taking me and my sister up to Disneyland."

"Monday is Washington's birthday, a holiday. That gives you three days. Make time to do the report. I can't let you off the hook. Do you know why?"

He looked down at his feet. "I know, I know," he mumbled. "You're teaching us responsibility."

"Right!" She leaned forward until his eyes met hers. "I care about what happens to you, Alex. And I know your dad does too. Just tell him what you have to do, okay?"

He smiled crookedly and nodded. "It's not really Washington's birthday until Thursday, you know. We should have a party."

"Party? We just had a Valentine party this week!" She shooed him toward the door. "Go home, Alex."

"Bye, Ms. O'Reilly."

Shortly afterward, Kendall stood at her doorway that opened directly to the outdoors. The school's earth-tone stucco buildings formed a wheel-shaped area. In the hub was the library. Surrounding it were classrooms like hers facing an inner courtyard of grassy plots and covered sidewalks. Across the way was another ring of classrooms also opening onto the circular courtyard. Completing the outermost ring of the wheel was a blacktop area and then playgrounds. It was a world unto itself, and to Kendall it was home.

She propped the door open and deeply inhaled the cool winter air thick with the scent of rain. The sun would be making its early descent into the Pacific behind a cloud cover again today, promising another wet jogging time at the beach.

Sitting in her chair she pulled on a long, ivory cardigan sweater, kicked off her sensible flats, sat down, and swung her feet to the top of the large desk. Her floral-print, mauve skirt draped along the drawers. Stretching her arms, she laughed out loud, smiling at the empty desks. She folded her hands and rested them on top of the braid at the back of her head.

Alex didn't leave pouting. That's progress! And Esteban got a hundred on the spelling test. Mindy raised her hand at least twice without coaxing—

"Is this Mrs. O'Reilly's room?"

The masculine voice startled Kendall. In one swift motion she jerked her head toward the doorway, flung her feet to the floor, and stood up, bumping a knee in the process. "Ouch! I mean, yes. Can I help you?" She slipped one foot into a shoe, kicked the other, and sent it skidding further under the desk. "Excuse me." She knelt down and retrieved it.

"Is she here?"

"Who?" Kendall stood.

"Mrs. O'Reilly."

"I'm Kendall O'Reilly. Ms."

"The teacher?" His curt tone indicated there was a problem.

"You know," she said in a joking manner, "just today I was reading over my job description and that's exactly what I'm called. Teacher." She stuck her gold-rimmed glasses on her face along with her best teacher-ish expression and strode toward him.

She didn't recognize him as one of her parents. Her first impression was that of an athlete. He was somewhat on the tall side; while not the bulging-muscle type, his broad shoulders filled the brown tweed sport coat and forest-green shirt in a solid way. Above the open collar, his face and neck had a strong, square shape and the healthy tan of one who spent much time outdoors. He had close-cropped, wavy hair the color of a shiny new penny.

She stopped in front of him, for a split moment taken aback at the undisguised sweeping appraisal by his hazel eyes. *Who is this guy?* "May I help you?"

He hesitated. His hands, stuffed in the pockets of his dress khakis, jingled change. An almost tangible energy seemed to emanate from him. "You're not what I expected," he announced in a blunt tone.

"Well," she gave him her best smile, the one that melted the most disagreeable of parents, "I hope I'm not a grave disappointment. Please, come inside. What can I do for you, Mr.—?"

"Jeremiah Zukowski." His hand engulfed the one she offered. "I'm—"

"Caitlin's father! How nice to meet you, Mr. Zukowski! I hope she's feeling better?" The girl had been absent since the Valentine's Day party three days ago.

He glanced around the room. "Physically she's fine. However, it seems there's another problem."

"Hmm. Sounds like we'd better sit down and talk." She led him toward the back of the room to a long table, gathering

10

her thoughts about his daughter.

The girl's wild blonde curls and sweet, round cheeks hinted that she must resemble her mother. She'd been in the class less than a month and was a bit of a smart aleck and behind in her work. Kendall chalked it up to being new and was giving it another week or so before calling her parents, hoping Caitlin would respond to her efforts.

"Here, this is our big person chair." She pointed to a high-backed chair, then sat across from him in a smaller one, shoving aside stacks of papers, and folded her arms on the table. "Now, what seems to be the problem?"

Like a fifth grader called on the carpet, he avoided eye contact with her and fidgeted. She resisted the urge to touch his arm like she would with a child to calm the restlessness. At last he looked at her and exhaled sharply. "Look, I don't know exactly how to say this, but . . . well, Cait refuses to come back to school."

"Why?"

"She doesn't like you." He shrugged a shoulder and tilted back in the chair. "Honestly, I expected an ogre. An extra-ugly one at that."

Kendall blinked, at a rare loss for words.

"I was wondering, Miss O'Reilly, do you ignore her?"

"No, not at all. Because she's new, I pay her close attention."

"Maybe too much attention? In a negative sense?" His voice wasn't deep, but a strong one that probably carried well outdoors. Inside these four walls, however, it was borderline gruff.

"I wouldn't say that. I've had to correct her a few times. She doesn't seem comfortable yet, and she acts out sometimes, making fun of others or being surly with me, but—"

11

His chair thumped down. "My daughter has never been *surly* in her life!"

"I'm certain she's only adjusting, Mr. Zukowski." Kendall smiled briefly. "It's difficult to jump into the middle of a school year with a group of strangers and feel at home when you're ten years old." *What an idiotic time to move the child!*

"What do you mean by surly?"

"When I say good morning, she scowls."

Caitlin's father looked at the ceiling, shook his head, and tapped a foot. "That hardly seems to warrant 'surly.' "

"Every morning?" Kendall noticed a fleeting resemblance when the man's eyebrows drew together, like now. Definite scowl. If his hair were longer, those short-cropped waves would be a mass of wild curls like Caitlin's, but not blonde. "And she's falling behind in her work."

"And when exactly were you going to tell us that?"

"It's nothing serious yet. I wanted to give Caitlin and me another week or so to get to know each other. I'm sure she'll respond favorably. I suspect she's a lovely, intelligent girl. She just doesn't want to share herself with me yet."

He abruptly stood. "I don't think she needs to. I'll talk to Lewis about moving her to another classroom."

"Mr. Zukowski—"

"I'd like to take her makeup work with me now. That is, if you give any to surly kids." The furrow between his brows deepened. On a man with such broad shoulders it was an intimidating look to behold.

Kendall bit her lip and walked to Caitlin's desk in the front, close to hers. *Lewis? He's already on a first-name basis with the principal?* She sat in Caitlin's seat, opened the lid, and pulled out some books, not looking at him. She examined a paper. "Let's see, a couple of students have been writing down the assignments—"

"I thought teachers made the assignments."

She looked up at him standing in front of the desk. "I do. I make them for twenty-four students," she explained in her soft, patient voice reserved for special moments. "And for Esteban I say them in Spanish. For Ling, I type them up so her aunt can more easily read and interpret them. I don't happen to know their particular Chinese dialect yet. For Chad I repeat them a minimum of three times and sometimes pin a list to his shirt because his ADD requires it. For Lisa, I make sure she's awake because she often falls asleep."

Kendall stuck the assignment papers atop the books, stood, and handed the pile to him. "And for absent children, I let the others help out by writing down what we do. Then I double-check."

"Thank you." The scowl had softened, as had the strong, outdoorsy voice.

She held his eyes with hers. "Mr. Zukowski, we do a lot of team teaching here. I have all three fifth grade classes for social studies and music. We get together for art and PE. I would have her for reading, no matter what class she's in. I wish you'd give this more time. I am absolutely certain it will work out."

There was a footstep at the doorway. "Jade, I see you found our Ms. O'Reilly."

Kendall didn't need to look toward the door to know that the principal, Dr. Lewis Thornton, had entered. *Jade?*

Mr. Zukowski turned toward him. "Well, it's either her or Pollyanna."

"Pollyanna? How so?"

"Quote, 'I am absolutely certain it will work out,' unquote."

The other man chuckled. "Ah, yes, there is a silver lining

for every cloud in Ms. O'Reilly's room. And she's been at this now for eight years."

Kendall leaned against the corner of her desk and clasped her hands. "Nine and a half," she murmured.

"I stand corrected, Ms. O'Reilly." Thornton turned his well-coifed, salt-and-pepper head back toward Caitlin's father. "Kendall has a fairly good idea of what she's doing, Jade. Why don't you come and observe her for a while next week with your daughter? Perhaps then you can understand why the rapport isn't there between the two and offer some pointers to Kendall. I'm sure we can work this out."

He shrugged. "Well, it seems that Cait will be in here for a number of subjects anyway, so I suppose . . ."

"It'd make my job easier, son. Juggling class numbers can get complicated." Thornton slapped Mr. Zukowski's shoulder, ushering him toward the door. "Will Tuesday work for you? Got any classes that day?" He called over his shoulder, "Stop by my office before you leave, Ms. O'Reilly."

They were out the door before she could offer her good-bye smile. With a slight shake of her head she walked around to her chair. *I guess some adults aren't part of the good-bye tradition.* But Caitlin most certainly would be.

Kendall smiled to herself. Interesting that the girl's dad had picked up on her penchant for optimism. Close friends called her Pollyanna, and not because her middle name was Anna. Well, Mr. Zukowski was at least an observant fellow, even if a bit stuffy. She just might win him over.

"Kendall, I cannot believe you referred to his daughter as surly," Thornton "greeted" as she walked into his office.

"I can't either, Lewis, but I did." She slid into a chair across the desk from him and shook her head. "It slipped out before I got into the part about her wonderful potential. I apologize, but it's not too strong a word. Caitlin hasn't smiled or been receptive in three weeks."

"You're too opinionated, young lady." He folded his arms across his impeccable, double-breasted black suit coat. "As I've said before, a little finesse goes a long way with our parents."

"I couldn't lie to him! First thing he asked was if I gave her negative attention. I had to explain why I've corrected her."

"Jade did not appreciate the word 'surly.' "

"I thought his name was Jeremiah?"

"Jeremiah Zukowski III. Jade is what his friends call him. It's short for something or other."

"How do you know him?"

"I'm a friend of his father's."

"Then you must know the home life. When I see such a somber girl as Caitlin, I wonder what goes on at home. What's her mother like?"

Thornton sighed noisily. "Jade is a widower and an excellent single parent."

Kendall felt an instant hollowness in her stomach. "Widower?"

"Didn't you read the file?"

"Uh, just the test scores."

"Well, then, you don't know much, do you? I suggest you do your homework. You realize, of course, that I will have to include this incident in your personnel file."

"This is an official reprimand?" She stifled a frustrated sigh. That meant she had to write her reply to what should have simply been an informative dialogue. *Once again a mountain grows from a molehill.*

He stood and patted his temples where the graying hair was slicked back. "Yes. Now I have to meet my, uh, wife for dinner. See you next week."

She turned at the door. "When did she die?"

"What? Oh, two or three years ago. Cancer, I think."

With a sinking feeling, she left.

Only two situations could plummet Kendall O'Reilly into a slump. One was realizing she had seriously lost track of a child. The other was when her own childhood memories grabbed her unawares.

By evening she knew this Caitlin Zukowski business was a double whammy.

She sat curled up on the couch, wrapped in sweats and a quilt, sipping green tea from a large mug, staring at the old piano—her mother's piano, her piano. She couldn't get warm. The dank Solana Beach winter seeped through the apartment's thin walls and through all the layers of clothes and blanket, seeping all the way into her bones.

The off-white vertical blinds were drawn over the sliding glass door that led out to her second-floor balcony. Lights were on throughout the combined kitchen/living area. In the short hallway the bedroom door stood open with lamplight shining through.

Once again she berated herself for not reading Caitlin's file, reliving moments from the past few weeks when she could have related differently to Caitlin had she known her mother was gone. Could she have been more tender? Should she have backed off a bit and not tried to force the youngster into an immediate rapport with her and the others?

What had *she* needed at that age?

Kendall closed her eyes but still saw her mother sitting at the piano playing Bach's "Arioso in G," their favorite. It was the last piece she had learned from her. She was eleven when she memorized it. Eleven when her mother died.

The piano was one of the few things she had of her mother's. She also had a ring. A love of music. A passion for teaching children. The things that counted.

But what had she needed in those early years? A dad. Hers had been there, but not really.

The doorbell buzzed, startling her. She shuffled in her stocking feet through the kitchen to answer it.

"O'Reilly, what gives? It's seven o'clock!" Her good friend Sara Terronez stood in the landing of the outdoor, covered stairway situated between their neighboring apartments.

"Oh, Sara, I'm sorry."

"You look sick, hon." She shoved the hood of the raincoat off her head and leaned toward Kendall. Her caramel-colored eyes widened. "Uh-oh. I've only seen this look maybe four, five times. You think you've lost one, right?"

She nodded. "I can't go."

Sara sighed and tucked her long, deep brown curls back under the hood. "I know. Go to sleep. Pollyanna will return in the morning ready to love that child back to the fold. We'll miss you, but I guess this means more pizza for me!"

Kendall couldn't help but smile. Her friend was a small bundle of fun-filled energy, always full of stories from the law office where she worked as a secretary. "Tell me about your week tomorrow?"

"Promise. Bye."

Chilled even more from standing in the open doorway, Kendall lay on the couch, pulling the quilt up to her chin, still full of the hollowness, too empty for anything meaningful or lasting.

Was Caitlin's dad like hers? There but not there? His restlessness and curt mannerisms, and that scowl, made him seem an extremely unpleasant man. Poor Caitlin. Jeremiah or Jade—whatever—Zukowski the Third would have to be shown the error of his ways.

The little girl needed to smile again, before it was too late.

Kendall's heavy eyelids closed, faint strands of the arioso echoing in her mind.

"Cait!" Jade folded the newspaper and slapped it on the lamp table next to the overstuffed chair where he sat after dinner. "I'm waiting!"

"Coming, Daddy!" Cait ran from the kitchen, her blonde curls bouncing, and skidded to a halt in front of him. "Grandpa and I just finished. You want some ice cream?" She planted a kiss on his cheek. When he shook his head no, she plopped cross-legged on the floor at his feet. "Okay, let's talk," she prompted, her large brown eyes, just like her mother's, bright with anticipation, dimples deepening with that smile that always squished his stern tendencies right into mush.

Surly? Jade cleared his throat. "Well, sweetheart, I met Miss O'Reilly."

"She likes Ms. She's not married."

"Right. Ms. Umm, she thinks you're a lovely, intelligent girl."

Cait nodded.

"And she knows it's really hard to be a new girl in school in February."

She nodded again, solemnly. "It really is."

"She wants you to come back, Cait. She smiles a lot, doesn't she?" He remembered the way her nose crinkled when she did.

"Yeah, she does."

He hooked his hands behind his head. "So, does she yell?" He thought of the giggle that bubbled near the surface when she first saw him, after bumping her knee and crawling under the desk to retrieve her errant shoe. He smiled to himself.

Caitlin shook her head. "When the boys get bad, she just talks quieter."

"And I bet they listen, huh?" He had listened when she set him straight about assignments with that soft but no-nonsense articulate voice. "She's not bad to look at."

"I think she's pretty, Daddy."

"She's very pretty." Jade recalled the sparkling dark blue eyes that bored through him. The peaches and cream skin so rare in this sun-drenched culture. The oval face framed by strands of wheat-colored hair loosened from a single braid. The feminine ears accented with small pearl earrings. She was probably the prettiest woman he had seen in years. It was a good thing she didn't teach at the high school. Guys would be asking her out.

"Even with the scar."

"Scar?" he asked.

"Right up here." Caitlin drew a jagged line along the right side of her forehead, at the hairline. "Sometimes her bangs cover it."

"Hmm. Didn't notice it. The room seems nice."

"Did you see those big, giant sunflowers on the bulletin board by the piano?" She spread her arms in a wide circle. "We made those to brighten up these gloomy, winter days, Ms. O'Reilly says."

He shook his head.

"Did you see my picture I drew?"

Again he shook his head. "What's in it?"

"Mountains. It's on the wall by that back door that goes to the library."

"I didn't have time to look around much. I saw the piano though. Does your teacher play that?"

"Yeah. Ms. O'Reilly makes music tons of fun."

Jade leaned forward, resting his arms on his knees. "Cait, why don't you like her?"

His daughter shrugged, and her bottom lip protruded. She

climbed up on his lap, snuggling her face into his shoulder. Small for her age, she still fit. "I miss Mommy."

He wrapped his arms around her, wondering at the illogical jump from school to Mommy. How he missed Deborah, especially at times like these! She would understand what the problem was and would know what to do. He did fine with teenagers, but this little girl stuff always eluded him.

Cait had been in third grade when Deborah died. Until last month they had always lived as a family in the San Bernardino Mountains, northeast of Los Angeles. Kindergarten through third were his wife's domain. First-day jitters, birthday treats, playground spats, room mother, field trip chaperone. His sister Elizabeth had helped out at the beginning of fourth. By fall of fifth grade, Cait seemed independent. Then came this move.

He was working, so his father had taken her to school that first day. If he remembered correctly, Dad had confidently handed her over to the principal, an acquaintance of his. It was all so practical. Logical.

"Sweetheart," he said into her curls. "I'll come visit on Tuesday. For the whole morning, if you want. Dr. Thornton said I could."

She sat up. "You will?"

"Sure." He nodded.

The dimples appeared. "Now can I have some ice cream?"

"Okay. Bring me some chocolate?"

"Daddy!" She squeezed his shoulder with two hands. "Your mus-kles will get all mooshy, and you won't be able to climb."

He laughed. It was an old joke. "Just one scoop."

She skipped into the kitchen, passing his father who called over his shoulder, "Two scoops for me, please, Caity-did."

"Okay, Grampy-do!"

He placed a forefinger at each cheek as he sank onto the couch. "She's smiling. Looks like you got it all straightened out."

Jade sighed. "Dad, we need a woman here. Why don't you get married? I've met three possibilities for you already in just one month. You're dragging your feet."

Reverend Jeremiah David Zukowski II chuckled. "Then I'd have to kick you out. This condo isn't big enough for four."

"Yeah, I guess we're stuck with each other for the time being." He looked at his father. At sixty-seven, the white-haired retired pastor still was a tall, impressive figure with a strong, baritone voice. Jade knew he was content. A widower for ten years, he had moved to Solana Beach five years ago to volunteer as visitation pastor for a large congregation. He thoroughly enjoyed the coastal area. "I think Cait just needs to settle in at school. It's taking more time than I imagined. Deb would have known."

"She would have." He nodded. "I peeked in a bit ago and saw Caitlin sitting at your feet. It reminded me of Mary listening to Jesus teach, giving Him all her attention, knowing He spoke words of life." He smiled. "You'll teach her the things that count, Jade. We can trust God to fill in those feminine areas that we don't understand. Maybe this Ms. O'Reilly will be a help. Do you think she's appropriate for her?"

Jade shrugged. "We don't have much of a choice. Guess faith will play a big part in this."

"Like it should with everything. When I saw Lewis last night, he didn't seem too sure about the woman. He hinted at other complaints."

"I guess you could say she's rather focused. Intense. She probably doesn't take much guff from him."

"He's focused too. Driven. They might not often see eye to eye."

"She got off on the wrong foot with me, but I think she knows her stuff. We'll just keep a closer eye on things. Also, from what I see of the makeup work, Cait's had more to do than she's let on."

"How old is this Ms. O'Reilly?"

"Well, she looks no more than twenty-one, but she's been teaching for nine years, so I'd say early thirties. And good-looking, to boot."

A smile spread slowly across his dad's face. "You noticed?"

Jade stared at him. His father knew he hadn't noticed in a long time. A very, very long time indeed.

Two

On Tuesday morning he realized she was more good-looking than he'd remembered.

"Good morning, Caitlin!" Miss O'Reilly grinned from ear to ear, stooped, and gave Cait a swift hug. "Welcome back! And welcome, Mr. Zukowski." She held out her hand.

"Thank you." Jade found himself grinning back at her as he accepted her firm handshake. She wasn't wearing her glasses today. Her long-sleeved dress was a deep blue that matched her eyes, and she wore again the small pearl earrings.

"Caitlin, we need to find a seat for your dad. Shall we have him sit at the table in the back? Or else," she looked up at him, stretching her neck in an exaggerated way, "we could put him in a little desk chair next to yours."

His daughter giggled. "He's too big for that."

"I agree. Better take him to the grown-up chair." Miss O'Reilly winked, then turned to greet another student. The long braid hung between her shoulder blades.

"What do you mean, too big?" he teased Cait.

"Oh, Daddy."

Surrounded by munchkin-sized youngsters, he followed her about the room. She hung her jacket along the row of coat hooks, then showed him her desk and drawing. The yellow sunflowers were huge and bright. The air smelled like schoolrooms always smelled of chalk and manila paper and thick, tempera paints and cleanser odor and glue and books. Shelves with neatly arranged books lined the back wall across to what must be the library door Cait had mentioned. Closed venetian blinds covered its window.

Abruptly his daughter told him he'd better sit down, gave him her dimpled smile, and scooted to her seat. A few seconds later the bell rang.

There was complete silence. Nobody even twitched a finger. Twenty-four kids and Miss O'Reilly sat at their desks with hands neatly folded. Jade pulled out his chair and sat as quietly as he could.

"Class," she said in a soft voice, "we have an extra-special visitor this morning. He's Caitlin's father, and his name is Mr. Zukowski. Let's give him our extra-special visitor welcome."

The entire group sprang to their feet and swung round to face him, shouting, "Good morning, Mr. Zukowski!" They whooped and hollered, waved their arms, and clapped. He even heard some whistles. An especially piercing one came from the front of the room where Miss O'Reilly stood.

Without thinking, Jade jumped to his feet, stepped onto the chair, and waved back. "Good morning!" he shouted at the top of his voice. He stuck thumb and forefinger at the sides of his mouth and let go his best whistle.

Miss O'Reilly's startled look gave way to a burst of giggles. Just when the group seemed on the verge of chaos, she held up a hand, and the laughter subsided. Jade sat back down along with the kids.

"We've never had anyone," she paused to catch her breath, "answer us." She clapped a hand over her mouth, and he heard a muffled fit of giggles erupt.

Static crackled from the speaker high up on the back wall. "Attention please," the principal's voice boomed.

Jade thought he heard a snort from behind the teacher's hand as the class stood for the Pledge of Allegiance. Announcements followed, during which she sat at her desk wiping tears from the corners of her eyes. She lowered her head to write, but he saw a smile tug at the corner of her mouth.

Miss O'Reilly's desk was in the front right corner of the room, facing the students. Just to the left of it was a window through which Jade could see a patch of sky and another classroom building across the sidewalk. In the left corner was the door. Along the wall at his left were closets and the row of coat hooks. Most of the right wall was chalkboard. Near the back, by the shelves, the low, upright piano angled out.

What wall space wasn't covered with bulletin boards or posters was painted a pale blue; on the floor was a nondescript thin carpet. It was a neatly organized room. Except for the inevitable scent, it was even cozy.

Miss O'Reilly stood now. He listened with half an ear as she took care of lunch details. Her mannerisms and tone of voice were efficient, no-nonsense, as if there were more important things to do. Her eyes were wide-set, almost like some sort of cat, maybe a tiger. No, more like a mountain lion with that tawny hair. As she walked down the aisle closest to him, he glimpsed the scar Cait had mentioned—high on her forehead near the hairline, white, jagged, and threadlike. She wore little makeup that he could tell. Her lips, smiling again, were glossy with a hint of pink.

He could not recall a teacher ever giggling. There were a

few who had laughed, rarely, but—

"SPELLING!"

He jumped at her shout. She stood grinning at the front of the room, her arms raised, hands clenched into fists, eyes wide, as if she were a cheerleader announcing the next cheer. He half expected her to do a back flip.

As if following some choreographed routine, several students moved about the room passing out papers. Someone laid a pencil and paper on the table before him. Within moments everyone was seated with pencils poised.

"Number 1."

He crossed his arms and leaned back.

Miss O'Reilly eyed him. "This is only a pretest, Mr. Zukowski. It won't affect your grade."

He picked up the pencil.

She strolled along the rows while pronouncing the words. When next to him, she leaned over his shoulder. "Thanks for your cooperation. We encourage 100 percent participation."

Gone was the smell of chalk and glue, replaced by the desert when the hot afternoon sun presses a dry, subtle sweetness from the mesquite, acacia, and sage. His mind began to wander.

"Mr. Zukowski?"

"Huh?" Jade looked up to see a dark-eyed boy sitting across the table from him.

"Trade ya papers." He brushed his long hair out of his eyes.

"Okay." They slid their papers toward each other.

"You got some blanks here."

"Oh, well, I, umm . . ." Jade cleared his throat. "I wasn't paying attention for all of them."

The boy grinned. "That's okay, you're just visitin'. You a good speller?"

"Well—"

"We're s'posed to use the books to check with. You can use mine if you want."

"Oh, I think I know these."

They worked silently for a few moments.

"You got seven right, Mr. Zukowski. That's good since you only did eight."

"What'd I miss?"

"Conscience."

"Isn't it *i* before *e* except after *c*?"

"Yeah, except for in *science,* and that's part of *conscience* cuz it's the knowledge of something and knowledge is part of science."

"Hmm. Well," Jade read the name on the paper, "Cory, you got eighteen right, make that nineteen with *conscience.* That's great."

"Thanks."

"GRAMMAR!"

She was doing it again, cheering for the next subject. Everyone scooted into position. Someone came by and handed him a grammar book.

"Page 152!"

Cait had probably never seen anything like this in her other school. He certainly hadn't seen it in all his years at school. He watched his little girl. She seemed to know what was going on. They must have shown her, just as they were showing him today, how things were done in Miss O'Reilly's class, making her feel welcome as they did him. Why would that intimidate her?

The teacher was reading to them now from a worn Superman comic book, pausing for the kids to identify verbs and such.

A short while later Lewis Thornton, the principal whom he had met through his dad, walked in.

"Excuse me, Ms. O'Reilly," he boomed as he strode toward the back. "Well, I see you found your way here." He stood across the table from Jade, half turned toward the class, hands on hips.

Jade nodded.

"How's it going?"

"Fine." He turned his attention back to grammar and noted that Miss O'Reilly had slipped on her oval-shaped glasses. The comic book had been replaced by the textbook. She stood stiffly behind a podium, separated from the kids, not moving up and down the aisles.

"Class," she said, "Dr. Thornton is here."

"Good morning, Dr. Thornton," the kids responded in subdued tones, not quite in unison, still facing forward.

The man nodded.

The lesson continued. Her smile didn't appear, and the room didn't feel quite as cozy. Even the construction paper sunflowers seemed to droop.

Thornton leaned over the table toward him. "Grammar can be a little dry, like spelling," he offered in a stage whisper. "But then, social studies is like that in here too." He rolled his eyes. "I'm sure your daughter will learn what she needs to know though. Let me know how you make out." Without another glance toward the class, he left.

Miss O'Reilly pushed up her sleeves and continued speaking in a monotone for approximately thirty more seconds. It took her another sixty seconds to divide the class into four teams and assign a grammar exercise to be done at the board as a race.

The smile returned, he learned something new about verbs, and Cait won points for her team. Soon the bell rang. "RECESS!" The cheer was back.

He stood and caught his daughter's attention as she lined

28

up at the door. "I have to go, Cait. If—."

"Okay. Bye, Dad!" And she was out the door.

Miss O'Reilly walked over to him. "I'd say your visit was a success, Mr. Z."

He smiled and shook his head. "In all honesty, I can't understand what was bothering her."

"Well," she leaned against the table and pulled off her glasses, "for one thing, I think she just needed you here to make it comfortable. Now that you know where she spends her days and it's okay with you, she has a new security. Do you want to talk about rapport?"

He met her wide-set eyes looking up at him in all sincerity. "You're joking, right?"

"No, not in the least."

"You obviously know what you're doing. I'm sure if I'd had you for a teacher, I wouldn't have misspelled *conscience* today."

She smiled, and her nose scrunched up. "My goal is that you have one."

He laughed.

"If you'd like, I can work with Caitlin after school for a few days. Unless she did everything I sent home, she could use extra time here. Some one-on-one might help her feel more at ease with me too. Hard as I try, she could very well still feel left out, coming in the middle of the year like she did."

"All right, thank you. How about tomorrow?"

"I'll plan on it. Now," she stood, "there's one more thing that will be a tremendous help for her."

"What's that?"

"If you chaperone our field trip."

He winced. "I thought only moms did that."

"Goodness no! Please, please come."

"Miss O—"

29

"It's a free visit to Sea World, in two weeks, March 5th. Plenty of time to rearrange your schedule, I hope? I promise, it would mean the world to her."

Chaperone fifth graders? "But—"

"Trust me, you'll make points with her—that'll make an incredible difference when she's a teen. When you have to say no, she can't date so-and-so, she'll know you care and she'll respect your opinion."

He pulled a notebook from his jacket pocket and checked the date, knowing full well his only out would be a nonrefundable ticket to Mars. He ran his fingers through his hair. "Well, I guess I could—"

"Oh, that's marvelous!" She clapped her hands together. "Thank you. I can't tell you how much I appreciate this. For her and for me. Is there anything else I can do for you?"

"Show me how you do that whistle. I always have to use fingers."

She laughed and shook her head. "Sorry. That's one of those things you either learn as a kid or never."

As they walked toward the door, he studied her profile. Until now he had never met anyone who could say *marvelous* and get away with it. "Tell me this, then . . . Are you for real?"

At the open doorway she touched her hair and briefly shut her eyes. "All right, all right, I have it highlighted—a little. It's mostly real though."

He chuckled. "No, I mean, you're a fun teacher. Except when Lewis was in here."

"You noticed?"

"Yeah, slightly."

She shrugged and peeked into the courtyard outside before answering. "He thinks my antics are silly, so I tone it down a little for him. Even with tenure, his opinion carries a lot of weight in regard to my career. So I try to keep him happy and still do what I know works with the children." Her eyes widened. "Do you think that's misleading? Does that make me not real?"

Jade smiled. "I don't think so. Do you keep that positive momentum going all the time?"

"There's a little ebb and flow to it, but basically, yes."

"Whew! Well, Miss O'Reilly, it has been a pleasure."

"In that case, call me Kendall."

They shook hands. "All right, Kendall. I'm Jade."

"I thought you said Jeremiah last week?"

"My parents named me after my grandfather and father, so the Jeremiah David got shortened to J.D. Then my little brother cut that down to Jade. It stuck."

"I'm sorry about your wife."

That threw him off guard. His throat constricted. Having this total stranger to his past offer such tender compassion out of the blue was unsettling. He swallowed but could only manage a hoarsely whispered, "Thank you."

"Mm hmm. Thanks for coming. See you soon!" She smiled and waved as he walked through the door.

"They're baaack!"

Kendall, grading papers at her desk after school, looked up and saw Greg Jones peering into her room. Maxine Carothers's face appeared behind his and added, "And you get one!"

"No way!" Kendall jumped up. "I had one last spring! You two promised." She pointed an accusing finger at the other two fifth grade teachers.

They looked at each other, then back at her and said in unison, "But they always like you best, Pollyanna."

She covered her face with her hands and groaned, hoping

it was a joke. *Another student teacher!* The door quietly clicked shut.

"Honey, you know it's not our decision," Maxine soothed.

"We'll help, of course," Greg added.

She peered at them through her fingers. "You're not teasing?"

They shook their heads. Maxine, a tall, stylish woman with silver-streaked, short black hair, sat down at a student desk. Her round face and brown velvet eyes wore a sympathetic expression. "Have a seat, baby."

She slumped onto the chair that Greg pulled out for her. He, too, looked sorrowful, his thin face drawn and the usually grinning mouth subdued. That in itself could easily mean he was in the middle of a practical joke, but Maxine wouldn't have allowed this one. He settled his lanky frame around another small chair.

The three had worked side by side for seven years and considered one another good friends. In spite of their different personalities, a synergy flowed between them that Kendall thought sprang from their mutual passion for teaching.

Greg was a family man with two preschoolers. He had moved to the west coast from Nebraska as a youngster. Maxine had arrived as a bride from Ohio with her Navy husband; they now had two sons in college. They were both as dedicated as she was. In her opinion, East Hills Elementary had the best fifth grade program in the county.

Kendall shook her head. "How did you find out before me?"

Maxine answered, "Just happened to be in Lewis's path at the right time. He asked me to be on that new curriculum committee. I was hoping for that. He didn't want me to have a student teacher at the same time." She raised her eyebrows. "He prefers you over Greg. Of course, I wasn't supposed to mention it before he got to you."

But of course her friend would.

"Ken," Greg said, "just don't try to clone yourself. This doesn't have to be a heavyweight issue. Let the girl do the required stuff—observe you and write some lesson plans and try 'em out. All you have to do is fill out the report and say she did swell."

The women looked at each other. Maxine chuckled. "What planet does he live on?"

"Right, Greg. I'll do just that."

"Seriously, we'll help. Share her more with us. Thornton won't know the difference."

Maxine added, "He's right, Kendall. You don't have to carry this burden all by yourself." She reached over and squeezed her arm. "We just heard something else in the office. The school board is considering rezoning. With those two developments scheduled to open soon, the population is shifting."

Greg shook his head. "They want to give our whole northeast section to Adams. We'll lose a fourth of our kids."

"Maybe not that much, Greg, but it's a given we won't need three fifth grade teachers here, since there's only two and a half classes coming up as it is."

Kendall said, "There'll be a place for us. Maybe we could move as a team to Adams."

"Well, ladies, team or no team, I'd go in a minute, as long as Thornton stayed here."

"What's he on your case about now, Greg?" Kendall asked.

"Nothing new." He shrugged. "I'm just growing weary of his condescending attitude. It seems like the team effort should start in administration."

"Hear, hear," Maxine said. "Like the good old days with

Lois." She referred to the principal who had preceded Thornton and moved away three years ago.

Kendall stood up and stretched. "Nothing to be done about it now. Wanna run with me, Greg?"

"No, I have to get home. The kids are sick. Steph will need a break."

"Say, Kendall, who was that man here this morning?"

"Man—? Oh, Caitlin Zukowski's dad. He's a widower, trying to be mom and dad."

"I thought there was an earthquake," Greg said. "Three kids ducked under their desks before we figured it out. Sounded like your special greeting got a little out of hand."

"Almost. You won't believe what this guy did. He answered it!"

"What?"

Kendall nodded. "Climbed up on the chair and yelled and whistled right back. I laughed so hard I . . . Hey, I got him signed up to chaperone!"

Greg's jaw dropped. "You got a dad to chaperone? Bus ride and all?"

"Yep."

"Umm-umm." Maxine crossed her arms and narrowed her eyes. "You *are* good, child. And he's single."

"So? What's that got to do with it?"

"And spontaneous and funny, from what you just said."

"Yes."

"And handsome as all get out."

"Is he?"

"He is. He came by the playground while I was on recess duty this morning." Maxine turned to Greg. "Mr. Jones, what are we going to do with her? We get a nice, single man laughing with her and she doesn't notice!"

"Well, Mrs. Carothers, she can't go on being single and

34

laughing alone. What does he do for a living?"

"Plays football." Maxine didn't skip a beat. "Yes, sir, he looks like a football player. Broad shoulders. Solid neck. I think he's that new member of the Chargers, using a pseudonym."

"Nah," Greg replied. "He's strong-looking, but not that big. I'd say a mountain climber. World-famous. He's taking some time off at the beach to write a book about it."

Kendall stared from one to the other. "The file didn't say what he does. It was blank."

Maxine took a breath, ignoring her. "Nice teeth. Thick, wavy hair, cropped real short."

"Healthy-looking, I thought," Greg continued. "Outdoorsy."

"Definitely her type. Probably eats lots of veggies."

Greg stood. "Come on, Max. Let's go find his phone number."

She took the arm he offered. "Goodness knows *she* won't." They strolled toward the door. "We'll set things up for her. She's just got too much love in her not to give some away and make room to get some back." They walked outside.

Kendall hurried to catch the door and called out, "He's a dad! I don't notice dads, remember? And I certainly don't date dads!"

Except for Mark. That was a long time ago though, during her second year of teaching when she didn't know any better.

Kendall stuck her foot on the bumper of her sunburst yellow Cavalier, leaned over, and retied her running shoes. While stretching out, she scanned the sky. The clouds were finally gone, leaving the promise of a visible sunset within the hour. Though the air was cool, her windbreaker and shorts should be enough. She headed down the short street that dead-ended at a low stone wall and the beach.

There had been nothing remarkable about Mark's physical features, certainly nothing like Jeremiah David Zukowski III. But he knew how to make her feel special, in a way no one else ever had. If she had a type, he was it—he knew Bach and good restaurants and had season tickets to the symphony.

She plowed through the soft sand and turned south on the wide, flat stretch of the Del Mar beach. Only a few people were scattered here and there, strolling or jogging. As usual, surfers were in the ocean. When her feet hit the packed sand just beyond reach of the waves, she began to run, falling into a rhythm in cadence with the coming and going of the rolling surf.

She deeply breathed in the moist, salty air. It was like an internal shower that could ferret out the day's overload of words and emotions and refresh her.

One thought stuck though. Mark. He hadn't come to mind for . . . years? That parting shot to Maxine and Greg, of course, was responsible for this reminiscing. He was the reason she put "dating dads" on her list of stupid things not to bother repeating nor to question why.

She had been teaching third graders. His little boy Benjy was a charmer and quite a troublemaker. Early in the fall Kendall had tried to reach his divorced mother with whom he lived. When her calls weren't returned, she called the dad and left several messages on his answering machine. At last he made an appointment and came in.

They communicated instantly, as if they had known each other for years. He was about her height, with blond hair, round wire glasses, an easy smile, and shifty eyes. She hadn't recognized the eyes at first. He was as charming as his son and swept her off her feet.

He invited her to dinner soon after that first meeting. He

sent flowers and took her to the symphony. His job was related to selling computer technology, and he always wore elegant suits. He listened to her play the piano. He was totally unlike the boys at Humboldt University.

Well, in all fairness she had been too focused on her studies to give them much attention. The scholarship was only good for four and a half years; she had to finish. And besides, she had spent too many years giving attention to the man who counted most in her life, and he had only tossed it aside.

Then Mark came along, showering her, the attention-starved girl, with gifts and smiles and hugs. She blossomed and fell deeply in love and never noticed that Benjy's behavior remained the same.

In the springtime when she expected a marriage proposal—he had hinted—he gave her instead a passionate kiss and then said good-bye. He had met someone else. Actually, she was waiting in the car and he had to go. Just like that.

And just like that Kendall very nearly lost all hope in life.

When she came to her senses, the school year was over, and the naive girl she had been was replaced with a young woman whom someone later pegged Pollyanna. She preferred rather to call herself a realist who could make things work out when they appeared hopeless—because she had spent most of her life doing just that.

Her roommate had recognized Mark's shifty eyes long before she had an inkling that they moved in such a way. Even Benjy's mother, his ex-wife, had laughed at her for dating him, warning her that he knew nothing of commitment—just look at their son.

And so she moved away from the hurt. She had lived near her childhood home in Eureka, almost as far north as possible in California, and decided to go as far south as possible, to the

San Diego area. She could still be close to her beloved ocean. Seven and a half years ago she found her teaching position, next-door to Maxine who had been there fifteen years, and Greg, a five-year veteran. It was a good move.

Mark faded and Pollyanna took on vibrant living colors. She made friends and occasionally went out with male friends on what could probably be called dates. Maxine and Greg's families became hers. She, often with good friend and neighbor Sara accompanying her, traveled during summers to other states, often incorporating research for her social studies lessons. She studied piano again and ran at the beach and loved the kids. The tough questions were answered; she'd found life.

As a teenager she'd felt a vague notion that she would someday want to be a wife and mother, to live as many others around her lived. Mark had kindled that feeling into a full-fledged dream, but she buried it when he left. No, to dream that was to dream of self-destruction. Perhaps marriage doomed for failure was a hereditary gene.

She considered herself fortunate though. Her one dream had come true—she was a teacher. And she was a good one, with the ability to give children a glimpse of their potential. She had immersed herself in that and in time found a deep contentment.

Kendall jumped now over a large pile of brown kelp and realized she was going too fast. Her breathing was irregular. The rhythm was lost.

She noticed that she'd already passed the long row of lovely beach homes. Across the wide stretch of sand to her left was a tall lifeguard station between two popular restaurants. People sat on the patio of the one, separated from sand by just a low stone wall. Glancing at the ocean, she saw the sun almost touching the horizon.

She slowed to a walk, then made her way up a bit to the soft sand and sat down. She would watch the sunset, jog through the dusk back to her car, and go home. Perhaps Sara would join her for dinner. Then she would grade papers and think through tomorrow's lessons and how to make Caitlin comfortable in them. In all that she would find again the rhythm.

"Bus? You didn't say anything about a bus, Miss O'Reilly!"

Kendall smiled sweetly at Jade and held up her palms. "There's always a bus involved with a field trip. We have seventy-five students to transport. I just assumed you would know."

They stood on the sidewalk outside the school. The early morning cloud cover was already breaking up. It promised to be a perfect 72 dry, sunny degrees. Students filed past them, climbing aboard the two buses parked at the curb.

"This is my first field trip." His low voice was full of exasperation. "I prefer to drive myself and meet you there."

"Oh, but we need you as chaperone on the bus too. It's our policy to have so many students per adult. There's less potential for problems that way. Excuse me." She leaned around him and ordered, "Matt, hands to yourself!"

Only a few students remained on the sidewalk. All the other adults were boarded too. It was time to go.

Jade didn't budge. "I don't do buses."

Kendall stared up at him now. There was an uncanny resemblance to someone. Maybe it was the way he tilted his head, his eyebrows knitted together and hands hooked in the back pocket of his jeans. Who . . . ? *Tony.* Jade Zukowski had undoubtedly been a similar, strong-willed challenge to his teachers as a child. Gently, she laid a hand on his forearm. "Jade, do bus rides make you ill?"

He turned his face toward the school, avoiding her eyes. "I have some Dramamine."

"That'll put me to sleep."

She took hold of his elbow and steered him toward the bus. "Sit right behind the driver. Keep the window open. It's just a straight shot down the freeway," she soothed. "No steeps hills or curves. Do you have your lunch?"

He shook his head and climbed the steps. She stayed right next to him and muffled a sigh. The note specifically told parent chaperones to bring their lunches. "Mindy, I need Mr. Zukowski to sit there. Thanks, hon. Find us a seat back there, okay?"

The girl slid out. Jade plopped down and reached for the window.

"Tony!" Kendall called above the chatter to the tall boy at the back of the bus. She crooked a finger and pointed to the empty seat beside Jade. Kneeling down, she rummaged through the knapsack she had stashed earlier under the front seat. She found what she wanted and nudged her reluctant chaperone, whose face was now sticking out the window. "Jade, here."

Slowly he turned toward her. His eyes were half shut and his jaw clenched tightly. She hoped he wouldn't say anything. She slipped a folded plastic grocery bag into his hand as Tony slid onto the seat next to him.

"Hey, how's it goin', Mr. Z.?"

"Mr. Zukowski, this is Tony." Reaching over her shoulder, she patted the bus driver's shoulder. "Ready, Jim."

Quickly, she made her way down the aisle, satisfied that Tony would talk the whole way and keep Jade's mind occupied, which should take his mind off his queasiness. In turn, having Tony sit next to the strong-looking man should keep him out of trouble.

Whew, she thought, *first challenge of the day hurdled!* And it hadn't even been initiated by a student.

"Ms. O'Reilly!"

Kendall walked over to one of the aluminum picnic tables where a group of girls sat waving to her. She was glad to see that Caitlin had been included.

Most of the morning had been spent with tour guides showing them behind the scenes at Sea World. They saw how the dolphins were trained and how stranded animals were rescued and cared for. Then the chaperones had taken their small groups to various exhibits. Kendall, with Caitlin and others, had enjoyed the penguins and polar bears. Now they had all met at a designated picnic area for lunch.

"You girls having a good time?" She slipped the knapsack from her back, took out a sack lunch, and stuck her cardigan sweatshirt into the bag.

"Yeah."

"Hey, I like your shirt."

Kendall glanced at the huge yellow sunflower that filled the front of her neon orange T-shirt. "Thanks. I figured if I get lost, you wouldn't have any trouble finding me."

A few of the girls talked at once. "We think Caitlin's dad is way cool."

"He is sooo handsome."

"What do you think, MISS O'Reilly?"

Caitlin laughed. "I keep telling him to call you Ms. Do you like him?"

Kendall smiled. "Sure."

A chorus sang out, "Oooh—"

"No, no, no," she protested, shaking her head. "Not like that. We need to feed him, girls. He forgot a lunch. If you have anything you don't want—"

Immediately her hands were filled with an apple, an orange, plastic-wrapped carrots, sandwiches, and cookies.

"Here," Caitlin offered, "my dad can have this. I just punched the straw through."

"I have an extra water bottle I'll give him. You drink your juice. Thanks, girls. Don't feed the seagulls."

She meandered through the groups of students to where the adults were gathering. Jade and Greg occupied one end of a table, sitting across from each other. She climbed onto the picnic bench next to Greg and set down the food. "Lunch, Mr. Z."

"What's all this? I'll go buy something."

Kendall and Greg looked at each other, then back at Jade and said in unison, "It's not allowed."

She added, "The kids will feel bad that they can't have hot dogs and ice cream and soda."

"But I can't take someone else's lunch."

"You have to. See Caitlin over there? All those girls donated it, and they think you are way cool. They might change their opinion if you don't accept their gift."

"Hmm. I suppose that would embarrass her, huh?" He pushed his sunglasses up on his forehead. "Well, thank you."

"Here." She slid a bottle of water over to him and half of her tuna sandwich. "How's it going with Tony?"

"We're getting along fine. My guess is he's about sixteen and still in fifth grade?"

Greg chuckled. "He seems like it. We appreciate you coming along, Jade. We were especially concerned about him and his friends. Another man in the crowd always makes a difference with those . . ." He cleared his throat. ". . . personalities."

Jade narrowed his eyes at Kendall. "I do seem to be the only dad here."

She shrugged. "I just said chaperoning wasn't only for

moms. Have you met all the moms, by the way?" She glanced down the table loaded with talking women.

"Yes."

"Jade was just telling me that he and his wife used to run a retreat camp above San Bernardino." Greg turned to Jade. "You were saying that teen groups came?"

Jade nodded. "And some young adults. There were formal groups from schools and churches as well as private individuals. We did family and teen camps too. We majored on rock climbing."

"Wow! Did you live there year-round?"

"Yeah. When it snowed, there was skiing, and we organized trips to the desert for climbing."

"Sounds great. My son would love it. He's just five. I've taken him up near Hemet, backpacking. Have you been there?"

Jade shook his head. "Not yet. I plan to. Cait always liked the wilderness, and camping too. And living in a log cabin in the woods."

Kendall watched Jade as they talked. He was handsome in a youthful, outdoorsy way. Clear eyes, green-flecked hazel. Straight nose. His neck was as solid-looking as the shoulders hugged by his short-sleeved, dark green T-shirt. His square jaw split into deep creases when his mouth curved into a smile. His voice was pleasant, low, and calm, an intriguing contrast to the energetic personality.

". . . Ken's already got hers."

"My what?"

"Master's," Greg answered. "Jade's working on his in counseling."

"Counseling? What type?"

"I'd like to work with teens, maybe in a high school setting."

"No wonder you're so good with Tony. Where are you going to school?" she asked.

"Westminster."

"The seminary in Escondido?"

Jade nodded. "I still have a ways to go. I'm just part-time now."

"That's wonderful."

"What's wonderful," Maxine interrupted as she walked up behind Jade, "is that we've made it halfway through this trip."

"Have you met Jade, Maxine?"

"Of course. As usual, you were off with the kids and missed half the lunchtime. He is a God-send, isn't he?" Maxine patted him on the back and squinted at Kendall. "Where'd you get that shirt, hon? I need my sunglasses to look at you."

Kendall checked her watch. "Just get us into our groups, Maxine. It's time for the Sea Lion and Otter Show."

"All right." She raised her voice and looked around. "Mothers and Mr. Zukowski, we'll head now to the Sea Lion and Otter Show, then the tide pool, and then Shamu at 1:30. Don't worry about keeping all the groups together. Just be sure to get your group to the exit gate by 2:15. And we are in agreement, no Happy Harbor, right?"

Several moms emphatically echoed, "Right!"

Jade stood and put on sunglasses with silvery reflective lenses. "What's Happy Harbor?"

"It's this fantastic playground," Kendall answered, "with suspended bridges and all sorts of unusual things. Kids adore it. Tony will beg to go, but it's too difficult to keep track of everyone."

"So I get to tell him no?"

She carried trash to a nearby bin, then slipped on her

backpack. "Or answer to Maxine."

"Maxine I can handle. It's you I want to keep clear of."

She raised her eyebrows.

"Well?" he begged.

"Okay. We'll skip the tide pool," she answered in a low voice, glancing at the parting backs of the others. "They get fifteen minutes max."

He grinned. "I knew it. Cait's in your group?"

She nodded. "Meet us at the squirting drinking fountains in the playground area."

An unplanned meeting occurred in the sea lion amphitheater, down in front, in full view of hundreds of spectators. It was the mime's fault.

Kendall had been sitting with her group of three boys and two girls near the center, about five rows up. Below them, the brilliant sunshine was reflected in the bright blue pool that ran the length of the stage. A mime, face painted white and wearing black pants and red suspenders over a white shirt, performed in front of the pool. She and the children were laughing at his pre-show antics as people strolled in looking for seats.

He studied the audience, then began climbing up the aluminum bleachers. With exaggerated arm movements, he pushed people apart and headed straight for her. He stopped a row in front of her and motioned for her to come down.

Kendall froze. She could easily clown around in her classroom without a single self-conscious thought, but this type of thing embarrassed her to no end.

The young man's expressive penciled brows and pouting red lips pleaded silently. Not knowing what to expect, she shook her head no, but the kids pulled and pushed her to her

45

feet amidst cheers. With his hand under her elbow, the mime gallantly escorted her down to the front, then gestured for the camera hanging around her neck. She gave it to him without protest. Whatever, just to get this over with. She knew her face must be scarlet.

He positioned her next to the chest-level, plexiglass-type wall in front of the deep, blue pool, then held the camera up as if to take her picture. He stopped and looked around, then walked clear across the front to the far side of the theater while she stood there feeling more ridiculous by the second. She watched him climb a few steps and from the crowd pull out . . . Jade.

She knew the applause and shouts came from her fifth graders. She really didn't know how much longer she could stand there. A moment later Jade grinned down at her, and the mime shoved them shoulder to shoulder. Once again he held up the camera, then put it down and went off looking for another victim.

Jade leaned over so she could hear him. "You're all red, Miss O'Reilly. Too much sun?"

She covered her face with her hands.

The mime returned with a little boy who obediently stood in front of them as if they were a family. Jade flung his arm across her shoulders and pulled her close and laid a hand on the boy's shoulder. A dull roar came from the audience. She smiled, and at last the mime pointed the camera and clicked it. He silently thanked them all profusely and handed the camera back to her.

The Sea Lion and Otter Show wasn't nearly as much fun as she'd remembered it.

"I don't like that stuff."

"But the kids thought it was great." Jade leaned around and caught her eye. They sat on a bench at the edge of the

Happy Harbor playground. "And I thought you'd do anything for your kids."

"Well, yeah, but . . . What time did we tell them to be back here?"

"Relax, Kendall. I'll keep an eye on my watch. Why don't you just sit still for a while and take a few deep breaths? I'll be right back."

She moved to sit cross-legged and glanced around. The air was sweet from the lush array of purple alyssum growing along the curb to her right. Palm trees swayed above her, and every sort of green bush and plant filled in the spaces between sky and sidewalk. From speakers hidden behind bird of paradise and azalea came muted strands of soft jazz. Earlier in the day it had been Vivaldi.

She did take a deep breath and closed her eyes. The entire park was like this. Glorious sea animals, flowers, blue sky, neatly swept walkways, people laughing, seagulls calling, the scent of churros. Churros? Her eyelids flew open.

Inches from her nose, Jade held the warm, sugar-covered donut stick.

Her jaw dropped.

He smiled. "Tony said you mentioned these were a favorite of yours and that this was a good place for them."

"Oh, thank you." She accepted it from him, grasping the waxed paper at the bottom, and pulled off a top section. "Here, have some."

"Thanks."

"Umm. This is a treat. I certainly didn't expect anything like this." She giggled, "Especially after I dragged you onto the bus."

"You're right. You certainly don't deserve anything after that." He reached for it. "Give it back."

"Too late. I'm just glad we're still on speaking terms."

"We're practically on family terms after that mime act."

"At least he didn't pull Tony from the audience."

"That would have been too weird." Jade laughed.

"You were like him, weren't you, as a child?"

"Like Tony? What, tall for my age?"

"No. You know what I mean. Full of excess energy and stubborn and spontaneous and, oh goodness, just a real challenge for teachers. Like remembering things like a comment about churros." She took a bite.

He stared at her. "Why would you say that?"

" 'I don't do buses.' And this." She set her jaw and drew her eyebrows together.

"Oh, that." He leaned back and crossed his arms.

"Don't get me wrong, I like Tony immensely. But next year at middle school some teacher with a hundred themes to correct is not going to have the capacity to enjoy him. He's headed for trouble." She wondered briefly if Jade had been in trouble as a teen. "So, is that why you're going into counseling, because you were like that?"

Beneath half-closed lids, he studied her. "It seems like an appropriate use of my experience."

"It's incredibly, absolutely the most perfect appropriate use of it." Kendall smiled at him. "Did you have to skip class to come today?"

"No." He shook his head. "Though I would have for Cait's sake. She's doing better, isn't she?"

"Yes. Since your visit two weeks ago and catching up on her work, she's been delightful. Today will cinch it. Thanks for coming."

"Thank you for inviting me." He glanced at his watch. "Eat up. They should be here in ninety seconds."

She broke the remainder of the churro in half, shoved one piece towards Jade's mouth, and popped the other in hers.

They were still munching silently when their two groups ran up, out of breath, faces red and laughing.

Jade stood. "Everybody here? Okay, which way, Miss O'Reilly?"

She pointed and swallowed. The kids, chattering among themselves, started walking. He put a hand on her shoulder. "Wait. You look like the cat that ate the canary. There's a little sugar on your face."

His sunglasses were on again; she couldn't see his eyes. She patted her fingers across her mouth.

"No, here." He lightly brushed at her cheek with his thumb. "Should we run?"

Tony and Caitlin had turned back to wait for them. "Running's not allowed, Mr. Z.," the boy pointed out. "Hey, Ms. O'Reilly, can we sit in the front row? Cait's never done that."

"Definitely," she answered.

They hurried through the park, then down the steps in the enormous Shamu stadium to an empty section of bleachers where all twelve of them could sit near each other. All but Jade sat just as the introductory music began. The blue pool, full of thousands of gallons of saltwater, loomed at about eye level behind a transparent wall just a few rows in front of them.

"These seats are wet," he complained.

Kendall pulled him down beside her and laughed. "Shh." She buried the camera inside her knapsack, stuck the pack on her back, and turned her attention toward the show. From the corner of her eye she saw the curious expression on his face.

The giant black and white whales were always a breathtaking sight. The trainers in their red and black wet suits swam with them and rode on them. The children were captivated. They oohed and ahhed and laughed. When Shamu sailed out of the water directly in front of them and plopped on his side, sending a splash the size of a small lake that showered them all, they squealed in delight, Kendall the loudest of all.

Jade calmly wiped at the water dripping from his hair. "I liked the mime better."

She laughed, squeezing water from the bottom of her braid. The man definitely had good dad possibilities.

Three

Fighting down the urge to grab the notebook that lay open on the counter and throw it across the office, Kendall plunged fists into her skirt pockets and took a deep breath. "We can't wait any longer. I'm signing her out."

"Thornton will hit the roof," Joann, the school nurse, murmured.

Kendall ignored the comment. It was true, but not out of the ordinary. What was there to say? Just another official reprimand added to her file.

The two women stood in the front office near the counter that separated the outside door from the two secretaries' desks. Ruth sat at one. Kendall referred to her as the real secretary, unlike Eleanor, the make-excuses-for-Thornton executive secretary who didn't get involved with the children.

Ruth picked up her phone. "I'll try that church number again. Maybe they were just gone to lunch and forgot to turn on their answering machine."

Joann sighed. "Seems the whole world goes out to lunch, except school secretaries, nurses, and teachers." She turned on her heel. "I'll go check on our patient." Her soft, white oxfords made a comforting squishing sound as she headed down the short hall that led from the main office to hers.

"Hello!" Ruth said into the phone. "This is East Hills Elementary School. We're trying to locate Jeremiah Zukowski."

Had it been anyone but Ruth, Kendall would have interrupted and reached for the phone, preferring to do it herself. Ruth, though, was efficient and smart as a whip when it came to communicating with parents. She was a large woman and could easily intimidate when necessary.

Ruth caught Kendall's eye now as she spoke into the phone. "Father or son, either one."

Kendall nodded.

"I see. Well, this is an emergency. Caitlin has been quite ill all day, and our nurse suspects appendicitis." She listened for a moment, then gave the school number and hung up.

"Where is he?" Kendall's voice rose.

Eleanor stepped into the office from a back hallway that led to the teachers' workroom and principal's office. "Tch, tch. Calm down, Ms. O'Reilly. Getting upset certainly won't help matters." She removed her half-glasses from her thin face and let them dangle from a gold chain around her neck.

"Caitlin needs to go to the emergency room *now*," Kendall replied. "Where is Lewis? It's 2:10."

Eleanor shook her head. Not one short, steel gray hair moved from its lacquered position. "Dr. Thornton and the superintendent had other business after lunch. His office said they'll be back shortly."

Kendall's fingernails dug into her palms.

Ruth added, "The church is trying to reach Mr. Zukowski. They think he is still visiting at the hospital—"

"Scripps?"

"Yes. In Encinitas." She winked.

"Great! I'll meet him there. Will you explain it to him

52

please, Ruth? I'm leaving in ten minutes—"

"Now hold on," Eleanor interrupted. "You're not going anywhere in ten minutes. You cannot transport that student without her parent's or Dr. Thornton's permission."

"Eleanor, they're not available, and her appendix could burst." While still talking, she picked up a pen and filled in the blanks in the notebook on the counter. Date, time of departure, student's name and parent or guardian. She signed "Kendall O'Reilly." "We have enough responsible adults around here to give permission." She walked to the door. "I have to tell Greg a few things."

"Just what makes you think you can leave your class in the middle of the afternoon? That's not allowed without a sub."

Kendall opened the door and looked back over her shoulder. "They're doing a special art project in Greg's room. The student teacher is in there, along with three parent volunteers." She noticed Ruth giving her a thumbs-up behind Eleanor's back. "They won't miss me for the last forty-five minutes of school."

"We could get sued."

Kendall gently shut the door behind her.

It took her less than ten minutes to speak with Greg, grab her purse and blazer, and push Eleanor's concerns out of her mind. Caitlin hadn't been well when she first arrived that morning and had progressively gotten worse. She didn't complain much, but by lunchtime Kendall knew she needed to see the nurse. Joann thought her symptoms were classic appendicitis and wanted to send her home. There were only two names and numbers listed on the girl's emergency card—dad and grandpa, home and church. Apparently there was no grandmother. When neither of the Jeremiah Zukowskis could be found and Caitlin was crying, Kendall had decided to take responsibility.

Now she and Joann quickly tucked Caitlin into the backseat of her car and buckled the safety belt around her. Eleanor hovered, complaining that the pillows and blanket were school property and shouldn't leave the building. Kendall promised to launder them and have them back first thing in the morning, then slammed her door and drove out of the parking lot.

"It won't take long, Caitlin," she soothed. "Maybe fifteen minutes. Your dad'll be there, and then the doctor will figure out why it hurts so much. You'll be better real soon, honey."

"Thanks," she whispered.

Kendall headed toward the freeway. Jade hadn't been reached yet, but Ruth would explain the situation. For a moment the teacher worried about leaving her class in the hands of that incompetent student teacher. It was good timing that one mother in particular was volunteering this afternoon. End-of-the-day details would go more smoothly with her help. And she'd give the kids individual good-byes.

Kendall concentrated on freeway traffic and soon pulled into a parking spot near the emergency room door. As she helped Caitlin from the backseat, a tall, white-haired man hurried toward them.

"Caity-did!" He scooped the girl up in his arms.

"Grampy," she whimpered.

"You must be Kendall?" He turned to her as she closed the car door.

"Yes."

"I'm Jade's father. Sorry I can't shake your hand at the moment." His voice was low and rich, almost like a radio announcer's. "Thank you for bringing Caitlin."

"You're quite welcome, Mr. Zukowski."

"Jeremiah. Shall we get her inside?"

"Then you don't mind if I stay?" She hated to just leave

54

and not be with Caitlin, especially if she needed surgery.

"Please, I wish you would." They walked toward the door. Caitlin's face was buried in his shoulder. "I never was very good when the children were sick. I often visit patients, but that seems to be a different thing."

"I thought Jade was here."

"No." He smiled down at her, his eyes sparkling. "It's the name. It happened all the time with my father, and after that, with my son. The most amusing complications were when there were three of us in the same town." He chuckled.

His gracious mannerisms immediately put Kendall at ease. "Mr. Zukow—Jeremiah, did you talk to the school secretary?"

"Yes. Ruth, is it?"

"Mm hmm. Did she explain the situation? That I needed your permission to bring Caitlin here?"

"And you have it, dear lady. Or had it, *in absentia*. I just got off the phone with her when I came out to the parking lot and saw you drive up." The automatic doors swished open for them. "I am so thankful it wasn't necessary to prolong this another forty-five minutes or so. Aren't you, Caity-did?" He kissed his granddaughter's forehead.

Kendall saw tears on the girl's cheeks, but she was smiling. *What a fortunate child*, she thought. A pang of sadness shot through her. She wondered what it would be like to be cared for in such a way.

Kendall sat on the edge of the hospital bed, holding Caitlin's hand and brushing hair from her warm forehead. The girl's blonde curls had lost their luster, and her pale skin blended with the white sheets.

"It'll be okay pretty soon, honey," she soothed while fretting to herself about Jade's absence.

55

Jeremiah entered and sat down on the other side of the bed. "Well, Caity-did, I just talked to Aunt Elizabeth. This happened to her when she was twelve. She said to tell you that it'll hurt after surgery for a little while, but not as bad as now." He took her hand in his two large ones.

"When's Daddy coming?"

Jeremiah swallowed. "Soon. He was a couple of hours away, so when you're all done, he'll be here. The nurse said he can spend the night right here in this room with you. Let's pray, sweetheart." He closed his eyes.

Kendall closed hers also and listened to the gentle cadence of the man's strong voice.

"Dear Father, thank You for loving us. We ask that You would hold Caitlin close to Your heart right now. Take away the pain. Don't let her be afraid. Bring her daddy here soon. Bless the doctor as he works. And bless Kendall for understanding that she had to bring her here in time. We ask these things in Your Son's name, Amen."

Caitlin smiled. "Thanks, Grampy-do."

Jeremiah kissed her cheek.

Kendall leaned down and kissed her other one.

"Thanks, Ms. O'Reilly."

Kendall and Jeremiah carried coffee mugs to a table near a window in the hospital cafeteria. It was already dark outside. Some hospital staff and visitors were scattered throughout the large room, eating dinner.

"I am so grateful that you brought her, Kendall. The doctor said if we had waited any longer, there more than likely would have been complications." Jeremiah eyed her over his coffee cup. "You are a rare teacher indeed."

She shook her head. "It was obvious that something had to be done." *Even if Lewis reprimands me for it.* "Where's Jade?"

He sipped his coffee and didn't look at her. She noticed that his jaw was square-shaped like his son's.

"I'm sorry," she said. "It's not my business."

"No, no, it's all right." He set down his cup. "I've paged him. Hopefully he carried the pager and had his cell phone nearby. By now he's probably called home and gotten the message I left on the answering machine. Or called the church. So many ifs . . ." His voice trailed off. "Today is his wedding anniversary."

Kendall closed her eyes.

"He takes it especially hard. It's his third alone. So he went to the mountains. He planned to camp there over-night."

She patted his arm. "I'm sure he'll be here soon."

"Sometimes he hikes in three or four hours from where he parks his jeep. But I'm fairly certain he carried the pager. And he knows I wouldn't beep him unless it's an emergency." He smiled briefly. "It's not like me to feel so anxious. Thank you for keeping me company. Are you sure you don't care for any-thing to eat?"

"I'm sure. I'm a little anxious myself." The twisted aching in her stomach didn't leave any space for food.

"Well, all we can do now is wait through this. You prob-ably have other things to do. Friends to meet, papers to grade?"

Kendall shook her head. "It can wait." There was some-thing about the soft twinkle in his gray eyes that beckoned to her. "If you don't mind my staying?"

He smiled. "Not at all."

She looked down at her mug. "My mother died when I was eleven. It gives me a sort of kindred feeling with Caitlin, I guess, although I was a little older. I can't leave her right now. Alone." She glanced at him. "I mean, she has you, but . . ."

It was Jeremiah's turn to pat her arm. "Adam was incomplete without Eve. I always think there's a yawning chasm in situations when the feminine is not represented. We need you here, Kendall. I'm a widower too."

"I'm sorry."

"It's been ten years, and I miss her. But God has given me good friendships and work to do."

"Are you the minister at the church?"

"No. I was a senior pastor in La Crescenta, just north of Los Angeles. That's where most of Jade's growing up years were spent. I retired about five years ago and moved here to help out a friend. He's the pastor. The church is growing. I fill in wherever needed. Most of the time I'm the unofficial visitation pastor."

"That's why you were here at the hospital?"

He nodded. "Visiting some church members. I know my way around most of the hospitals and nursing homes in San Diego County. I was on my way out the door to head downtown when the church's call came. Caitlin was going home with her new friend Hannah for a while this afternoon."

"I'm so glad we caught you."

"I am too. Tell me about your teaching. How long have you been doing it? My daughter, Caitlin's Aunt Elizabeth, teaches in Phoenix."

They chatted through two cups of coffee.

"Well, shall we go back upstairs?" Jeremiah suggested.

Kendall walked comfortably at his side through the hallways. She had never met a man as gracious as he was. Back in the waiting lounge they sat in mauve upholstered chairs, facing each other across a magazine-strewn coffee table. No one else lingered in the cozy room. Lamps cast a warm glow on the soft watercolor paintings hanging on the walls.

She laid her purse and blazer on the chair next to hers.

"Jade told me that he's studying for his Master's in counseling."

"Yes. He's quite gifted in communicating with adolescents. I think his choice is a wise one. It suits him. Did he tell you about the camp?"

"A little."

"It became too much for him after Deborah died. Last summer he was able to sell his share to a young couple. He started commuting to Westminster and looking for a job in this area. When our youth pastor resigned, I recommended Jade for the position."

"He's the youth pastor?" She wouldn't have guessed this, though she wasn't sure why. Perhaps he wasn't square enough to fit a pastor's role.

"Well, temporarily anyway. They want to go through the process of interviewing applicants, but that takes time. The other man left suddenly, and Jade was available and willing to do it on an interim basis. Housing was no problem because I had space in my condominium. My wife and I bought it almost fifteen years ago for our retirement. She wanted to be sure all the children and grandchildren could visit at the same time."

Kendall thought Jade's situation sounded rather indefinite for a thirty-something with a child. "So, he's one of the applicants?"

"Oh, yes." Jeremiah nodded. "He'd like to be hired permanently. It's a job that fits him like a glove, and he can take quite a few classes while he does it."

She remembered Caitlin's response to her grandfather. "I would imagine your granddaughter enjoys living with you."

His eyes twinkled as he smiled. "She's a delight to me. I know their stay is temporary, but I'm thankful for it."

"I'm sorry I didn't meet you when she first started in my class."

"I am too. Her first day of school coincided with a number of urgent things that needed to be attended to, and Lewis Thornton offered to take care of her introductions, so—" He shrugged. "A mother wouldn't have been so inattentive."

Kendall shook her head in agreement. "You know Lewis then?" she asked, curious about the principal's personal life.

"Yes, he's—"

"Dad!" Jade burst into the room. "Where's Cait?"

Jeremiah stood. "She's fine, son. She's in surgery."

Jade covered his face with his hands.

"It's all right, Jade. She's fine. It won't be long now. Sit down."

Instead he ran his fingers through his hair, hooked them behind his neck, and paced. He wore jeans, a plaid flannel shirt, and a thick, beige vest. His face crumpled in a look of rage as he muttered, "I can't believe this! O God, help us!"

Kendall hoped he wouldn't jam a fist through the wall.

"Son, it's all right. Take a deep breath." Jeremiah laid a hand on his shoulder and steered him to a chair. "Sit down."

He sat and took a deep breath, leaning forward with his arms on his knees. Then he saw her. "What are you doing here?" He looked up at his father. "What is *she* doing here? This room is for family only. She's not family. She's just a teacher."

"Jade . . . Kendall is concerned. She brought—"

"Oh, I know. Lewis told me." He glowered at her. "He left word for me to call him."

Stunned beyond words, Kendall could only look back at him.

"Don't look so innocent, *Ms.* O'Reilly. You brought Cait here without permission." His eyes narrowed. "Without permission you took over responsibility for *my* daughter. Who do

60

you think you are? You're her teacher, not her parent, or even a friend!"

She stood then, reaching for her purse and jacket.

"Jade!" his father admonished.

She passed the two men, hurried out the door, and made a quick left turn. She didn't think of where she was going. She didn't really see where she was going. As if on their own accord, her legs simply carried her away from that twisted face spewing the barrage of insults at her. Through a red haze she spotted an exit sign and found a stairwell. What floor were they on? It didn't really matter. Her legs wouldn't stop long enough for an elevator anyway.

By the time she stepped outside, her heart raced from the exercise rather than from the anger. It helped. She gulped in the cool night air and looked around. This wasn't the entrance she had come through earlier this afternoon. Where was the car?

She pulled on her blazer, unsnapped her purse, and rummaged for the keys in the dim light shining through the glass doorway.

"Kendall . . ."

She looked up to see Jeremiah walking through the door.

"I apologize—"

She held up a hand. "Jeremiah, I don't allow my students to make excuses for each other. Please don't try to apologize for your adult son. He's terribly upset. I know I shouldn't take it personally."

He stared at her a moment. "Well, may I walk you to your car?"

"Please. I don't have a clue where it is."

He smiled and took her elbow. They walked along a sidewalk. "You're shaking."

She waved a hand in dismissal. "I'm a little upset."

"You did the right thing, remember that, and I will always be grateful to you." They rounded the corner of the building and walked down a few steps toward a parking lot. "If I may, I'd like to say just one thing to explain Jade's overreaction."

Kendall didn't reply. She didn't really need to hear anything. She didn't want to get any more involved in this situation. Now that Caitlin's dad had arrived, she could leave. Not that the girl was in the best of hands, but at least they were *family* hands and they were available. Between the two of them they should be able to cope with events. Caitlin probably wouldn't know too much until morning anyway. Maybe her aunt would come then.

"Jeremiah, I don't need to know any more. Jade's right—I'm just her teacher."

"All right—we'll leave it be. Is there any chance—please tell me if I'm asking too much—is there any chance you could come visit Caitlin at home? I know it would mean a great deal to her."

"Are you sure it would be all right with her dad?"

"I'm sure."

"Well," she smiled, "I do always make home visits in this sort of situation."

He returned her smile. "I thought you might. Thank you."

Kendall rang the doorbell. She noticed there was no decorative wreath hanging on the front door of the Zukowski condominium. No potted plants along the flagstone front steps either.

She looked around. It was an old group of buildings, but nicely kept with a profusion of large-leafed subtropical plants and bushy oleander dividing the small grassy front yards, creating the illusion of private spaces. Like her apartment area, tall eucalyptus trees formed a border along the avenue. Their scent mingled with that of scrubby pines in the warm late afternoon, a welcome leftover from a rainy winter season. She noticed a large bunch of yellow daffodils blooming at the far left corner of the yard, along the base of the beige, stucco wall, and wondered if Jeremiah's wife had planted those long ago.

The door opened, and a wave of rock music rolled out. Jade stood in his stocking feet and stared at her. A rosy tinge deepened his tan face.

"Hi!" she offered with a tight smile. If he asked again what she was doing here, this would be difficult.

"Uhh, hi." He wore jeans and a navy blue T-shirt with *Chargers* across the front in large gold lettering. The short sleeves were rolled up.

Remembering Maxine's comment about his being a member of the football team, she smiled to herself. "I have assignments." She held up her armload of books. He made no response. "For Caitlin."

"Oh." He glanced over his shoulder. "That music—" He turned to go, then called back, "Come in."

She stepped inside, pulling the door shut behind her, and noticed steps directly to her right. Jade strode to a bookcase situated along a wall that formed the banister of the staircase.

Beige-colored carpet covered the steps and the floor of the room. Along the same wall as the front door was a fireplace; a comfortable-looking couch, loveseat, and chairs were arranged around it. A sliding glass door covered much of the far wall. Toward the back of the room was a rectangular dining table and chairs. Beyond that was a counter and open kitchen area.

The music faded into background noise.

"DC Talk," Jade said.

"Dee cee what?"

He lifted a shoulder. "A group the kids like."

A pastor and rock music? "I just talked to your father. He said it was all right to stop by now."

"He did?" He hooked his thumbs in his back pockets. "He left for the store. Some of the youth group kids are coming over soon. They eat a lot . . ." He stopped talking.

"I won't stay. Here." She held the pile of books out toward him. "It's self-explanatory—"

"Cait will want to see you." He bit the bottom corner of his lip and glanced sideways, toward the fireplace.

She let the silence grow awkward. He had dug this rut, and he could very well pull himself out. He wasn't a fifth grader.

"About the other night . . ." He made eye contact now. "I was out of line, Kendall. I'm sorry. I didn't mean what I said."

She let her breath go and realized she had been holding it. "That certainly is good to hear." She smiled.

"After I settled down, Dad explained the situation." He shook his head. "The way Lewis phrased things, and not knowing if Cait was okay, and being stuck on the freeway . . . I'm sorry—I'm making excuses, but there are none. Let's go check on the patient. Give me those." He relieved her of the books and bounded up the stairs, two at a time.

The man could be charming. Kind of a grown-up version of Tony's charm, not turned on just to get his way, but genuinely thoughtful.

"I was going to call you." Jade smiled over his shoulder at her from the top.

"Yeah, right. Next year?"

"I couldn't find your number?"

"I'm in the phone book under O'Reilly, K."

"Uhh, no answer?"

"Functioning answering machine."

"Soon then." He headed to the open door on the left.

"Chicken."

"Hey, Cait! Look who's here!" He stood aside to let her enter first.

"Ms. O'Reilly!" Caitlin grinned from what looked like a fluffy sea of purple. She wore a grape-colored sweatshirt and pants. A lavender comforter covered the single bed she sat on. Surrounding her was a cluster of pillows in various shapes, sizes, and shades of purple. The wall behind her was a pale lavender. A colorful mountain of stuffed animals sat at the foot of the bed.

"Caitlin!" Kendall strode to the bedside and gave her a hug.

"She brought you some work, Cait." Jade set the books on the desk beside the bed.

The girl groaned and leaned back amidst the pillows. Her skin was still pale, but her blonde curls were shiny again, and her eyes sparkled.

"Aww," Kendall sympathized, "you don't have to do it today. I can just show it to you, okay?"

"Okay. Wanna see my scar?"

"Do you mind if I don't?"

Jade laughed. "Now who's chicken? It's a pretty cool scar, huh, Cait?"

"Yep."

"Uhh, that's okay." She glanced around the large bedroom. There was a bookcase and an armchair near the dresser. "Your room is beautiful."

"Thanks. I love it." Her eyes widened. "It's the *master* bedroom, and I have my own bathroom."

"Her grandpa wanted me to have it, and I wanted him to keep it." Jade smiled. "So we thought we'd call it the *missy*

65

room and give it to Cait. She's already planning her first big slumber party."

"Well, I'd say you have a pretty special dad and grandpa."

"Nope." Jade leaned past Kendall to ruffle his daughter's hair. "She's the special one. I'll let you two get to work."

"You can stay."

"Do I have to?" he asked in a serious tone.

Caitlin giggled. "He's afraid of you, Ms. O'Reilly."

"Well, Mr. Zukowski, you're not required to stay at this time. However, I do expect you to help with this. I can't be here every day."

"Why not?" Caitlin asked.

"Actually, the school provides a tutor who will come—"

"Instead of you?" The girl's mouth trembled.

"Normally." *But she's not in the "normally" category.* "But if you'd rather not have a stranger, I can do it." *She doesn't need another stranger or disruption.* Kendall looked up at Jade. "Is that all right with you? I could come maybe Tuesday, Wednesday, and Thursday, either at 4 or 7-ish. Will she be out about three weeks?"

He nodded. "This is asking too much. If there are regular tutors—"

"It's not too much. You're only a few miles from my place, and the school's between us." Kendall touched his arm and turned him toward the door. "Scoot. You're interrupting."

"Yaayy!" Caitlin clapped.

Sometime later Kendall sat at Caitlin's desk next to the bed and eyed the 5 by 7 framed photograph while the girl did a few math problems.

"That's my mom."

Kendall smiled at her. "I thought so. She's pretty. Her eyes are soft brown like yours. And her face is shaped the same." Round cheeks. Dimpled chin.

"She had blonde hair when she was little too, but then it got brown."

What had Jeremiah called her? *Deborah*. She certainly was attractive. Her hair was very short. She looked athletic. In the photo she leaned against a pine tree, and sunlight filtered through to her face. "Do you have your dad's curls?"

Caitlin nodded. "Mom was real tall, so I probably will be too. She came up to Daddy's nose, not like you. And she was stronger too."

"Stronger?"

"Yeah, she climbed the rocks all the time, just like Daddy. She wasn't big like him, but her leg muscles were just as strong. She showed all the teenagers how to climb." Caitlin rolled her eyes. "She *didn't* work in the kitchen."

"Did someone else do that at your camp?"

"Yeah. Cassie and Nate did that. Chuck and Tina helped with the climbing and hiking. We all helped keep the cabins fixed up. Mom was a teacher too."

"Really?"

"Yeah. She taught the Bible studies. Daddy mostly talked to the kids, not like a teacher."

"Oh." Kendall felt saddened. They sounded like such a wonderful family, even if they did live in the mountains and climb rocks for a living. Why did it have to happen?

Caitlin leaned over and rummaged through a desk drawer. She sat up and laid a pile of papers in Kendall's lap. "I'm sorry, Ms. O'Reilly. I ripped it."

She picked through torn bits and pieces of pink construction paper. "The valentine?"

"I ate the candy hearts." Two big tears rolled down her cheeks.

"Oh, sweetie." She slid onto the bed next to Caitlin and put her arms around the girl. Every year Kendall made personalized Valentines for her students. Evidently, Caitlin didn't like hers for some reason . . .

Valentine's Day and the party. That was the week she was absent and Jade had come to school and said the girl didn't like her. "What happened?"

She shrugged and sniffled. "My mom used to make me valentines."

Kendall hugged her tightly. She remembered an acquaintance of her mother's attempting to take over the piano lessons. The woman's stern face appeared in her mind. Pages torn from a piano music book strewn on the floor, beneath the piano bench. Nobody could teach her like her mother. Nobody would. "Well, I'd sure be mad enough to rip up a valentine too." A tear slid from the outer corner of Kendall's eye. She brushed it away and kissed the top of the mass of blonde curls.

"Really?"

"Really. If I would have known, baby, I never would have made it. Your mom loved you like nobody else can. That valentine just made you miss her a whole lot more, because I was trying to do what she did." No wonder Caitlin despised her. "It was something special between the two of you and I interfered with that."

"You're not mad?"

"No, not at all. It's okay. Don't worry about it."

Someone cleared his throat. They looked up to see Jade standing in the doorway. "The kids are here. Do you want to come down, Cait?"

"Yeah! Can Ms. O'Reilly stay?"

"Well—"

Thunderous footsteps could be heard approaching. Two teenage girls brushed past Jade. "Caitlin!" They rushed to her with arms open wide.

Kendall moved out of their way to see a boy and another girl enter.

"Hey, it's Ms. O'Reilly!"

"Nick? Susie? My goodness, you're all grown up."

"Steve's here too. And Pam and Missy—remember, from Mr. Jones's class?"

"Sure. They came in for reading. Great! What are you all now—sophomores?"

"Juniors."

"Juniors? No way!"

Nick headed to Caitlin. "Wanna ride downstairs, squirt?"

She laughed and grabbed the back of his neck for a piggyback ride. "We're having spaghetti, Ms. O'Reilly. Stay, please?"

"Well—"

"Oh, yeah, you gotta stay," the teens chimed in as they moved through the door like a herd of cattle.

Jade still stood by the door, his brows pulled together in that frown that was becoming familiar. Maybe the charm was just for certain moments after all.

Kendall turned and gathered the school books and papers into a pile along with the valentine pieces on the desk. "We got a good start. I'll come by Tuesday. Does 4 or 7 work best for you?"

"Make it 7. I'll be in class, but Dad'll be here."

"All right." She walked past him. "Good-bye."

At the bottom of the steps she was bombarded by five of her former students, all speaking at once.

Jade's father stood behind them and announced in his rich voice, "Ms. O'Reilly, your presence is requested at this gourmet dinner."

"Requested?" one of the boys said. "It's demanded!"

What fun to visit with these kids! If it weren't for that

frown following her down the steps—

"I'm sure," Jade's low voice was at her shoulder, "Ms. O'Reilly has other things to do."

How would you know? She bit her tongue.

"Nah, she never used to have a life without us, right, Ms. O'Reilly?"

Stevie said that. He had been a Tony. She knew he didn't mean it disrespectfully. The truth was, he was right. Interacting with students was her life. She smiled. "You're right, Stevie—oh, I bet you're Steve now! But I'd be in the way here. This is your group—"

"I think they want you to stay." Jade laid his hands on her shoulders and nudged her aside so he could walk around her. "You won't be in the way," he added quietly.

She didn't think his eyes meant it, but she wasn't about to pass up a meal with her kids because of someone who wouldn't say what he really meant.

Jeremiah cooked the pasta, but everyone else had brought spaghetti fixings. The dinner was informal, with the group of eighteen teenagers eating wherever they could find a seat. Kendall sat outside on the patio with some of her former students and caught up on their lives.

After dinner she helped Jeremiah clean up in the kitchen while everyone else sat at the far end of the front room. Although the entire area was open, the kitchen was separated by distance and a counter with cupboards above it. So she and the older man were able to visit without disturbing the meeting.

She watched Jade with the kids. The energy she had sensed in his presence seemed almost palpable now. He was in nonstop motion. If he sat, it was only for a few moments with his arms gesturing or legs bouncing. His strong, tanned facial features were expressive.

"He's talking about rock climbing," Jeremiah observed. "He's taking the group in a couple of weeks. Can you tell it's a passion with him?"

Kendall nodded. "Mm hmm. How long was he involved with the camp?"

"Since he was sixteen."

"Sixteen?"

Jeremiah chuckled and dried his hands on a towel. "More or less. He was always an energetic, inquisitive boy. By the time he was a teenager, his mother and I couldn't keep pace with him. We heard about Lion's Trail Camp. They advertised wilderness challenge and confidence-building. We sent him for a month. He learned all about backpacking, camping, and rock climbing and gained the self-esteem and sense of responsibility he needed. It was as if he'd found his place in this world. He met Deborah there that summer too.

"The owners took him under their wing, hired him for weekends and summers. They encouraged him to go to college. He and Deb got married while they were in school, then gradually took over the camp. Eventually they were able to buy it with another couple."

"What did he major in?"

"Physical education and history." He poured two cups of coffee and handed one to her. "It's decaf. He actually received a teaching degree, although he didn't plan on using it. His heart was in the camp and working with teens there."

"Is his heart still there?"

Jeremiah was silent for a moment. "Well, perhaps a part of it. The part that includes Deborah. It really was a team effort. He couldn't replace her or do it—physically or emotionally, especially since Caitlin came along—without her. No, that chapter is closed for him. He'll keep going to the mountains

71

though, sometimes with the teens, sometimes alone when he needs to sort through things. Do you mind cutting these brownies?"

"No." She accepted a knife from him. "Caitlin seems to be part of the group."

"They're good with her. As far back as she can remember, she's been sitting in on planning sessions like this."

A shrill whistle pierced through the condominium, followed by a chant of "O-Rei-*lly!* O-Rei-*lly!*"

"I think you're being paged." Jeremiah smiled.

Kendall gave him a puzzled look and stepped around the counter. "For what?"

Jade motioned to her, and she walked over to the group. One of the girls stood up and said, "Have a seat."

"Ms. O'Reilly," Steve said, "will you chaperone our trip? Please?"

"Please, please," others chorused.

"Camping and rock climbing? Uhh, I don't do camping and rock—" She glimpsed Jade's grin and clamped her mouth shut. *"I don't do bus rides."* But this is different! "I can't—"

"Why not?"

"I—"

"It's just from Friday about noon 'til Sunday morning," Jade explained. "The kids have midterms and get out of school early. Some parents are going, and I have two friends who'll help with the climb. We need one more adult, and the vote is unanimous—they want you. It's a free trip to the mountains . . ." He raised his eyebrows, waiting for an answer.

"Can I think about it?"

There was a loud groan from the kids.

"That's not like you, Ms. O'Reilly," Susie, one of her students, said. "You were always up for anything." Her lower lip protruded in an exaggerated pout.

"Yeah." Pam added, following her friend's lead. "Guess you just like fifth graders."

Missy added, "You used to be my all-time favorite teacher."

Kendall burst out laughing. It was so exciting to see her little girls grown into lovely young women. "I can't cook, and I can't deal with bugs or snakes—"

Jade laid a strong hand on top of her head. "Rule number one, we never say 'I can't' about anything."

She looked up at him with a frown. He was sounding too much like her.

Jade walked beside her through the darkened neighborhood to her car parked a block down the street. "Kendall, I hope you don't change your mind."

"If Thornton will get me a sub for one day, I guess I won't renege."

"That shouldn't be a problem. His son is part of the group."

"Really? I don't know him."

"He was the dark-haired boy with glasses, average height. Anyway, once he tells Lewis about the whole group wanting you to come, he'll understand."

"Are we talking about the same Lewis Thornton?" At her car, she stepped into the street and unlocked the door. "Does he go to your church then?"

"Has for years, I guess. That's how Dad knows him."

"I see." She looked at him across the low car. He had his elbows on it and was leaning forward. "Jade, is it all right that I go even though I'm not part of your church?"

He shrugged a shoulder. "My friends aren't part of it. They're necessary for the climb. I'd say, from the kids' response, that you'll be an integral part of the experience."

She shook her head. "I don't know the first thing about camping."

"You run."

"How'd you know that? And what does that have to do with anything?"

She could see a smile cross his face in the dim light. "Greg told me. Or was it Maxine? Anyway, what it means is that you're probably physically fit for hiking and climbing. Climbing is done mainly with the legs. And it's not just about the physical anyway. The kids respect you, and your input will help me encourage them. I'm not sure what to expect from the parents who are coming."

"Whose idea was this?"

"Your friends."

She smiled. "I hadn't thought of them in that way before, but I suppose that's true. Now that they're growing up, we can become friends. They were in class my second year here."

"They think your first name is Ms."

She giggled.

"That's what I need on this adventure."

"What?"

"Your giggle."

She eyed him for a moment in silence, thinking how to best phrase her concern. "Well, don't give me such a hard time then."

"Hey, I apologized—"

"I'm not talking about at the hospital. That one I understand. I'm talking about tonight in Caitlin's room. I don't think it's my imagination that you seemed opposed to me staying for dinner."

Jade drummed his fingertips on the car top.

In the nighttime hush Kendall heard distant freeway

traffic. The scent of eucalyptus played tag with a faint, salty, damp ocean breeze. The fingers stopped their drumming.

"I don't know . . ." He rested his chin in his hands. "Seeing you sitting there with Cait, holding her . . ." He closed his eyes. "For a split second her mother was back and everything was okay. But she's not, and I reacted like it's your fault that I thought she was."

Like Caitlin and her valentine, she thought. She definitely didn't want to be in the middle of this situation. She was just her teacher, and that's where she belonged.

He looked at her again. "I can't be a mom to her, and that makes me furious."

"But you're there, Jade. Just stay there. With her. You know what I mean?"

He nodded slightly.

Kendall opened her door. "I have to go."

In a few quick strides he was beside her, then closed the door as she climbed inside. He tapped on the window. She turned the key and lowered the window.

"What size shoe do you wear?"

"Seven. Why?"

"I'll find some hiking boots for you. Bet you don't have any?"

She shook her head and started the car.

"Thanks, Kendall." He rapped his knuckles on the door and stood back.

She gave him a thumbs-up sign and drove away.

Jade stood transfixed in the open doorway of the classroom. The kids had been dismissed a while ago, and the room was empty except for Kendall sitting at the piano. Her music permeated the air.

He watched her play. She was turned slightly sideways

from him. Her eyes were totally focused on her fingers skimming across the keys.

Her wheat-colored hair was in its usual braid, and loose strands hung about her cheek. The pearl earrings covered her small earlobes. She wore a long, pale yellow sweater over a yellow print skirt. Her glasses were on.

The music slowed now. It sounded familiar. Music Appreciation 101? The sad, haunting melody filled him like music seldom had.

The tempo sped up again. Now her fingers were flying up and down the keyboard. There was a carefree feeling with it. He felt an excitement in the notes that raced about the room.

She slammed her palms onto the keys. "Oh!"

"Bravo!" Jade clapped loudly.

"Oh!" she exclaimed again, jumping in surprise.

"I didn't mean to scare you."

"My fault." She spun around on the bench to face him. "I should lock the door when I do this. Come in." Her face was flushed, and she was out of breath.

He sat down at a desk near her and set on the floor the pair of boots he'd carried over his arm. "For your hiking pleasure, Ms. O'Reilly." He untied the laces. "I couldn't find any climbing shoes, but these will work for what we're doing."

"That was fast service. Didn't I just see you last night?"

"I have to make sure I lock you into this. Did you get a sub?"

"Well, I put in a request for one." She slipped off her right flat and tried on the boot. "It's kind of big."

"You need to wear thick socks. I have some you can use."

"How's Caitlin?" She put her shoe back on.

"A little tired out today, but she's doing homework now and wants to see you tomorrow."

"Okay." She brushed bangs off her forehead. The white,

pencil-line scar near the hairline made a pronounced contrast with her fair skin.

"So what were you doing?"

"What—? Oh, the music?"

He nodded. "It sounded familiar."

"Beethoven's *Moonlight Sonata*." She looked frazzled, not her usual calm and collected self.

"Would I know that?"

She smiled. "The first movement is a familiar tune." She hummed a few bars.

"Right. It was great. What were you playing before that?"

"How long were you standing there? It was probably Bach's 'Jesu, Joy of Man's Desiring.' You may recognize that from church."

"And what was that fast stuff right before you quit?"

"That was still the Beethoven sonata. The third movement."

He thought she was lightening up. "Do you do that often?" He wiggled his fingers across an imaginary keyboard. "Play real fast, then smack your hands down?"

She giggled. "Just when a student teacher drives me up the wall."

"You look like you need to talk."

"What I need to do is run, but I just won't have the time today." She winked. "Spent too much time with a bunch of teenagers last night, but at least I got dinner out of it. And now," she sighed, "I have to figure out how to undo what my little helper did today."

"What did she do?"

"Oh, Jade, you don't want to hear this."

"Sure, I do."

"What is this, research for one of your counseling classes?"

He heard the sarcasm in her voice and studied those bright blue eyes for a trace of trust. There didn't seem to be any. "No. I'm just wondering how a student teacher can chase away Pollyanna."

Her eyebrows shot up; she looked perplexed. She carried the boots to her desk, keeping her back to him. "I don't think she cares about the children. There's no passion in her. But she will graduate and she will find a job and—oh!" She plopped onto her chair, shuffled through a messy pile of papers, and held one up. "Look at this. This—*this* is her lesson plan." Her soft voice rose. "I don't care so much that I can't read it, or even that there's no point to it, but she didn't put any flesh on it. There was no feeling, no warmth, no breath when she did it!"

Jade glanced at the indecipherable pencil scribblings. "Can't you teach her?"

Kendall removed her glasses and rubbed her eyes. "How to love the kids? Not in a million years."

"Has she been here long?"

"Only two weeks. Seems like two *years*."

He leaned across her desk until she had to look him in the face. He smiled. "Maybe you'll rub off on her."

She blinked. "Well, I will teach her how to write a lesson plan, and I will teach her that she is never, ever to laugh at a child. Those are unacceptable in my classroom." Kendall bit her lower lip in thought for a moment, then smiled. "And if she doesn't catch on next week, she can sit in a corner for the next nine. I can do that. Because I will not allow her to jeopardize my fifth graders' well-being and development."

"Bravo!"

She gave his shoulder a playful punch. "Thanks. What do I owe you for this therapy session, Dr. Z.?"

He straightened. "How about a climb?"

"Deal." She stretched her hand across the desk.

He shook it, noticing its smallness and how slender the long fingers felt.

"I don't have a clue as to what I just signed up for."

"Three-fourths of the kids don't either. You'll do fine. We take inexperienced people all the time. Did you get the information sheet?"

"No."

"I'll get one to you, so you know what to pack. We're going to Hemet, just a couple hours' drive. It's not quite a Class 3 climb—" He saw the vacant look on her face. "That's simple enough for beginners, but we can learn how to use gear on it. And there's nearby camping. El Capitan it's not."

"That enormous vertical block in Yosemite?" The vacant look was replaced by one of horror. She shuddered. "I hope not. So, what's the attraction? Why do you do it?"

"What? Climb?"

She nodded.

Jade turned around a student desk chair and straddled it. "Got a few hours?"

Kendall smiled. "How about the short version? And what is it about it that helps you relate to teenagers? I'm guessing that's why you take them."

"You're right." He thought a moment. "Why did you agree, just now, to climb?"

"Umm, I have a bad habit of agreeing to a challenge without thinking." She paused. "That's probably it, the challenge."

"Exactly. With climbing, it's always a challenge. You're forced to stretch yourself, to push yourself beyond self-imposed limits. Teens need that. It's an adventure, a living on the edge that doesn't involve drugs or alcohol or whatever. I climb to get away from myself and to find myself.

It works that way with the kids too. They find the stuff they're made of. If they don't make it to the summit, they learn there was success in what they did do."

"Fantastic! Then again, it makes me feel inadequate." She began stacking the mess of papers on her desk into neat piles.

"How's that?" He noticed her face was almost perfectly heart-shaped. The mouth that so easily smiled was proportionate, not too full or narrow, the nicely shaped lips defined with a hint of pink. Nothing like Deb's mouth, full and generous . . . He mentally braced himself for the ache that would inevitably roar through him now. *Take every thought captive*—

"Well, I don't spend any time with teens. I'm not sure how well I communicate with them."

Her humility amazed him. He had watched—what was it, four, no, five—former students rally around her as if she were a superheroine. The impression she had made on them at a young age was staying with them through adolescence. They had made it obvious that they still communicated with her. "Kendall, they're just a little bigger than fifth graders."

Those blue eyes bore into him now. They sparkled like sunshine dancing on the ocean. "But they think about different things now. They're driving and dating and studying chemistry—"

Jade held up a hand. "Whoa! Didn't you drive and date and study chemistry?"

"Well—"

"You don't have to be a heavy-duty counselor. Like I said last night, just be their friend. And giggle."

"Okay, okay."

He stood. "Good. Pollyanna is back and I can go."

She followed him toward the door. "Why do you call me that?"

"For the obvious reason. You are eternally optimistic.

You see the best in everyone, in every situation." He stopped at the door. "The old movie was a favorite of Cait's and her mom."

"Oh." She stuck her hands in the pockets of her skirt. "It's just so odd. Close friends call me that, but you and I only met a few weeks ago."

He marveled again at her lack of self-awareness. "Guess that makes me a close friend." He grinned. "Do you know you're like that?"

"It's just me, so—" She shrugged. "I don't notice."

She was a gem. "God certainly made you one special woman. And I am glad Cait's in your class."

Kendall looked down at her foot and shoved a scrap of paper with it. "Tell her I'll see her tomorrow and not to worry about finishing everything I left."

"Are you sure it's not too much of an imposition on your time?"

"My goodness, no." She smiled up at him now. "She's a priority for me."

"Dad told me about the loss of your mother. I'm sorry."

"Thank you. It does give me an empathy."

"Well, thank you. Good-bye."

"Bye. Thanks for the boots." She closed the door behind him.

Jade walked along the sidewalk between the buildings toward the parking lot. He had never met anyone like Kendall. She wasn't like Deb in the least. Physically, she was inches shorter and much slighter of build. There seemed to be a fragility about her. Since she was a runner, though, she probably had the endurance for a short climb.

There was an engaging liveliness, a spontaneity about her, a contrast to Deb's more solid, bold ways. There was a similarity, however, in her selfless giving to young people, in her relating to them. He suspected that Kendall drew from deep within herself, unlike Deb who had depended on Christ for strength. *Amazing,* he thought again.

Dear Father, show her the limits of her human goodness and ability. Bring her into Your family. In Jesus' name, I thank You.

Four

"Remember when Jimmy got locked in the courthouse bathroom?"

They roared and clapped their hands as Kendall, Susie, Missy, Pam, Steve, Nick, and a few others enjoyed the countless remember-whens. Tears dampened the girls' cheeks, they laughed so hard. Steve rolled off the log he was sitting on and kicked his feet in the air.

Nick burped. "Oops, excuse me! Too many hot dogs."

"Hey, Kendall, remember how Nick used to barf all the time?" Steve asked.

She nodded. "That's the year I learned to never leave home without a plastic bag."

"Remember Snoot the snake?"

They roared again.

"Especially the time he got loose! Ms. O. spent the entire afternoon standing on her desk."

"Not the entire afternoon!" she protested.

"And then Jones came in, and he climbed on top of the piano!"

"It was Mrs. Carothers who finally caught it."

Jade sat down on the log next to Steve. "Sounds like fifth grade with Ms. O'Reilly was quite a year."

"Oh, it was," agreed Pam. "Be glad Caitlin has her for a teacher. She's the best ever."

Nick added, "I still remember state capitals and how to spell *conscience*."

"Thanks." Kendall smiled. "You were an extra-fun group." She scooted the short beach chair closer to the bonfire and hugged her knees to her chest. Her jacket and the fire were fairly warm, but any other heat had fled with the sun two hours ago. "This is a first—reminiscing with students. Doesn't seem like enough time has gone by for this to be happening."

Missy leaned toward her and winked. "Guess that makes you feel really old, huh?"

Kendall gave the girl's cap a playful yank. "Didn't I tell you I was only sixteen when I graduated from college?" She caught Jade's incredulous glance. "Not really!"

"I don't think Kendall will ever be old," Pam observed.

"If I had three Jimmys in one class I would grow ancient overnight."

They laughed.

"Anybody want s'mores?" Nick asked. "I see marshmallows on those sticks."

The teens jumped up and hurried to the picnic tables where the food was served. Jade sat in Missy's vacated chair, next to Kendall. "Snoot the snake?"

"It was Jimmy's." She giggled and rolled her eyes. "This is so much fun, Jade. I'm glad I came."

"Not afraid of teenagers anymore?"

"I never said—" She saw the fire reflected in his eyes and recognized the candor without a hint of mockery. "No. They're just bigger fifth graders. With a lot more understanding."

"Right. Did you get in on the demonstration this afternoon?"

She shook her head. She had helped the mothers organize the food and supervise the dads as they completed what the kids had started—setting up the tents. "I was told I would sit in some sort of loopy seat and a rope would be tied to it. That I should put all my weight on my legs and balance with my arms. And even though my fingernails aren't long, they would probably get chipped to nubbins. Did I miss anything?"

He chuckled. "Not a thing. You're a quick learner."

"You're absolutely perfect with these kids, Jade." She had watched him instructing them, joking with them. They obviously respected him, and not just because he was bigger than any of them. His dad had been right about his gift of communicating with adolescents. "I hope you get the job."

"Dad must have told you?"

She nodded. "When will you know?"

He shrugged a shoulder and poked at the fire with a long stick. "They put out the word last month. They'll probably wait another six weeks or so. They've had a couple requests for applications, I guess."

She couldn't understand why they didn't hire him on the spot. "What are they looking for that you don't have?"

"Well, my future Master's in counseling is an asset, but it's in the future. They can wait for the cream of the crop. It's a large, well-respected, well-organized church." He smiled at her. "Close to the ocean too. If someone with more education or experience is interested, maybe someone with a more stable family situation, they'll want to talk to him."

"Who's 'they'?"

"A committee, a cross-section of the congregation. Lewis is head of it.

"Lewis Thornton?"

85

He nodded. "My guess is he's—how should I put it?—on the thorough side."

"He is that. I would imagine the quality time you spend with his son will score you some extra points."

Nick stepped over to them. "Here you go, Ms. O."

He handed her a graham cracker with squished marshmallow oozing out the sides. "Umm," she said, "the chocolate is melting just right. Thanks."

"Want one, Jade?" The boy squatted on the ground behind them.

"No, thanks."

"Guess I'll have to eat it then. Did he tell you he climbed El Cap, Ms. O.?" He bit into his s'more.

Kendall swallowed and stared at Jade's profile. "You did?"

"When he was nineteen," Nick mumbled through his mouthful, "with that other guy Jerry over there."

"Nineteen? Nineteen! No way. Did you really and truly?"

Still facing the fire, he glanced at her from the corner of his eye and murmured, "It was just there, this rock of all rocks."

Goodness, she thought, *no wonder his parents couldn't keep up with him.* She could imagine him an energetic child, like Tony, but beyond that he and his head-on-collision approach to life frightened her. Maybe teens needed that type of challenging personality. Maybe that's why teens didn't interest her and did in fact frighten her. It was all so . . . so out of control.

He was grinning at her now. "You going to eat that?"

"What?" She saw the s'more dangling from her fingers, shook her head, and held it out to him.

He accepted it and popped the whole piece into his mouth.

Guitar music came from across the fire. The chatting groups quieted down, and the musician, one of Jade's friends, started singing. Kendall didn't recognize the song, but others joined in. Jade's strong voice rang out in clear tones.

After a while the upbeat music gave way to slower melodies. A few were repeated choruses, easy to follow, all containing words like *Jesus, worship,* and *praise.* They finished with "Alleluia" sung over and over in a haunting tune. A hushed, restful feeling lingered as they made their way to the tents. Kendall found herself humming the last song as she stared up at the black sky that looked like a canopy of a zillion stars flung over the pines.

It was her first-ever camping experience, and except for the pleasant weenie roast, everything had an unfamiliar feeling about it. She knew Jade and her five former students but no one else. The hiking boots felt thick on her feet but were a welcome stability on the rocky ground and an added layer between her and those snakes she was sure were slithering about just out of sight.

The exhilarating musical stroll through the cool, fresh air gave way to a stifling canvas scent as she entered the tent she shared with a mother, two girls, and Susie. She had borrowed a sleeping bag from her friend Sara, and the mother had provided a cot for her, so the arrangements weren't impossibly uncomfortable. The campground's restroom was passable for two nights.

A short time later she sat on the edge of the cot, in the semidarkness of the tent, brushing out her hair and watching the girls shine their flashlights around the floor littered with clothing and sleeping bags.

"Nope, no snakes, Ms. O."

"Thanks, girls."

Jade's reminder as they had left the fire about a 6 A.M. wakeup call and the importance of being mentally alert for the climb cut short the girls' unavoidable giggling time. Not quite short enough, however, to suit Kendall. As the last flashlight clicked off, the loud whispers began.

"He's hot!"

"Totally."

"I like his eyes. They are so dreamy-looking with those half-asleep kind of eyelids."

"Yeah, and the dark, thick eyelashes that kind of curl like his hair."

Oh, no. They're talking about Jade. I don't think this is appropriate, especially for a church group.

"What about his broad shoulders? He looks like that wall of rock we're going to climb."

"I saw him in shorts once. He'll wear his climbing shorts tomorrow. Wait 'til you get a load of his leg muscles!"

"Girls!" the mother's voice reprimanded across the darkened tent. "He's at least thirty-four years old. Probably close to Kendall's age. Hey, you're single, aren't you?"

She groaned and put the pillow over her head. "Good night, girls."

Their muffled laughter was the last thing she heard. Drifting off to sleep, anticipating the unknown challenge of tomorrow's climb, she sensed a vague nagging at the back of her mind.

Sometime later she jerked awake. Over the soft breathing of the others, she heard distant howls. Coyotes or mountain lions? Like the unseen animals, that anxiety she couldn't pinpoint cried faintly, dampening her usual enthusiasm toward a new adventure and keeping her uncomfortably awake for a long time. What was that all about?

"Your turn, Kendall." Jade grasped the harness at her waist, checking the knots one last time. "I'll meet you at the summit. Ready?"

She nodded. "Sure."

He didn't think she looked ready. Up close like this, he saw dark circles under her eyes, as if she hadn't slept well. Her hair was in its familiar braid, but the pearl earrings were missing from those small lobes. The smile was infrequent, forced.

"Remember, keep your weight on your feet. Balance with your hands. Just move smoothly, a short distance at a time." He kept his voice low, even, reassuring and maintained eye contact, making sure she understood the words she'd heard him say almost a dozen times already this morning. "There's no hurry. And you don't have to do this."

She blinked. "But I want to. I really want to."

"I know you can do it." He glanced up the 110 feet of rock face. Out of sight, his friend waited. "Jerry will belay you. Just walk up to him. He's holding the rope the whole way." He tugged at the rope tied to her harness. "And remember, he's protected, he's anchored to the rock. You can trust him and the rock. Okay?"

"Okay, got it."

He watched her eye the rock, a wary look on her face. She still seemed hesitant to start, and he wondered how else to phrase what lay before her. She wasn't a teenager; she imagined in a different language. "Kendall, it's like your piano. There are places for your fingers and your toes. You'll find them intuitively. They'll flow together, and you'll make the music. You'll play the sonata."

She threw him a brief smile, then turned and found a foothold a few inches up. Planting her right foot on it, she lifted herself and leaned forward, balancing with her hands. Her slender arms beneath the short-sleeved yellow T-shirt moved gracefully. The loose-fitting jeans she wore allowed her legs to climb with ease as she continued.

"Kendall," he called, "stick your bottom out more."

"Mister Zukowski!" Her head whipped around and she looked down at him. "That's no way for a *pastor* to speak."

"Sorry," he laughed. "It's the best way I can explain it."

He heard faint chuckles behind him. They came from those who had chosen to picnic rather than climb—a few of the girls, all of the mothers, and one of the dads. With a clear view of the rock face, they sat and watched the climbers.

It was a perfect morning for a climb. The sun, still low in the sky, warmed the rock. No wind blew. Jade and Chuck and Jerry, fellow wall rats, had checked out the area a few weeks ago in anticipation of bringing the kids here. It was a new place for them, although they had climbed together for years and often worked with groups like this. When their schedules permitted, these guys had often helped him out at the camp.

This rock was 110 feet of steep terrain with one short stretch vertical enough to challenge, but not enough to intimidate. It was a doable climb for the beginners that allowed them to learn about belaying, ropes, and protection, about how to grasp the dime-thick edges, how to trust the solidity of the rock. The kids were all equipped with sit harnesses. If anyone slipped, they would fall only a short distance before they would be securely anchored from a seat rather than from just their waist. And once they reached the summit, an ideal area for rappelling nearby would set them down a short hike from the campground.

Jade continued looking up. The structure of the rock was such that they were able to run two climbing lines simultaneously. With Chuck and Jerry each belaying one, he was free to send off each kid just as he had Kendall, triple-checking knots and instructing one on one. To his left now he saw Scott Thornton, last of the teens, about thirty feet from the summit. He knew Chuck was up there, facing out, the rope leading to the boy taut around Chuck's back and in his hands, Chuck no doubt talking the whole time, telling the others his endless climbing stories.

To his right Jade watched Kendall. She was doing well, without uncertain pauses or strained movements to prompt him to call out suggestions. Under his direction, she had studied the others ahead of her, spotting through binoculars the infinitesimal holds.

They would eat an early picnic lunch at the summit. Jade anticipated their reactions—faces flushed with the excitement of what they'd just accomplished, their eyes bright with vision into a world of dimensions they'd never imagined before. They would talk and laugh, show chipped fingernails, recount details of looking down, not looking down, toeholds seeming to sprout from the rock. The emotion of dancing on air would be hinted at, unable to be wrapped in words. Some would express a finished attitude; some would beg to return next week to find a higher, steeper challenge.

It was always that way after a climb. And tonight, around the campfire, they would give thanks and think of fear and impossibilities and faith—of the solidity of the one true Rock.

Jade prepared to self-belay. In spite of the fact that this spot was as easy to climb as the steep stairway at the Del Mar beach, he had to be a role model for the kids. He knew that watching him free solo could encourage the boys' hot-dogging instinct. So he would climb carefully, deliberately, with rope anchored to the ground.

That would also help him guard his attitude that too easily slipped into cockiness, both on and off mountainsides, when he wasn't paying attention. He had learned the hard way at seventeen that climbing was a surefire way to keep that tendency in check. The fall he suffered had been a wakeup call that spoke louder than getting kicked off the football team.

What really got his attention was falling sixty feet, gouging his leg on a piton along the way, and dangling 200 feet aboveground, all because he had hurriedly hammered his protection into what he knew was rotten rock in the belief that it was his skill that kept him on the rock, not the gear. Jerry had been below him, in his usual solid belay position, and saved his life.

Just then Kendall screamed. Jade looked up just as she jerked to a stop in midair. She couldn't have slipped more than a few feet, but even at that, sitting on air eighty feet aboveground was terrifying for the novice.

"Kendall!" Jerry yelled from above. "You okay? I've got you."

She scrambled, her feet quickly finding a toehold, her hands clawing at the rock until they found enough to cling to.

"Kendall, I'm coming," Jade shouted, dropping the rope. In one fluid movement he was on the rock, free soloing. He climbed swiftly, his natural aggression taking over, obliterating all thought of anchoring himself. "Jer, you okay?"

"Yeah. Take it easy, bud! We're not going anywhere. Kendall," he said soothingly, "that's a tough spot, but you can do it."

His friend continued to encourage, but she didn't respond. No movement, no words. It took Jade almost ten minutes to reach her.

Slightly below her, he studied the rock to her left until he found what he needed. Carefully he made his way closer, then wedged his fingers into the crack about at her knee level. He pulled, his fingers finding another hold, his left foot resting on a tiny, rounded protrusion. Stopping just above her, he jammed the toes of his right climbing shoe sideways into the crack. He could stay in this position for a few minutes, easy. "Hey, Kendall. You're doing great."

Directly above them, smooth rock shot straight up. If she

had studied closely for holds, she'd probably also given fear the opportunity to seize control. She was at the crux of the climb.

"Kendall." He looked at her now. Her forehead was pressed against the rock. Her eyes were squeezed shut. She drew jagged breaths through clenched teeth. "Hey, open your eyes. I'm right here. You won't get hurt."

Still she didn't move.

"Take a deep breath. Deeper. Yeah, that's good. One more. Okay, look at me."

Her eyelids opened, but he didn't think she saw him. She stared straight ahead. Her face was a death-white.

"Good. You're really doing great. This is just a tough spot, but you can do it."

The scar on her forehead stood out, a bright white slash against her colorless face. Dirt smudged a cheek, and beads of perspiration dotted her upper lip. Her breathing was still uneven. Fainting would not be good.

"Look at me."

Like a blind person, she turned toward his voice, not seeing.

"You're okay. This is just part of climbing. No big deal. Remember, Jerry's holding you. You won't get hurt. It's just like playing music." He hummed a few bars of the familiar part of the sonata he'd heard her play. "Play the sonata, Kendall. You can do it. I know you've got it in you. You're tough. I'll climb right beside you, okay?"

She blinked at him now. It was better than nothing.

"All right. Take a deep breath." He took a deep breath himself and hoped he could get her to continue. *Lord, give her strength. Help her conquer this, whatever "this" is.* "Okay, good. We'll go up together."

Her left leg started moving involuntarily. Sewing machine

leg, some called it, a violent up and down motion like the needle on a sewing machine. He knew it wouldn't stop unless she moved soon.

"That happens sometimes. It'll go away. Shift your weight a little to your right foot. See that spot?" He nodded with his head. "Slide your left foot—"

A whimper escaped her, and her breathing became stiff gasps. "I c-can't. I can't move."

"That's fine. You don't have to go up. Don't feel bad. We'll just go down."

"I can't!"

"Yes, you can. Jerry will let you down. We've done this dozens of times." The ache in his forearms warned him that he, too, had to move soon. He called up, "Jer, we're going down."

"No problem. Tell me when."

Kendall's leg was still shaking. He thought it odd she wasn't crying, just whimpering softly. The look on her face was beyond fear; it was more like one of terror. He'd never seen this on the rock before. "I'm going down right beside you. Just spread your feet shoulder width, lean back in the harness, hold the rope, and walk down backwards."

"I c-can't."

"Kendall!" His harsh tone was intentional. He had to get her attention. "Yes, you can! It's the only way I can help you. Now, let go of the rock. Hold the rope."

No response.

"Look at me!"

She lifted her eyes to him.

"You gotta trust me and Jerry. Can you trust us?"

She shuddered.

"Jerry's strong, and he's anchored in solid. He's done this with me, and I'm a lot bigger than you are. You're like a feather pillow on his rope. You won't get hurt, okay? Do you trust me?"

She nodded slightly.

"Move your left hand to the rope." He slid his foot from the crack. He had to move. "Now, Pollyanna! That's it. Good. Now the right hand. That's it. I'm going down with you. Move your feet apart a little bit. Okay, Jer!"

His friend slowly let out the rope. Kendall's first steps were more of a dragging until she got the feel of it. Jade down-climbed, an arduous task of finding in reverse the holds he'd used for his ascent. He remained a short distance to her left, talking to her as much as he could while concentrating on his own path.

It took almost twenty minutes to reach the ground. He grasped her waist, steadying her, then worked at untying the knots. Her fingers dug into his forearms as if they were a rock hold and she needed to balance. He glanced at her face. It was expressionless.

"Hey, we're down!" He wrapped his arms around her. "Talk to me, Pollyanna. You okay?"

No words came from her, just that ragged breathing. She began to sink, and he helped her sit on the ground, then finished removing the ropes from her, talking softly the whole while.

"Everything's all right. Nothing's hurt. You'll be fine."

She held her head in her hands. He saw trickles of blood on the knuckles of her right hand. Her jeans over the right knee were torn.

The hiking group arrived on the scene then and surrounded her. They helped her to her feet, encouraging her, offering to drive her back to camp and telling him good-bye.

Jade watched them walk off, two of them supporting Kendall between them. In all his years of teaching, no one had ever become totally stiff with fear like she had. He shook his head in amazement and in relief, letting out a breath he hadn't realized he was holding.

"Yo, Jade!"

He waved up at Jerry. He knew his friend would belay him. He also knew he didn't want to climb alone this time. He tied the rope to himself.

The remainder of the day was uneventful in comparison, but it was the fulfilling time he had prayed the kids would experience. Late that afternoon, back at the camp, he learned Kendall hadn't emerged from the tent. While the group prepared for the evening activities, he went in search of her.

Through the pines a short distance from the campfire area, he paused outside one of the girls' tents that he thought was hers and said, "Knock, knock."

No answer. Stepping closer, he peered through the netting and saw she was asleep on the cot. Concerned that she was ill, he quietly slipped inside. She slept on top of the sleeping bag, still wearing the torn jeans and rumpled yellow T-shirt. Wisps of hair from the braid lay across her smudged cheek. Band-Aids covered three of her knuckles. Her breathing was regular, her color more normal. She appeared to be in a deep sleep.

His heart felt heavy. What had happened on the rock? How could he have so totally misjudged her ability? If she feared heights, surely she wouldn't have gone, would she? What—

Father, I ask that You would comfort and strengthen her. Help—

His earlier prayer for Kendall popped into his mind, and he caught his breath. He had prayed that she would meet her limits.

Oh, holy and merciful God. Is this Your answer? Already? Is

96

this the limit of her human goodness, her human ability?

As always when faced with such direct communication, Jade was overwhelmed with an awe that prompted worship. He left the tent and softly sang praises to God as he walked along the pine needle-covered trail, wondering what path Jesus would lead her down next.

In the dawn's cold, Kendall sat bundled in the sleeping bag, sipping coffee, her feet propped on the ring of stones surrounding the fire pit. She had stoked the embers, adding kindling and logs to get it going. She felt rested, which made sense after sleeping for almost fifteen hours. When she had awakened a short time ago, it was still dark, but she got up, changed clothes, washed her face, and brushed out her hair. Here and there a bird chirruped good morning.

She pondered yesterday. She had missed lunch, dinner, and last night's campfire and singing. That much she knew.

The nagging from the night before started again, tugging at her memory for attention. She responded automatically, shoving it further into the recesses of her mind, firmly shutting doors, burying memories deeper.

"Good morning."

She turned to see Jade making his way toward her. "Good morning." She held up the plastic pot she had carried over from the shelter's kitchen. "Want some coffee? It's still hot."

"Smells great." He ducked into the screened-in shelter and emerged with a mug.

He looked wide awake and warm in jeans, red turtleneck, and heavy vest. Two days' stubble shadowed his face, a shade darker than the coppery hue that covered his head.

"How are you feeling?" he asked.

She poured coffee into his cup. "Grateful to you."

"You're welcome."

She set down the pot and looked at him. "And extremely foolish."

"No need. Climbing isn't for everyone. That's okay."

"I'm not much of a chaperone for you either."

He sat in a chair next to hers. "Well, everything went fine after we lost you, but I'm sorry you missed out."

"I really am too."

"You were climbing well. What do you think triggered it?"

She shrugged. "I remember going up. Jerry was so nice and helpful, and it was pretty exciting. Then things just went fuzzy." That nagging feeling crept along the edges of her thoughts again, along with the sensation of falling. She ignored it. "Until I heard your voice." *Play the sonata. Play the sonata.*

He nodded. "I kept thinking about the part where Pollyanna falls out of the tree."

"You didn't," she laughed.

"No, I didn't." He smiled. "I had a few other things on my mind."

"Well, thank you. Goodness, saying thanks hardly seems adequate for saving my life."

"You weren't in that kind of danger. It wasn't that big of a deal."

"It felt like it was. I think I owe you and Jerry big-time."

"Nah. It's just part of our job. Like you taking care of Cait. We're even now."

"They're hardly in the same category. I suppose I could start referring to you two as my knights in shining armor."

"I don't think so. What else do you remember?"

"Music. You were humming, weren't you? And I remember holding onto the rope. And riding in the van back here, drinking something somebody handed me, and then going to sleep." She did remember a sense of letting go, of trusting a calm voice, of holding onto a man who promised he wouldn't let her get hurt. Jade, of course. She lowered her eyes. "Guess I'm afraid of heights and didn't know it."

"Fear is powerful. It can make us forget things or not be conscious of them, even to the point of not knowing what it is we're afraid of."

"I am so sorry."

"There's nothing to be sorry for. You tried, and that's the best anyone can do."

"Did the kids have a fantastic time?"

"I think everyone said 'awesome' at least three times." He grinned. "It was great."

She listened and laughed as he described everyone's reaction to yesterday's adventure. They finished the pot of coffee as the sky brightened.

"Last night we talked about how living by faith is like rock climbing." His eyes sparkled. His coppery hair shone in the slanted shafts of sunlight pouring through the pines. "It helped them put handles on what they hear in church. In one sense Jesus is the Rock, a solid constancy to lean on, a love that never lets us down. In another sense life is like a rock, and God expects us to work at climbing it. He doesn't promise that it's easy or that we'll know what's at the top, but He provides the toeholds just where and when we need them."

"Why doesn't He tell us what's at the top?"

"Well, ultimately He does with the promise of living with Him in heaven if we trust in Jesus His Son. But the peaks along the way can be difficult to reach. If we see all the impossible protrusions blocking our climb, we'd get too discouraged. We only need to see one at a time, learn from it, get our faith strengthened by it, and move ahead. It's like your sonata. If you put your fingers on the right keys for the notes that are written, the result is beautiful music. Just one note at a time, it doesn't sound like much. But a group of them played together makes a melody and tells you to keep playing, there's more to come." He chuckled. "I never thought of that analogy until now."

"I've never heard religion talked about like that before."

"I think it's more about getting to know God better rather than an organized institution with a set of rules. Do you go to church?"

She shook her head. "My mother took me after she got sick. She seemed to need to get close to God, probably because at that time she knew she was dying." She looked into the fire. "My dad would get mad though, and then she got too sick to go anyway." She remembered her mother's weak voice telling her that Jesus loved her. *But I was eleven, and my mother died, and it didn't make any sense.*

"Hi."

She looked up to see Scott Thornton approaching. "Good morning."

The boy had black hair, like his dad's must have been before graying. She had only seen him wearing glasses, but they weren't on yet this morning.

"Hey, Scott," Jade said. "You're up bright and early."

"So are you two." He raised his eyebrows.

"Old folks do that, right, Kendall?"

She punched Jade's arm. "Speak for yourself, Zukowski."

Scott coughed. "Is there coffee in that?"

Kendall shook the pot. "Sorry. I'll go make some more." She stood and stretched. "Think I'll start breakfast too. We're having pancakes. Want to help, Scott?"

"I don't think so. That's women's duty."

Kendall thought she saw a smirk on the boy's mouth, but she suspected he wasn't joking.

"Whoa, Scott!" Jade chuckled. "You better duck. *Ms.* O'Reilly is liable to throw that coffeepot at you." He stood to follow her. "I'll help."

"No," she protested. "Remember? *I'm* taking care of *you* now." She strolled off. Giggling, she turned and bowed. "My knight in shining armor." *And besides,* she thought, *that poor boy is in desperate need of your counseling services.*

Five

"Sara, why don't you run your errands and pick me up later? I just want to check on the sub's comments, see how the day went without me. Next week's lesson plans may need adjusting."

The two women strolled through the empty school grounds. It was Monday morning, the day after Kendall's weekend camping adventure, and the first day of spring break. Dressed casually in jeans, they planned to go to lunch and an antique mall after stopping in her room.

"No, I want to stay." Sara smiled. Her chestnut curls were pulled back in a ponytail. "I like coming to your room. I haven't been here for ages. It's so cozy. And I'm in need of a dose of fifth grade nostalgia. Work was just too much last week."

"Trust me, it couldn't hold a candle to rock climbing." She flipped through her ring of keys, selecting the one for her classroom door. "It's great that your boss let you have this week off."

Sara shrugged. "Couldn't give up our tradition, even if the boss is new and his big court date's next week. Our time is set in concrete, or whenever your spring break falls—Wow!"

Kendall had just pulled open the door. Speechless, she surveyed the room, barely recognizing the place she'd left on Thursday.

"Wow," Sara repeated. "What was I saying about cozy?"

"That silly, silly student teacher, Jennifer."

"She did this?"

"Well, she and the sub are responsible, I'd guess. They were the last ones here. The custodian probably wasn't in Friday afternoon."

"If he was, I think he would have turned right around and walked out."

They picked their way slowly through the room. Desks were out of the rows and not lined up with chairs. Papers and books were strewn everywhere. Chalk drawings and writing filled the boards. The podium was at the back of the room. Mobiles hung crookedly from the ceiling, some torn. The piano lid was open. Cabinet doors hung ajar. The empty bulletin board she had given Jennifer charge of was still empty. Her desktop was obliterated from view.

Kendall wheeled her chair from a far corner over to her desk and sank into it with a loud, disgusted, "What on earth!"

"Where do we start?"

"I don't know. I do not believe this!"

Sara grabbed the trash can and immediately began stuffing papers into it. "You take care of your desk, hon. I'll work on the rest. We'll have this place in tiptop shape in no time, then we can officially start our week off. Mind if I turn on the radio?"

An hour later, with jazz softly playing, the room was almost back in shape when Kendall unearthed a piece of mail under her desk calendar. She dug around, finding more. "Sara, somebody brought in my mail. Isn't that a federal offense, or at least inappropriate procedure, which when it comes to *my* mail is just as serious? Wait—what's this?"

Noticing that one return address was the district superintendent's office, she ripped open the envelope and quickly skimmed a formal letter. "They can't do that," she whispered. She felt like she'd just run a marathon.

"Kendall? What is it?"

She handed her friend the letter.

Sara leaned against the desk and read for a moment. "They can't do that, can they?"

They stared at each other. Kendall said, "I don't think so. I don't know. Oh, I can't think straight."

"Uh-oh. Hold on, Pollyanna. The letter says that if they change the school boundaries, you only have enough kids for two fifth grade classes next year, right?"

Kendall nodded.

"So it's not decided yet." She held out her arms as if that answered everything.

"No, it's not. They'll vote before school's out in June about the boundaries. Or finish their study or whatever it is they do to turn people's lives upside-down. Do you know how many of our families will be affected?"

"Nope. But there's plenty of time to work this out."

"What if it's true though? What if there are only two classes and because I'm low on the totem pole I get transferred to—where does it say?"

"Eighth grade social studies. It's your minor, remember? You're good at it."

Kendall's eyes widened. "Eighth grade?"

Sara shook her head. "You're right. It's not you. Why don't we call Maxine or Greg?"

"They both left town."

"Ruth?"

"She wouldn't know about . . . The union! This is union

stuff, Sara." She yanked open a desk drawer and found one thing in its place, the school district directory. She thumbed through it. "I'll call the mediator." Hope coursed through her veins again.

"Who's that?"

"He's at the high school. What's his name? He's the band teacher. Here it is. Ian Edwards." She strode to the wall phone provided in every room and dialed for an outside line. "I hope he's in town."

He was, and was quite understanding. They arranged to meet later in the week. She hung up the phone and looked at Sara who stood on a chair, trying in vain to reach the dangling mobiles.

"So what did he say?" She jumped down.

"Well, it may mean a change, but nothing as drastic as eighth grade. He mentioned that there are bound to be retirements in this building or in another elementary, and I'll get first crack at those. We're meeting for lunch on Thursday to discuss my options."

"Why would they send this letter?"

"Ian says it's a formality they have to follow." She sat back down at her desk. "They can't pink-slip me because I have tenure, but they have to offer me something even in advance of a potential change like this. And there's a good chance the boundaries won't change. I am so relieved."

"Me, too." Sara hopped onto the now-clear corner of the desk. "I can't get those mobiles straight."

"Miss Jennifer can do it. She's about three feet taller than you. Long legs."

"That makes her 8'2". Want me to fill that bulletin board? It's probably time for your San Diego unit, right?" She was of Mexican descent and always enjoyed providing Kendall with information on San Diego's Spanish heritage.

"Student teacher job. Thanks anyway."

Sara's dark eyes studied her. "You still look concerned, Poll."

"I have to get used to this idea of changing classrooms and grade."

"That is sad, but you know you can do it. You really didn't expect to be here forever, did you?"

"A part of me did. Remember those teachers who would say they taught parents of your classmates? I had my mother's fifth grade teacher. And almost everyone had an older brother or sister who had the same teachers."

Her friend shook her head. "Dark ages, hon. You have to live in the same neighborhood for more than a generation. Nowadays people don't stay in one district from kindergarten through high school, let alone generations."

Kendall sighed. "You're right, of course. Well, I need a vacation. I'm taking this planning book home and working on it later."

Sara gasped in mock horror. "That's not allowed, Ms. O'Reilly! What if you're too ill to come to school next Monday?"

"Fat chance," she laughed. "Have I told you recently how many unused sick days I've accumulated?" She quickly stacked folders and stood.

"You're tempting fate when you talk like that."

"Do you believe in fate, Sara?"

She gave her a puzzled look. "I suppose, in a way. Why do you ask?"

"There was a lot of God-talk this weekend, and it just got me wondering."

"Right now I'm wondering if it's fish tacos I hear calling my name." Sara cupped a hand to her ear. "I think they're saying, 'Come quickly to Rubio's.' "

Kendall laughed and wondered if Jade had discovered Rubio's yet.

Jade slid a Bible commentary from the bookstore shelf and browsed through it. It was a newer one, not in his father's collection. He was searching for another resource for a paper he was working on for his doctrine class.

He liked the store he was in, even though the religion shelf contained more New Age and Eastern thought books than Christian. It was located upstairs in a non-enclosed mall in Del Mar, close to home, open from early in the morning until late at night. The old-fashioned wooden-floored aisles were wide, providing plenty of space to roam and stand while reading, although the store wasn't huge. Music played softly in the background. Classical. Violins and stuff like that. The homey smells of wood and books and some herb-scented potpourri and freshly brewed coffee mingled.

The coffee came from the delicatessen area separated from the books by a wide, open doorway. A high, wooden counter with stools ran along the large plate-glass window, facing the second-level, covered walkway. Scattered tables and rung-back chairs stood between this and the display case of pastries. Daily newspapers were strewn here and there, available to everyone.

He stuck the book back in its place. Thirty-two dollars for a questionable version of the Gospels wasn't part of the budget. He eyed the parenting books. Maybe there was one on how to be a mother even if your name was Daddy.

Cait was doing as well as could be expected, being pretty much confined to home. This week was his break from school, coinciding with hers, for which he was grateful. It was good to be able to devote extra time to her. He had convinced Kendall before leaving the mountains not to tutor her when

107

he was available. She seemed to appreciate the fact that he was willing and able to fill in.

Besides, after her response on the rock, he knew she would need this week to recover. Whatever that unearthed fear had been, it would certainly have drained her energy reserves. Her ability on Sunday to function—she had cooked, conversed, attended the worship service, and helped clean up the campsite with her usual friendly attitude—must have certainly left her on empty. That fifteen-hour sleep would have helped, but—

He blinked at the open book in his hands, bringing back into focus the table of contents. It didn't look like answers to his questions about mothering from a male point of view. What would Deb do with Cait after surgery? *Lord?* He breathed the question into a prayer and replaced the book.

He found the dictionary he wanted. His dad's old one didn't include three words for which he needed Webster's perspective. Strolling toward the cashier, he spotted bright sunflowers painted on the front of a box of note cards. He picked it up, turned it around, looked inside. Cait liked sunflowers now. And she liked to write notes to her aunts . . .

He smiled. Deb would buy it for her. *Way to go, Daddy-Mom,* he congratulated himself as he waited in line, looking over toward the coffee shop. A cup of java sounded good. Cait would probably like one of their pastries. *Two in two minutes. Hallelujah.*

From the corner of his eye he saw a slender hand move in a familiar way. He turned his head and saw Kendall sitting in the coffee shop area, facing his direction but looking at the man across the small wooden table from her. As usual, she was animated, emphasizing what she said with graceful hand gestures, almost as if her long fingers put musical notes to her words. Her eyes widened, and, as always, that smile tugged at her mouth.

"Sir, may I help you?"

The cashier's voice broke into Jade's reverie. He swallowed. "Uhh, yeah." After paying for his things, he entered the coffee shop. Kendall spotted him immediately, smiled, and waved. He circled toward her table, detouring from his path to the pastry counter.

"Jade! How are you?" She glanced at her companion. "Ian, I'd like you to meet Jade Zukowski, one of my students' parents. Actually, my knight-in-shining-armor parent."

The man shook his hand. "Ian Edwards. Nice to meet you. You must be the climber. I hope you're a supportive parent too?"

"Supportive?" Jade noted the man's grip was strong, though his hand was soft; an indoors hand. His blond hair was pulled back into a short ponytail. He wore a beige, V-necked sweater, and appeared tall. "Of what?"

"Of Kendall." Ian smiled toward her.

She looked up at Jade. "There's a chance I'll lose my job—well, get transferred anyway. Ian is our teachers' union mediator—and high school band teacher."

Musician. That's what he looked like—the arty, bohemian type. And apparently not the boyfriend type. "Why would they transfer you?"

"Oh, school boundaries may be changed, and then only two fifth grade teachers would be needed at East Hills." She shrugged. "It happens."

"But," Ian intervened, "we can negotiate for her best interests." He winked at Kendall. "So any parental support will be helpful. I take it you've been pleased with her work?"

"No question about that," Jade answered. "My daughter has never had as good a teacher as Ms. O'Reilly. *I* never had as good a one. I appreciate her influence more than I can say. I would imagine the vast majority of parents would agree."

"If your endorsement is typical, and I assume it is," another wink in her direction, "we should organize a letter-writing campaign. Or a petition. Kendall, would you be able to contact parents, ask them to send letters to the administration on your behalf?"

"I'm having my annual class weenie roast next Friday night. Usually most of the families attend."

"Why don't I come?" Ian offered. "We'll turn it into a 'We Love Kendall' bonfire."

Two bright pink spots colored her cheeks. "That's not necessary, but we could talk to all of them at once and ask for support. We'll be at the beach, in Solana, from 6 until 9." She turned to Jade. "I hope you'll be able to bring Caitlin?"

"Of course. Well, I'd better get going." There seemed nothing more for him to say, and he was beginning to feel like an intruder.

"Nice meeting you, Mr. Zukowski."

Kendall touched his arm before he turned. "Caitlin's doing all right?"

"Yes. Thanks for asking. We're doing math this afternoon. See you."

While waiting for his coffee, he noticed the two of them leave. He wondered at the workings of the educational system. It seemed a shame that this exceptional teacher would be required to leave her classroom. She hadn't appeared upset, but he knew it must be a troubling situation for her.

Outside in the parking lot he noticed Kendall walking by herself near where his car was parked.

"Kendall," he called.

She turned and waited for him to catch up to her. "Hi again," she said.

Seeing that expectant face waiting for him reminded him of the early morning she had watched his approach at the camp, when her hair had laid softly on her shoulders. "Hey, I'm sorry about this potential move. It seems a shame."

A look of surprise flitted across her face. "Thank you. I'm sure it will work out for the best. It might be time for a change, a new challenge." She laughed, her nose crinkled up. "One that's not related to a rock."

He grinned. "Speaking of rock, you'll probably be getting a phone call soon, from the youth group. They want to invite you to their next gathering."

She slapped a hand to her forehead. "Oh no, not another climb?"

He noticed that only one bandage remained, on the forefinger, though the other knuckles were still scraped and red. "No. Church. Not nearly as intimidating. Sunday is Easter, and we're having a special service, with the kids doing the music and everything. Except for the sermon—my dad's doing that. They all thought it was so great having you on the campout, they've been trying to figure out how to get together again."

"Really?" Her face lit up.

"Really." *She's so unaware,* he thought, *so . . . childlike.*

"I'd love to hear your dad speak. What time?"

He winced. "Six A.M. It's the sunrise service."

"My favorite time of the day."

Of course. "Not mine. Do you know where the church is?"

"Yes. May I ask you a favor? I need wood picked up for the weenie roast. Someone is donating it, but they can't deliver it."

"No problem."

"Great. Thank you. I'll give you the address next week.

111

Well, your coffee is getting cold. See you later." She turned to go.

"Can you still play all right?" he asked.

"What?"

"The piano. With your knuckles like that."

She glanced at the back of her hand. "Oh, sure. It doesn't interfere. I still can't play that sonata, but this doesn't have anything to do with that." She smiled and waved. "Bye."

He watched her walk to her yellow Cavalier and climb in. *Can't play the sonata? I thought that's what she was playing that day at the school.*

Kendall sat at the old upright piano in her apartment, took a deep breath, and started the third movement for the—what was it?—sixteenth time that Friday morning. Like the fifteen times before, for that matter the twenty years before, she quit a few minutes later in frustration. She would never, ever get it right!

She strode through the combination living and kitchen area and yanked open the door.

"Sara!" Her friend sat outside on the top step. "Why didn't you come inside?"

"Oh, I love looking out over the eucalyptus trees at our almost-view of the ocean—"

"You have such a good imagination." The ocean was three miles away, hidden behind hills.

"Yes, well, and listening to you play through the open windows." She stood. "And besides, I didn't want to scare you by walking in. I've seen how intense you get with that piece."

"If my mother could know this legacy of frustration, she never would have attempted teaching Beethoven to a ten-year-old."

"I've heard you play it through."

"Not the way it should be. Anyway, I was coming over for a cup of tea. Want one here?"

"Sure."

They walked into Kendall's apartment. After preparing a pot of tea, they carried mugs out to the balcony and sat on the two white resin chairs, facing the east and the morning sun.

Sara propped her feet on the railing. "It *is* a great view, even if you can't see the ocean."

Tall eucalyptus trees dotted the landscape, and an orange grove was visible on a distant hillside. This time of year, after winter rains, there was more green than brown. From the second story, the apartment overlooked a row of covered parking spaces. Drab gray fences and thick, deep green oleander bushes hid neighboring backyards from view, though red-tiled rooftops could be seen. Traffic noise was muted.

"If you have to move, Kendall, I think I'd like this east side better than my hot western one."

She chuckled. "Sorry to disappoint you, but chances are good I'll still have a job close by."

"Well, I'd much rather have you than the morning sun. So was this Ian guy helpful?"

"Yes, extremely. He wants to document my positive influence at the school, talk to happy parents and former students, maybe even chart their progress after fifth grade. And he's looking into possible retirements and other transfers."

"Sounds rather ambitious. What's he like?"

"Friendly, extroverted. We talked a lot about music, of course, since he's the band teacher. I enjoyed his company."

"And?"

"And what?"

Sara raised her brows. "And what's he look like?"

"Oh, he's good-looking in a bohemian sort of way. You

113

know, longish hair, creative, artistic way of relating. Unconventional outlook. Definitely attractive. And he's single."

"Maybe he'll ask you out."

"Well, that would be all right. He was fun. But rumor has it his dating schedule is rather tight."

"You haven't been out for a while, have you?"

"As in with a guy?" Kendall shrugged. "A few months maybe. I'm not counting—and you don't need to either. You know I'm too content to be lonely." Her friend had heard this before, and they both knew it was not an exaggeration. "So how was your mystery man date last night?"

Sara stared down into her mug. "I love you like a sister, Pollyanna, but sometimes I feel as if you're a priest and I'm at confession, and that annoys me." She looked up. "Sorry, but it does. It's not your fault—it's just the way you are."

Kendall didn't reply. Her friend would ramble for a bit, then eventually tell her the problem.

"I'm twenty-eight, and I'm lonely, and there is an absolute dearth of eligible, appropriate men out there. I know you don't care, you're so totally fulfilled with teaching and men have only let you down, so why bother with them." She set her mug on the table between them and held up a hand. "Correction. Not *let* you down, *trampled* you down. And I agree, men like your dad and Mark should be locked up and not allowed near females." Now she was wringing her hands. "I've met someone who's not like them. Problem is, he's not eligible. There, I've said it."

"Oh, Sara. He's married?"

She nodded. Her soft, brown eyes pleaded for understanding.

Kendall bit her lip. Sara had always agreed with her that dating a married man was full of potential dangers, not the least of which was unbearable pain. Unnecessary pain. And they would never do it. "How did this come about?"

"It's Terry."

"Your ex-boss?"

She nodded. "We've been friends for seven years. His kids are almost grown, and his wife is a witch."

"Maybe that's because he's not being her friend. I'm sorry," she apologized, seeing Sara's jaw drop. "I don't know the situation."

"It just . . . it just happened."

"He's probably about forty, huh?"

"I know what you're thinking. He's the typical age, midlife crisis, and all that. But we're friends, and I have loved him for a long time that way. And he's leaving her."

"When?"

"Soon. When their son graduates in June."

Kendall sighed. How could Sara be so blind? "I can't pretend like this is just fine."

"It happens all the time, Kendall. Wake up. It must be all that church talk at your campout that's making you judgmental like this. How can you say flat out that this is wrong?"

"It was talk about God, not church. And I didn't say it's wrong, but I do know it's not right, because more than likely you'll get hurt. I don't want that to happen."

"I know."

"Just his leaving you to go home to his family will hurt you, every time. It's not fair to you or them. And what if this is just a temporary spat with his wife? If he can break his promise to a wife, what kind of man is he? What if . . . Oh, Sara, you know all this."

"This is different. I can feel it. We've known each other so long. Last night was our first real date. I didn't want to hide this from you."

Kendall shook her head. "I wouldn't want you to. I'll try

not to keep bringing up what I don't like about it." *I'll just be here for you when you cry.*

"Can I tell you what we did?"

"Sure."

She listened with only half her mind, wondering how she could change her friend's decision. She found herself wishing she could slip inside Sara's heart and influence her, give her another view of this situation, a view full of wisdom—

"So we're going to dinner tomorrow night. You don't mind if I cancel our plans?"

"Of course not. They were tentative and nothing special. Anyway, I probably want to stay home. I have early Sunday morning plans."

"Sunday morning?"

"I'm going to a sunrise service."

"Church?" Sara's eyes widened in surprise.

"Yes. Jade invited me for the kids, then one of the girls called." She told her about seeing Jade at the coffee shop.

"I suppose even I would go to church if my knight in shining armor invited me."

Kendall laughed. "Or your parents." Sara always went when she visited her family back in Los Angeles.

"That's true."

"So why don't you go anymore? You grew up going."

"It didn't mean anything to me. When I moved down here on my own, I didn't see a reason to keep it up."

"Jade doesn't talk much about church. When he was with the kids, they talked about having a relationship with Jesus like He's a real live person. They prayed like they were having a conversation with Him."

"Do you believe in God?"

"I think there must be a Higher Power who created all of life, and I've read that there's enough historical evidence to prove Jesus was a real person. But I don't see a connection. And I don't think He cares about our everyday stuff, like they prayed about."

"I don't either," Sara agreed. "I suppose God exists, but church seems like a tradition for old folks. Why are you going?"

"Well, for one thing the teenagers go, and I'm curious what the attraction is for them. Also because they asked me. Probably Caitlin will be there too."

Sara rolled her eyes. "I know, I know, if it involves kids, that's enough reason for you."

She smiled. "And I really like Jade's dad, Jeremiah. He's doing the sermon. I thought it'd be interesting to hear him."

"What about Jade? Do you like him?"

"Yeah, I think I do." She giggled. "Besides the fact that he saved my life, he's a nice guy."

"Well, that makes two for you."

"Two what?"

"Two possible men to date. Ian and Jade."

"Hold it, Sara. Jade is completely off-limits. He's a dad, like Mark was. It makes for complicated, messy relationships. I'm concentrating on his daughter. Discussion closed." She stood. "I need to run. Are you coming?"

"Sure. If you'll still be my friend."

Kendall gave her a hug. "Nothing will ever change that, Sara."

"Hey, Sara, looks like you'll get to meet Jade," Kendall puffed as they jogged side by side at the ocean's edge.

Sara followed Kendall's gaze down the beach. "That's him?"

"Um hmm."

"He's taller than I expected. More slender too, but strong

looking. Really broad shoulders."

Kendall focused her attention on the clear blue sky, ignoring Sara's running commentary. The salty air carried a hint of warmth already.

"My goodness, I've never seen legs like that. Those muscles—"

"Shh!" Kendall slowed to a walk, as did Jade coming toward them. He wore long, black mesh shorts and a faded red T-shirt with white lettering, *Lion's Trail Camp*. A white outline of a mountain cut through the words.

"Hello," she called, catching her breath.

"Hi." He stopped in front of them, also out of breath, and smiled. "We seem to be on the same schedule. We should ride together and save gas."

Kendall returned his smile. "We could. This is my good friend and neighbor, Sara Terronez. Sara, Jade Zukowski."

The two shook hands. "Nice to meet you, knight in shining armor."

He teasingly gave Kendall an exaggerated frown. "Same here, Sara. Are you a teacher too?"

"No. I'm a legal secretary downtown. I need to thank you for saving Kendall's life."

He grinned. "You're quite welcome."

"Do you run here often?" Sara asked.

Obvious nosiness, in Kendall's opinion.

"I just discovered it."

"It's a good wide spot," Kendall intervened. "High tide doesn't matter most of the year."

"I usually go to that area north of here, where those steps are on the bluff. Oh, I mentioned to Cait about you maybe coming to church. She'd like to sit with you."

"That'd be great."

"I have to be with the kids. If you come about 5:45, she

can meet you just inside the front door."

"All right. I'll be there."

"Feel free to bring Sara too." He turned to her friend. "If you'd like. Well, have a good one." With a wave, he jogged off.

The women resumed their run.

Her voice uneven with the thumping of shoes against packed sand, Sara exclaimed, "Kendall O'Reilly, you are ridiculous! He looks like Adonis."

"That is a mythological character."

"Trust me, that's what Adonis looked like. And he's magnetic. A magnetic Greek god."

Kendall sighed loudly. "Mark was magnetic."

"You ought to throw your dad-dating rule out the window, girl."

"In the first place, Sara, he hasn't asked me out."

"Women can ask men out. It's acceptable nowadays."

"No, thanks. Feel free though."

"Are you kidding? The way he looked at you, he won't even remember he met me. And in the second place, you were going to say?"

Kendall's chest tightened. "Nothing." A familiar pang twisted, rearing its ugly head, reminding her why she had made the rule, why she ached for her friend who was more than likely headed for the same agony. She looked toward the ocean.

"Well," Sara continued, "I just wonder what a guy like that is doing in church."

"Why don't you come with me and find out?"

"I think I will!"

Kendall smiled. She would be glad for her friend's company in a strange place.

Six

Bach as well as Caitlin greeted them early Sunday morning in the foyer.

"Ms. O'Reilly!" The girl wrapped her arms around Kendall's waist.

"Good morning, sweetie." She stooped to hug her. "How are you feeling?"

"Lots better."

"I'm so glad. This is my good friend, Ms. Terronez."

"Hi, Caitlin." Sara smiled at her.

"Hi. We can go sit down now. It's not crowded this early." She raised her eyebrows as if emphasizing the word *early*. "So we can sit anywhere."

They followed her into the sanctuary, where a teenage boy handed them bulletins. The Bach music, louder now, drew Kendall's attention to the front, where a lovely rendition of "Jesu, Joy of Man's Desiring" poured from a grand piano. She recognized the pianist as a teen from the camping trip.

Sara nudged her and whispered, "She sounds like you."

"No, she's extremely good."

They sat near the front on a cushioned pew, Kendall between Caitlin and Sara, behind a middle-aged couple. It was a large church with center and side aisles. Lining both sidewalls were tall, stained-glass windows. The ones with the east view were beginning to brighten, the colors glimmering vividly.

The simple decor was contemporary, with a forest green carpeted dais and fragrant potted Easter lilies at the base of a large, wooden pulpit in the center. The piano was off to the left, an organ to the right. Beside the organ, facing the pulpit, were a few rows of pews, probably for a choir. The walls were bare except for a single, large wooden cross hung at the back of the dais. Soft, indirect lighting shone on it.

The pews were almost half full. Kendall was surprised to see so many people out at this time of day. A group of teens now emerged from a door behind the piano, three boys and three girls, all wearing white dresses, shirts, or slacks. A boy sat behind a set of drums; the others carried instruments and stood at music stands. She saw a flute, two trumpets, a saxophone, and an oboe. As the drummer started a slow beat, the pianist moved to a keyboard and joined in with the others. The tempo quickened, and from the back of the church came the sound of singing. The aisles filled with young people, all dressed in white, voices raised in loud, excited song as they moved as one toward the front.

The energetic group of at least forty gathered on the steps in front of the pulpit, hands clapping, smiling faces glowing as if they were cheering their basketball team on to the state title. The scene mesmerized Kendall. After a time the thought struck her that the music was not meant to entertain the audience. The kids' attention seemed focused elsewhere, not on their performing. They were just singing together, not in a polished unison, and they looked so joyful and . . . innocent.

She felt bubbly inside, and when the congregation was asked to stand and sing the words printed in the bulletin, it seemed natural to do so. She heard Sara's voice join in with hers. They sang about an empty tomb and a risen Christ and a glorious morning. Three songs later they sang a slower melody, and the teens sat down in the first few center rows.

Jade's father, Jeremiah, stepped up to the pulpit. Other than wearing a suit and tie, he didn't appear different than how she remembered him. His prayer was like in the hospital, a respectful conversation with God. What must have been his sermon was spoken in the tone he'd used with her in the kitchen. Coupled with that rich baritone voice, he was easy to listen to.

He too spoke of a glorious morning and an empty tomb and a risen Christ. And then he said, "Sometimes we forget the point. Why did Jesus come? Why was there a cross and a tomb? Why did He die, and why did He leave the tomb?"

Kendall had wondered the same.

"Let's go back to the creation of man. God gave Adam and Eve a free will so they could choose whether or not to live as He told them. Simply put, when they chose to disobey God, they placed their own wills above His, and thus sin entered human nature. The result of that sin nature has been death—total spiritual and physical separation from God.

"Throughout history, as documented in the Bible, God taught His people that He requires a sacrifice of a perfect being to atone for our sin. He loved His creation and wanted the fellowship restored. He promised that in time He would send the Messiah, the Savior, His Son, to bring that to pass. Until then, perfect animals were sacrificed, symbolic of the perfect One who would come later to pay the debt once and for all.

"Specific prophecies told of Messiah's coming and what He would do, what would happen to Him. Jesus fulfilled them all. As He Himself predicted to His disciples, He was crucified, but three days later His tomb was empty. Impossibly empty except for the fact that He had conquered death—He had paid the price God required.

"There is more eyewitness evidence on the life of Jesus, including the empty tomb, than there is on Julius Caesar. We may ask then, where does faith come in? Faith means accepting His life, death, and resurrection as a completed work of salvation. Today we still have a free will and must choose to either live the way He tells us to or do it our own way. Human nature is still a sinful nature, imperfect, choosing its own way, and it still dies. But because of the work Jesus Christ did, death does not have to be eternal separation from God.

"Jesus said, 'Whoever finds his life will lose it, and whoever loses his life for My sake will find it.' The Bible teaches that if we simply accept the gift of Jesus, acknowledging that He is Lord and has made full payment for our sins, we are saved from death, saved to spend eternity with Him. And that eternity begins the moment we accept Him. We can be with Him here and now and forever.

"Without Jesus, we cannot be in a right relationship with God. You can come into that relationship today. Shall we pray?"

Kendall automatically bowed her head, amazed at the logic of it all. She had never heard this kind of stuff before. She remembered being yelled at from the pulpit to get saved, but never from what or to what or why. *Choices against God equals wrong equals a need for sacrifice equals the purpose of Jesus. Hmm. This makes sense.*

"Ms. O'Reilly . . ." Caitlin tugged at her sleeve. "Dad said to bring you to the patio out back. We have donuts and juice."

"Thanks." She glanced at Sara who nodded. "Show us the way."

"Kendall! Sara!" Jade waved to them.

They wound their way through the crowded patio to where he stood at the far edge, near a table laden with goodies. It was a lovely early morning, the air thick with eucalyptus scent from the surrounding trees.

"Oh, Jade," she gave his forearm a quick squeeze, "the kids were absolutely incredible."

He grinned. "Here's the one responsible for that. Bethany Delaney, miracle music woman, meet Kendall O'Reilly and Sara Terronez."

Sara shook her hand first. "They were fantastic."

Kendall looked down into a perky face that resembled the young people, full of joy and innocence, and said, "You're remarkable. Why aren't you teaching at our high school?"

Bethany laughed. "No way. They're *required* to go there. This place is a choice, and they're usually glad they're here."

"Well, I'm sure you make them feel that way."

"Thank you. Oh, you must be the Bach lady."

She raised her eyebrows, puzzled.

The woman turned to Jade. "Right?"

He nodded.

"It was his idea that we include the Bach before the service because he was so impressed with your playing."

"I was impressed with the girl's playing. It was beautiful."

"It was. And appropriate since Bach wrote his music to worship God. Well, nice meeting you two." Bethany turned to Jade, briefly grasping his hands. "See you later." She walked away, her long white dress flowing behind her, thick auburn curls bouncing on her shoulders.

"Would you like some coffee and donuts?" Jade asked.

Kendall noticed he wore dark trousers with a white polo shirt. His eyes sparkled in the slanting sunlight; his tan face appeared freshly shaven. "I prefer juice," she answered.

Sara moaned and helped herself to a donut. "She has disgustingly healthy eating habits."

Jade laughed, picked up two paper cups of orange juice, and offered her one. "I'm glad you came."

"Thanks." She accepted the cup. "This is a special place."

He smiled down at her. "I think so."

"Kendall."

She turned to see Jeremiah approaching. "Hello." They shook hands.

"And you must be Ms. Terronez, according to my granddaughter."

"Sara. I enjoyed your sermon. I've never heard one quite like that."

He laughed. "I hope that's good?"

"Oh, it *is* good," Kendall answered. "Thank you for helping me understand some of the concepts you spoke about."

"You're quite welcome. I want to invite you two to our Easter dinner—Colonel Sanders is cooking it, and we're taking it to La Jolla Cove this afternoon. My other children and grandchildren are in town and will join us."

"Well, Kendall's free," Sara offered, "but I'm afraid I have plans." She sounded sincere. "Thank you for asking."

Her eyes widened at Sara's answer. Her friend had plans? And *she* didn't? Well, she didn't, but—

Jade laughed. "Kind of puts you on the spot, doesn't it, Kendall? Don't feel obligated, but I hope you'll come."

"Why?" she challenged, shifting the spot elsewhere.

125

"Because Cait says you're really good at soccer." He sobered. "I need you, Ms. O'Reilly."

She couldn't help but laugh at his serious expression and clasped hands. "For soccer?"

"It's an annual event. Dad's getting slow." He glanced at Jeremiah. "Well, you are. And Cait's on the injured list, and my nephew had the flu last night."

"Soccer," she repeated.

He nodded.

His dad added, "We're meeting at the Cove about one o'clock. All the food is taken care of. Please stop by if you have time. I'd better go. Nice meeting you, Sara."

"Bye," she replied, then turned to Jade. "She won't come unless she can bring something. She makes incredible from-scratch brownies."

He looked surprised. "From a health nut?"

"Yeah, strange, I know."

"Okay, she can bring those."

"Hey, you two." Kendall stepped between them. "Do you mind if I get in on these plans?"

"Not at all." Jade took the empty juice cup from her hand. "Make your brownies, and I'll pick you up at 12:30."

"I'll drive myself."

"Okay. We'll be in the grassy area, ocean side, between the clump of trees and that little shelter nearest the snorkeling area. See you!" He walked off.

Somewhat frustrated, Kendall greeted a few of the kids she knew as they made their way through the crowd to the parking lot. Once alone, she exclaimed, "Sara, you could have let me think for myself."

She waved a hand. "Oh, you would have started wondering if it was a dad date."

"It isn't, is it?"

"Polly, his dad asked both of us." She chuckled. "But it will get you two together. Who knows? Maybe . . . if that cute little Bethany isn't going along. She could be why he hangs out here."

"She *is* cute. But this *is* his job, Sara. I can't figure out the soccer comment. We finished that PE unit before Caitlin moved here." She unlocked her car door. "By the way, what are you doing today?"

"Well . . ." She looked at her over the top of the car. "I was supposed to wait in case Terry called." She frowned. "But I'm going to go visit my folks."

Kendall smiled. "Good choice."

"I told Mom I wasn't coming for Easter dinner, but I think I've got time to make it." Her parents lived about ninety minutes away. "Do you want to come with me?" They climbed into the car.

She considered it for a moment. "No thanks. You know how I love the Cove, and I need to finish some things for class."

"Kendall, I feel kind of clean or something after being here."

"I know what you mean." She wished she had a home to go to like Sara did.

La Jolla, a wealthy San Diego community, was crowded, its usual condition for a sunny, holiday afternoon. Tucked between I-5 and the Pacific, it was home to the University of California San Diego, the Salk Institute, Scripps Institution of Oceanography, endangered torrey pines, high-tech firms, exclusive restaurants, and boutiques. Its Cove area was situated where the California coast looped straight westward a short distance before curving back to its southern path, creating a protected area for caves, long-distance swimmers, snorkelers, seals, and dolphins. Above its high, rocky shore were grassy areas that provided magnificent, unhindered views of coastline to the east, endless ocean to the north and west.

Kendall parked her car on a side street packed with condominiums, halfway up the hill. Two blocks away, at the top, lay a business district. A couple blocks down the hill was the Cove area. Anticipating a soccer game, she wore jeans, T-shirt, and tennis shoes with a sweatshirt tied around her waist in case clouds rolled in. She carried the pan of brownies, still slightly warm from the oven.

The moment she rounded the corner and eyed the vast expanse of ocean glittering like lapis lazuli, the light breeze caught her, filling her with a unique scent she thought existed only here. The combination of moisture and greenness and earth and sprouts seemed to seep through her pores, filling her with a sensation of growth, of life itself. Closing her eyes for a moment, she inhaled deeply, then crossed the street.

A sidewalk lined with 100-foot tall palm trees ran to the right and left. She crossed it and a grassy area and headed toward the ocean. Turning right on the sidewalk that ran above the sea, she strolled along the wooden railing that provided a leaning spot above the cliffs. Most of the rocky shoreline here was too steep to climb down, though further ahead was a more gentle slope leading down to tide pools.

The Zukowski adults were easy to spot. They were all tall with curly, copper-colored hair, with the exception of Jeremiah with his shock of white hair. Caitlin and Jade waved to her. She watched Jade lean down and saw his daughter grab hold of his neck for a piggyback ride down the sidewalk to meet her. He too wore jeans and a cream-colored T-shirt.

"Ms. O'Reilly!"

Kendall reached up and gave her a one-armed hug. "Hi, sweetie!"

Jade looked over his shoulder at her. "Hi."

"Hi, Jade."

"How many miles away did you park?"

"Oh, not too many. Isn't this a gorgeous spot?"

He nodded as they headed toward his group. "We've tried to come here every year on Easter since Mom and Dad bought the condo."

"We even come when it's cold, huh, Daddy?"

"Yep. Do you want to walk, Cait?"

"Okay." She slid from his back. "I'll meet you there."

"Don't go too—" He shrugged as she ran off. ". . . fast. I can't keep her down."

"How's she doing?"

"She tires easily, rests awhile, then takes off again like that. Well, are you ready to meet my family?"

"Sure. Who else is here?" she asked.

"Just them."

"Just family?"

He nodded. "One sister, two brothers, three in-laws, four nephews, three nieces, Dad, and Cait."

Kendall felt uneasy. "Jade, why am I here? I thought there would be other friends around."

"I think my dad's sweet on you."

She giggled.

"Seriously," he stopped walking and waited for her to do likewise and look up at him, "you're an honorary family member. He wants everyone to meet the special lady who has made such a difference in Cait's life. And he suspected you don't have family around here, so he thought you could join ours for today." He smiled.

She took a deep breath and exhaled an "Oh."

"So, if that's too heavy for you, you can leave," he reached for her pan, "but give me the brownies."

"No way." She turned and hurried on. "I have to ask that Reverend Zukowski how he raised a knight in shining armor. Maybe he could teach a seminar to our parents at school."

A moment later they reached the group. Before Jade could introduce her, a tall woman with a long, curly ponytail the color of a shiny new penny threw her hands in the air. "Kendall!" She gave her a big hug. "Thank you for taking care of Caitlin. I'm Elizabeth. This is my husband Dave."

Kendall grinned and shook their hands. "You're very welcome."

To her surprise, everyone's greeting was just as warm. The sisters-in-law hugged her, the brothers Sam and Mike took her hand in both of theirs, Jeremiah hugged her, and two nieces called her "Aunt Kendall." Except for a baby, the children appeared around Caitlin's age or younger. All of her uneasiness quickly melted away.

They ate soon after her arrival. She sat between Jade and his sister at the picnic table and tried to keep everyone's name straight. Seven of the eight children sat on blankets nearby. The eighth, a little girl less than a year old, sat on her mother's lap.

"Kendall," Elizabeth said, "I didn't hear how you liked the rock climbing trip?"

"Oh, the campout was great, but I discovered I am *not* a climber. Halfway up I froze. Jade had to get me down." In a teasing manner, she batted her eyelashes and gently patted his shoulder. "He's my knight in shining armor."

His brothers hooted and threw wadded napkins at him. They resembled him with those short, coppery waves of hair, dark-lashed hazel eyes, strong-looking straight nose, square jaw and neck. All of them had a curious straight line of an upper lip that barely curved when they smiled and a slight space between the two front teeth. Jade's laugh lines creased more deeply, perhaps because he was the oldest. He wasn't quite as tall as they, and his strong arms that filled his T-shirt sleeves didn't bulge like theirs did.

Jade raised his voice above the laughter, "You guys are just jealous, you muscle-bound Neanderthals who can't even do a chin-up, let alone climb!"

The bantering continued back and forth until the small, blonde sister-in-law Annette, the one with the child on her lap, asked, "So, Kendall, how long have you and Jade been seeing each other?"

She caught his eyes widening in surprise and imagined they mirrored her own. They stared at each other for a speechless moment.

He turned to his sister-in-law and said in a matter-of-fact tone, "Since right after Valentine's Day. And we saw each other on her field trip too."

Continuing his literal reply about *seeing* each other, Kendall added, "Then we saw each other at the campout, of course."

"And then today after church," he concluded.

"Oops!" Annette grinned. "I thought you were dating. You're such a striking couple."

They looked at each other again, burst into laughter, and began offering opinions.

"He looks like a tree. An oak tree."

His jaw dropped. "She's looks like a, like a, well, like a sapling."

"Sapling?" She looked back at his sister-in-law. "He's just Caitlin's dad."

"She's just Cait's teacher."

"We hardly know each other."

"We're not even friends."

"And he climbs rocks, of all things."

"She doesn't climb."

She looked at him. "Definitely not my type."

"Ha! Definitely not my type."

Caitlin squeezed between them. "But Daddy thinks you're pretty."

Laughter erupted around the table, Kendall the loudest of all as she noticed scarlet creeping up Jade's face.

A short time later, with brownies devoured and food packed away in baskets and coolers, the children and women climbed down to the tide pools. The soft, worn, sandy-colored rock area sloped gently toward the water, giving way to dark, jagged rock that formed crevices and deep impressions. The tide pools would be completely covered whenever the incoming tide pushed the waves over them.

Now, however, the tide was receding and the scattered pools were approachable. Kendall and the others made their way carefully over the uneven rock, scrunching down here and there to peer into the dozens of separate little watery worlds teeming with hermit crabs, sea anemones, tiny fish, and barnacles.

Annette apologized again to Kendall. "You know I'm so busy with the baby . . . I don't catch everything . . . I just figured . . ." She shrugged.

"That's understandable," she assured her. "After all, I am the only non-family person here. But actually it was your father-in-law who invited me. Caitlin's special to me, and I assumed there would be other friends here, so it was easy to say yes."

"You don't have family in the area then?"

"No. I was an only child, and both of my parents are dead.

My life is teaching." She knelt and trailed her fingers through a tide pool. There was a gentleness about Annette that made her seem familiar. Kendall enjoyed talking with her. "I do have friends who often include me on holidays, but everybody went out of town this week."

"Well, truthfully I was hoping Jade was seeing you. I think he needs someone like you."

"Oh, he's fine. He does a good job with Caitlin. And he seems so busy with the youth group, plus going to school."

"I know, but his temper's back. A female companion might help smooth his rough edges again. His immediate reactions can be harsh."

"I saw that at the hospital. He wasn't there when they started Caitlin's surgery and when he arrived . . . whew! I got out of his way fast."

"He wasn't there?"

"No, but Jeremiah was, and it was an emergency, so they couldn't wait."

Annette's eyes filled with tears. "Kendall, he wasn't there when his wife died."

She shifted from her knees and sat down, tide pool forgotten. "Oh no."

"He was off in the mountains. He desperately needed a respite, and the doctors said he had time. It was awful."

"No wonder he reacted the way he did. He must have been frightened out of his wits, hearing that Caitlin was so ill and he couldn't get there quickly." That's what Jeremiah had wanted to tell her, but she wouldn't let him. Sympathy for Jade drained energy from her.

A memory of being carried from her mother's bedside flashed through her mind. *Let me stay!*

Annette sighed. "Well, that one can almost be overlooked, but Sam—"

"That's your husband, right?"

She nodded. "I'm married to Samuel. Nicole is married to Micah. Then there's their sister Elizabeth." She grinned. "Mom and Dad Z. loved biblical names. Anyway, Sam is concerned. He sees shades of old tendencies coming out in Jade. Since Deb went home, there's been no one to draw his attention like she could."

Kendall glanced at her. "Went home?"

"You know . . . to heaven. It seemed too early for her to go, but God knows what He's doing, no matter how awful it looks from our viewpoint. Deb loved Jesus, and she was so sick."

"What happened?"

"It started with breast cancer and spread. They thought they caught it in time, but . . ."

"I'm so sorry. My mother had that too."

"Did your grandmother?"

"No one ever told me. All my grandparents were gone by the time I was in high school, and they lived in Idaho anyway, so I didn't know them well." She noted Annette's concerned look. "I know it could be hereditary. I keep up with exams."

"Good. Oh, dear, those boys are going too far." She stood and followed them.

Kendall looked up to see Jade making his way toward her. For a brief moment she wondered if her dad had ever looked that young and energetic and alive and . . . solid. She couldn't remember him that way. In spite of his loss, Jade didn't appear hopeless. His lapses, those angry reactions, seemed only momentary distractions from a focused life. Why couldn't her dad have been . . . ?

Maybe it was simply his personality. Or was it something else?

He knelt beside her at the tide pool and smiled. "Ready for

soccer? That group next to us just left, so there's more space now."

"Any time."

"Don't go yet. I have to check on these little buggers here." He plunged his hand into the water and scooped up a hermit crab. "They are so amazing."

She smiled at him, amazed that a man would feel that. "You know what impressed me this morning? Well, besides those teenagers and their music."

"What?"

"The logic in your dad's talk. I've always believed there must be a God. And I've read enough history to know that Jesus lived. The finding of the Dead Sea scrolls in 1947—such ancient copies of biblical writings—and the thousands of New Testament manuscripts in existence. Whew! That's proof enough. But I never got the connection between God and Jesus. Like your dad said, what was the point?"

He studied the crab in his hand. "Do you understand the point he was trying to make?"

"I think so. Is it that God said He would send a way to know Him better and Jesus fit the bill?"

"Yes. Do you believe that? Do you believe in Jesus?"

"Sure. What's not to believe?" She was puzzled. Hadn't she already said she thought He was real?

His eyes held hers. He looked as if he wanted to say more but instead just slowly smiled. "Not a thing, Kendall O'Reilly." He set the crab back into the tide pool. "Let's round everybody up. You'll be on *my* team, won't you?"

She stood with him. "Are you any good? I don't want to team up with a bunch of losers."

"I only allow winners on it." He dried his hands on his jeans. "Your little friend Tony told Cait you were awesome.

That's why you got asked."

She wrinkled her nose at him. "That boy certainly is a talker. Were you like that?"

He laughed. "Most of my school day was spent alone out in the hall. When I had a chance, I made up for all that quiet time!"

When Jade's nephew kicked the soccer ball between the goal markers, Kendall yelled, "We won!" and lifted her arms in triumph.

"We won!" the kids screamed.

He hugged her then. He didn't intend to, it just happened. Instead of the usual high fives, with Kendall on the team everyone hugged everyone. She started it, hugging his nieces and nephew and Caitlin who left her chair to join the celebration. He was in the middle of it and . . .

And he hugged her. It was a quick embrace, nothing inappropriate, but it left him with an impression of softness and femininity and the dry sweetness of mesquite and sage.

"We won!" she yelled again. "I can't believe it." She laughed up at him. "All the kids and you and me . . . This is so much fun!"

He smiled. Of course they won. The other team was made up of non-competitive women, his football-playing brothers, and an unathletic brother-in-law. Dad had sat this game out with Cait. And Jade had Kendall on the team who was competitive as well as athletic in spite of her slight build.

She chatted now with the others. She easily fit in, adding her own sparkle to his favorite group of people. They welcomed her, as he knew they would, and from their response they obviously enjoyed her.

He knew too that they would pray for her, that they would ask God to help her know the reality of Jesus beyond the intellectual understanding she'd spoken of.

He always enjoyed it when his family got together, traveling from Phoenix, Los Angeles, and Santa Barbara. Spending Easter together was tradition; the other holidays were sporadic, being at the mercy of conflicting schedules.

"Jade, I need to go home." She tied a purple sweatshirt around her waist.

Purple—Cait would like that. He picked up the soccer ball and tossed it toward a large canvas bag full of toys. "You can't yet. We have to watch the sunset. It's tradition."

Her brows knit together as if she were weighing something in her mind.

"Please?" he asked and immediately wished he had kept his mouth shut. Why didn't he want her to go yet? It was a good ending to a good day. She was just Cait's teacher. If she called him on it this time, asking why like she had about the picnic invitation, he wouldn't be able to talk his way out of it.

"Okay."

"Okay." He rushed his words. "Cait and I like to sit above the tide pools. Is that all right?"

She nodded.

"Cait," he called to his daughter who stood near the picnic table munching on snacks with her cousins. "Coming to the wall?"

She shook her head, her mouth full, probably with a cookie.

Dad stood next to her. "We'll come in a bit."

He noticed Sam walking in the direction of the street, his arms filled with a picnic basket, blanket, and diaper bag. Three little kids later, his brother was more interested in getting into the car than watching a sunset. Micah, the photographer, was setting up his tripod at the railing. He would want the clearer view here. His sister appeared to be in the middle of a serious conversation with Annette and Nicole.

"Well, at least I'll get to sit with you to watch the sunset."

Jade looked at Kendall. She giggled, her nose all crinkled up. He stopped himself from telling her he had been watching quite a few sunsets by himself in recent years. She'd probably quit smiling. "Do you mind if we go over there? It's really the best spot."

"I've always thought so too." She turned and headed toward the sidewalk.

Strolling near the railing, they passed photographers, parents with youngsters in tow, and hand-holding couples. The crowd had thinned.

An elderly, white-haired couple beamed up at them. The woman said, "Hello. We couldn't help noticing your lovely family."

"Why, thank you," Jade replied.

The man grinned and took the woman's hand. "Elsie and I often brought our children here when they were young, playing games just like you did today. God richly blessed us in those times."

"We enjoyed watching you," his wife added. "It brought back such good memories. You're such a handsome couple too. Which children belong to you?"

What a great couple! Jade threw his arm across Kendall's shoulders. "All of 'em!"

To his surprise, she protested, "That's not true!"

The couple laughed and stepped around them. "Enjoy the sunset. It looks like it should be a good one."

Jade dropped his arm. She wasn't smiling at him. Her nose wasn't crinkled up. They continued in silence until they reached the low stone wall above the tide pools. "How about here?" he asked.

138

She sat down on the concrete top and swung her legs over. He stepped over the wall and sat down beside her. Her legs dangled, too short to touch the ground. They stared out over the ocean. The sky was a deep cloudless blue, the sun low on the horizon. A faint breeze blew. The surf dully pounded in a rhythmic whoosh.

"Jade, that wasn't true."

"They knew that."

"I mean . . ."

He glanced over at her. There were goose bumps on her arms. Her face was pale. Her mouth was set, the lower lip tucked inside as if she were biting it. "Are you cold?" he asked.

She fumbled with the sweatshirt tied at her waist, then pulled it over her head. It caught on her braid. She yanked it out, smoothed down the shirt, then brushed loose strands back from her face.

"You mean what?" he prompted. He wasn't sure what she was upset about, but she certainly seemed angry.

"I mean, none of it." She took a deep breath and kept her eyes toward the ocean. "None of it was true. It's not my family."

"Yeah, it is. Honorary."

She shivered and didn't respond.

"What's wrong, Polly?"

That did it. She glanced at him and bit her lip again. She pulled her feet onto the wall and wrapped her arms around her legs. "I don't know."

"Do you want me to help you figure it out?" She was hurting, and he thought it might have something to do with not having a family. It probably wasn't the moment to talk about being in God's family.

She shook her head.

"Did I mention I'm working on my Master's in counseling?"

No response. Teasing didn't help.

"What can I do?"

Her face crumpled, though no tears came.

He scooted closer to her and put his arm around her shoulders. It seemed the only way to offer comfort. She stiffened, but he was glad she didn't pull away. He silently prayed for her. By the time the brilliant orange ball of a sun slipped into the ocean, she was leaning against him.

"Beautiful, huh?" he asked, wishing there was a reason they could remain sitting this way for a while longer. He couldn't think of one. Reluctantly he dropped his arm and stood. "Ready?"

She nodded and swung her feet to the sidewalk.

He wondered when she would find her voice. In the growing dusk they headed back to the picnic area.

"Sorry." Her soft voice was husky.

"For what?"

"For getting all drippy."

"Everybody needs to get drippy now and then. Are you okay?"

"Mm hmm." She cleared her throat. "Thank you. Do you mind walking me to my car?"

"Of course not."

Her shoulder brushed against his arm, then her hand slipped around his elbow. "My knight in shining armor."

A warmth filled him. It was a joke, but he liked the image. She was a damsel in distress, and he had comforted her. Maybe he should drive her home, walk her to her door . . .

Or maybe he should watch the sunset by himself next time.

$\mathcal{S}$EUEN

That La Jolla sunset had been just a bit too much for Kendall.

The sweet elderly couple's reminder that she had no family—and certainly was without a mind-set to ever have one—was inadvertent, of course, but her drippy, syrupy reaction to it was abominable. And then to be fearful of walking alone in the dusk to her car just three blocks away in a busy neighborhood was the ultimate absurdity. Jade probably thought she was a helpless, conniving, silly female looking for a shoulder to lean on or something worse, like a relationship.

She'd make certain she was nowhere near Jeremiah David Zukowski III when the sun set tonight, Friday, the night of the weenie roast for students and parents.

She watched him now as he walked toward her down the beach, his arms full of split wood, that solid, all-American look about him.

No, it was older than America. It was an ancient air of slaying dragons and rescuing the innocent and having the strong character that he carried so effortlessly on those broad shoulders. A larger-than-life knight in shining armor . . .

She pressed her lips tightly together, stifling an involuntary sigh.

Jade came from the direction of a long, paved ramp that led from the lifeguard station and parking lot. Wide enough for the guards' jeep, it was the only way down between steep cliffs.

She sat in a low beach chair, feet propped on the concrete ring that encircled a fire pit. The ocean whooshed in rhythmic intervals a short distance to her right; bluffs towered at her left. To the north and south the bluffs jutted out, creating an enclosed, relatively small beach area. High tides would cover the narrow strips of sand beyond, but at low tide the route was open, and one could walk to Del Mar or Cardiff by the Sea.

Today, the first of May, Solana Beach wasn't crowded, leaving plenty of space for her children to race about and not disappear from sight or disturb others. They wouldn't want to swim either; the water was still too cold except for a few brave surfers.

Jade approached. He wore jeans and a faded army-green, short-sleeved sweatshirt. A green that would bring out the color in his eyes. He smiled. "Hey, great night for a weenie roast."

"It sure is. Need some help?" she asked.

He dumped the wood into the fire ring. "No. I recruited a couple other dads up in the parking lot."

He should have been out of breath, but he didn't seem to be. "Where's Caitlin?" she asked.

"She's coming with Hannah's family. She went home with her after school. I'll head back up and get another load."

"I need to get a picnic basket out of my car."

"I'll get it, if it's got your brownies in it."

She laughed and pulled her keys out of her jeans pocket,

holding back the words about the basket being too heavy for her. She really could have made another trip and dragged it down herself. "It does. Thanks. My car's the—"

"Yellow Cavalier." He took the keys from her and grinned. "Saw it." He sauntered off as two more families arrived.

As usual, most of her students and their families attended the annual class beach party. Twenty-one were there with at least one parent as well as siblings. They brought balls and rackets, Frisbees, fold-up tables, blankets, numerous picnic baskets, coolers, and chairs. They talked a lot, laughed a lot, ate a lot.

To Kendall's surprise, Ian Edwards showed up as most of the adults mingled near the roaring fire. Clouds had gathered on the horizon, blotting out the last warmth of the sun.

She waved to him as he approached, then stepped away from the group. He looked attractive in a navy blue Nike running suit.

"Kendall!" He smiled and gave her a friendly hug.

"You came!" she laughed.

"Of course. I wanted to meet your fan club."

"Well, I hope that's what it is. Do you want a hot dog or brownie?"

"Bleagh!" His handsome features contorted. "No thanks. Did you learn anything at school this week?"

She shook her head. "Thornton seems to be avoiding me."

"I'm sure it's a conflict of interests for him. He doesn't want to lose you, but his influence won't count for much if boundaries change." He shrugged, then smiled and took both of her hands in his. "But you do have a first grade teacher in the building who is seriously considering moving to L.A. with her husband who just got transferred there. What do you think about first grade?"

Impulsively, Kendall threw her arms around his neck and shrieked, "I love first grade!"

Ian laughed. "I thought you might. Now, can I talk to the fans?"

"Sure."

She made her way to the concrete ring and stepped up on it, with a hand on Ian's shoulder for balance. "Moms and dads, may I have your attention? Thanks. This is Mr. Edwards. He's the high school band teacher and a mediator for the union. It seems I'm in need of a mediator, so he'd like to talk to you." She jumped down.

"As you may know, the district boundaries could change, and your school wouldn't need three fifth grade classes. If so, Ms. O'Reilly may have to be transferred."

A loud groan went through her families.

Ian laughed. "That's what I thought I'd hear. She can use your support right now. If you could call the board members or write them a note before next Tuesday's meeting, it will greatly help keep her at East Hills or Adams if there's an opening. And please come to the meeting. That would be the most impressive show of support. I'll be negotiating for her, so I'd appreciate anything you can tell me about her. Thank you."

Kendall was immediately bombarded with questions and comments, as was Ian. By the time he left, the sun had set unceremoniously behind the clouds. She escorted him across the beach to the bottom of the ramp with effusive thanks.

He laughed. "You're very welcome, but it's not over yet. We could plan a celebration anyway though. Why don't we go to that outdoor concert on Hospitality Point next Friday?"

She caught her breath, then squealed, "They're doing Bach. Oh, Ian, I would love that!"

"All right." In the dim glow of a parking lot lamp, she saw

his smile. "It's not the best of circumstances for you, but I must say, I'm certainly glad it happened."

Her jaw dropped.

He stepped closer and put a finger under her chin. "Because I'm enjoying getting to know you." His lips brushed hers briefly. "I don't know anyone else who would react to Bach that way."

Kendall swallowed.

"We can do dinner after the concert?"

She nodded.

He chuckled. "See you Tuesday."

"Good-bye."

She watched him walk off.

"Kendall."

She saw Jade and Caitlin approaching in the dark.

"Cait's tired, so we'd better go now. Can I carry anything up for you?"

She cleared her throat. "Uhh, n-no."

"Here are your keys. I almost forgot I still had them."

She reached for them, but her fingers didn't quite get a grasp, and they dropped in the sand.

Jade stooped. "Sorry."

"My fault. Caitlin, did you have a good time?"

The girl wrapped her arms around Kendall's waist and squeezed. "The best. Thanks, Ms. O'Reilly."

"You're welcome, sweetie. Have a good weekend."

"Here you go." Jade took her hand, then placed the keys in her palm with the other and closed her fingers around them. "You're cold. Go back to the fire. Great weenie roast!"

"Thanks. Oh, and thanks for bringing the wood."

"You're welcome, Ms. O'Reilly. Bye."

"Bye."

Grateful that no one else was close by, she trudged slowly

through the sand trying to recover from her embarrassment. Jade and Caitlin must have been near enough to witness the kiss. Maybe it was too dark though. Anyway, it was a just a quick, friendly one.

But it was nice.

Later that evening Jade sat at the kitchen table and dialed Lewis Thornton's number.

"Lewis? This is Jade Zukowski."

"Hello, Jade." His voice was boisterous, friendly. "How are you?"

"Good, thank you. I'm calling about Kendall O'Reilly."

"More problems?"

"No, quite the opposite. I heard she may be transferred away from East Hills."

"There's always that possibility. Did she tell you?"

"Yes, and I know she'd prefer to stay where she is rather than go to the middle school."

"Well, Jade, it's too early to tell what will happen. Much depends on the district boundaries." His voice had taken on a condescending tone.

Jade didn't want to discuss the details, so he got to the point. "I'd just like to put in my two cents' worth. I think she's an asset to the school, and it would be a shame to lose her."

Lewis didn't respond.

"I thought it might help your decision if you knew parents support her. I can't be at the board meeting because I have a final that night."

"Well, ultimately it's not my decision—it's the board's. It really needn't concern you. Your child will be going on to middle school next year."

"Yes, but I feel I owe it to Kendall to voice my support."

"You owe her?"

"She's been a tremendous help to my daughter."

"And that's it?" He chuckled. "I mean, after all, she *is* an attractive young woman."

Jade clenched his jaw. "I'm merely interested in her teaching."

"Well, I will make a note that you think she should remain at East Hills in spite of the problems you had with her earlier."

"I appreciate that. Thank you."

"Of course if she stayed, you wouldn't run into her again at the middle school, would you? Oh, by the way, the church committee is no longer accepting applications. We'll be getting to the interviews for youth pastor soon and give you a call."

"That's good to hear. I'll see you Sunday. Good-bye."

"Good-bye, Jade."

He pushed the Off button and shook his head. *That was an odd conversation. Lewis almost sounded as if . . . But why wouldn't he want to retain her at his school?*

He leaned back in the chair and tapped his fingers on the table.

His dad's words came to mind then, something about Lewis not sure of Kendall being appropriate for Cait. And he remembered how Kendall had changed her demeanor when the principal was in the room, because he preferred it that way, she'd said. It appeared that perhaps there wasn't a good working relationship there. Strange. They both seemed so competent.

Father, I ask that You grant wisdom to Lewis. Lead Kendall to wherever she needs to be to hear Your voice. I pray that it's at East Hills, but . . . You know best, Lord.

The high school gym was full. Folding chairs faced a long

table where the school administrators and board members sat just in front of the stage. Apparently there was a healthy interest in the looming possibility of changed district boundaries. Kendall estimated at least 200 people were present, and she was thrilled to see many of her parents there. She felt a twinge of disappointment when she couldn't find Jade in the crowd. So much for contemporary knighthood.

She waved to Ian across the room. He looked extra-nice in a tan sport coat and tie. A number of teachers were present, though Greg Jones had refused to come, convinced he couldn't make a difference. She sat next to Maxine Carothers and shredded the program in her lap.

"Calm down, baby," her friend soothed. "According to this agenda, it'll be a while before they get to faculty business."

It was a *long* while. Two and a half hours later, a recess was called. The heated boundary discussion seemed at a standstill.

Ian came over and put his arm around her shoulders. "It won't be long now. Hang in there. The board will go into executive session to discuss personnel. When your name comes up, we can go in. Okay?"

She nodded.

Most people left. Most of her parents walked past her, apologizing, promising to continue with calls and letters if necessary. They were working people with young children and baby-sitters to pay. She thanked them all.

Another eternity passed before she and Ian were summoned into the library. Members sat around tables that had been pushed together, forming a large square. The atmosphere felt less formal here; faces were relaxed. They had the freedom to discuss openly, knowing their words wouldn't be printed in tomorrow's *Union-Tribune*.

Lewis Thornton was given the floor. He estimated next year's class sizes and concluded that with or without boundary changes, class changes were inevitable. Some grades were increasing, others decreasing. He proposed some different split classes, which would accommodate all the teachers except Kendall O'Reilly. He recommended that she be transferred.

Kendall felt a knot tighten in her stomach.

A board member asked, "Let me clarify . . . If there are boundary changes, you'll probably need less teachers than you have now. Even if there are no changes, you will need one less teacher. And whichever happens, you recommend transferring Ms. O'Reilly?"

"That's correct." Thornton nodded.

Ian was granted permission to speak. He explained that her desire was to be given the opportunity to remain at East Hills. He knew of a possible first grade opening. He asked that the board would allow Ms. O'Reilly to pursue that avenue.

Thornton pursed his lips before replying. "Mr. Edwards, I realize that legally she has that right, as soon as an opening becomes available and is posted. However . . ." He coughed and glanced at her. "Ms. O'Reilly, I had hoped you would see the reasonableness of this situation. There are no openings at East Hills or Adams at this time. You minored in history, which the middle school needs."

"But if there's even a hint of a possible opening, I'd much prefer elementary," she replied. "Can't this wait?"

"Well . . ." Thornton coughed again. "There are extenuating circumstances in your personnel file." He pulled papers from a briefcase on the table and turned toward the others. "I have here documented complaints by parents during the past three years. These can be verified by my secretary." He began reading names and dates and phrases about not enough homework, having favorites, ignoring a child, being incompetent in math. "I have concluded that Ms. O'Reilly is not suitable for my building."

Ian stood. "Dr. Thornton, these are minor infractions, everyday occurrences. I'm sure the board has received kudos triple the number of these."

He ignored him. "The latest complaint is from Mr. Zukowski whose child felt so intimidated by Ms. O'Reilly's treatment of her that she refused to attend school for a week in February. Ms. O'Reilly was subsequently rude to Mr. Zukowski, for which I reprimanded her. This was the same student whom Ms. O'Reilly later transported on the freeway without parental or administrative permission."

A member asked, "What was her reply to that?"

Thornton read from a paper she recognized. "Quote, 'Under the circumstances I believed it was a matter of life and death. I take full responsibility for choosing on the side of life,' unquote."

Kendall noticed one of the women smile briefly.

"Lewis," a board member said, "would you say Ms. O'Reilly's file contains more reprimands than the average?"

"Oh, without a doubt. I have another serious concern that I haven't had the opportunity to discuss with her, but it should be included here. With her response, of course."

The president looked at her. "Do you mind, Ms. O'Reilly?"

What else can Thornton say? At least she could reply. She shook her head.

"Go ahead," the president said to him.

"There was an appearance of inappropriate behavior during a recent camping trip with a group of high schoolers. We're not here to judge one's morals, but since my son observed the father of one of her students leaving her tent while she remained alone inside, I feel I have the right to question the appropriateness of that behavior. They were also seen together early the next morning, before dawn."

Kendall was livid. She felt herself trembling. "I don't know what you're talking about."

"Late the second afternoon of your campout?"

"I was asleep. Alone."

Ian blurted, "These are insinuations, Dr. Thornton, and they should not affect her job in any way whatsoever."

"Nevertheless, I prefer not to have this renegade influence in my building. She is an adequate teacher and will do fine perhaps with one subject, with older students."

The president interrupted, "We need a break. Due to the fact that it's past midnight, I'd like someone to move that we table this discussion as well as the other personnel changes and then schedule a special meeting for two weeks from tonight. Do I have a motion?"

Kendall flew from the room and outside to the parking lot. There she stomped past a row of cars, then back again, furious at what she had just witnessed. A few minutes later Maxine and Ian appeared. Oblivious to others walking nearby, she shouted to them across the lot, "I cannot believe that!"

Ian hurried to her and grasped her arm. "Kendall, stop. He didn't say anything that made any sense. I talked to a couple of members. They all got phone calls supporting you. It'll work out."

She clenched her fists and gritted her teeth but still couldn't regain the self-control that was usually at her fingertips. She heard her own normally soft voice screech at decibels she would have thought impossible for her. "Yes, I took her to the hospital! She could have *died* if I hadn't!"

151

Maxine's strong arms pulled her close and held her tightly like a mother would with an hysterical child, muffling her shouts.

"I don't even teach them math. It wasn't *before* dawn! I'm not perfect! I—"

"There, there, baby. We know. We know."

With great effort, she quieted down. "Did Ian tell you?"

"Yes. I'm glad I drove you here. I wouldn't want you on the road in this condition. Are you okay now?"

She straightened and nodded.

Ian wrapped his arms around her. "Kendall, I'm sorry I didn't see that coming. What's that man got against you anyway?"

Maxine answered for her. "She's too independent and very good at what she does. Mind you, she doesn't break his rules, but she certainly does ignore the man. Come on, honey, let's go home."

"It'll be okay," Ian soothed. "Trust me?"

She nodded, her face buried in his shoulder.

"I'll pick you up Friday at 7, all right?"

She returned his hug. "Yes. Thanks, Ian."

He smiled and patted her cheek. "Bye."

In the car, Kendall groaned. "What was all that about, Maxine? I haven't done anything wrong. Those complaints weren't representative of my teaching. And the way Thornton twisted things around, I feel so . . . dirty. What will people think?"

"Nothing, Pollyanna. You have the reputation of a good, honest person."

"But he has planted a huge seed of doubt. He's cast shadows. I just don't believe this is happening."

"What was that business about his son and, I take it, Mr. Zukowski?"

Kendall shook her head. "I don't have a clue. As far as I know, Jade was nowhere near my tent. I slept that whole afternoon and night. When he saw us in the morning, we were drinking coffee at the fire and the sun was up."

"You know what this goes back to, don't you?"

"Unfortunately, yes. Thanks for covering for me with Ian. It wouldn't do any good dragging Thornton's name through the mud, regardless of what he's done."

"You're right. Even if that's what he just did to yours. I am so proud of you, baby."

"You've taught me well over the years, dear Maxine." She smiled at her friend and mentor. "I have never been so angry though. I doubt I'll sleep tonight."

"I'll pray for you. You know, that Ian's kind of cute, ponytail and all."

Kendall smiled. "You are so prejudiced! Well, at least I have Friday night to look forward to. At the moment, I think I could request a sub for the next six weeks."

As expected, she did toss and turn, finally getting up at 4 A.M., arriving at school at 6:30. It would be a long day.

She sat at her desk, sipping coffee, trying to focus on the day's plans rather than last night's board meeting. The door opened, and Greg stuck his head in.

"Hey, Ken."

"Hi, Greg."

"Max told me what happened. It stinks, and I'm really sorry. I think we should *all* get out of here."

She shrugged. "I don't want to."

"Whew. You've got more stamina than is good for you." He shook his head. "Send your class over after lunch. We'll do some extra science together. I'll put Miss Jenny to work, and you can read a magazine."

She smiled. "Thanks, Greg. That'll help."

153

"See ya." The door clicked behind him.

A short time later there was a knock. "Come in," she called.

Jade stepped inside. Kendall was unprepared for the avalanche of conflicting emotions that rolled through her. Unexpected delight at the sight of him was quickly overtaken by embarrassment and hurt and finally anger.

"Kendall, what happened last—"

"Why weren't you there?" she snapped. Her hand flew to her mouth, too late to catch the words. "Oh, I'm sorry."

He strode across the room. "No, I'm sorry. So, what's the status of your job?"

"They ran out of time to decide. They'll have another meeting in two weeks."

"I would have been there, but I had a final I couldn't miss. I told Lewis that when I gave him my vote of confidence for you."

She felt confused. "You talked to him, supporting me?"

"Sure." Jade sat down in the chair next to her desk. "I called him the night of the beach party. He said he'd make a note of my support. You know what I think. Without you, Cait and I would be in deep yogurt." He looked closely at her face. "You do know that, don't you?"

She bit her lip. Yes, she did know that, but . . . "He didn't mention anything about support from anybody. He just talked about your complaint about when Caitlin—" Her voice cracked. It was the tenderness in Jade's eyes . . . But she would not cry! She could not afford to do that and lose all control in this situation that was quickly developing into a nightmare.

"Are you serious? Were your families there?"

"It was almost midnight. Only a few could stay. We were in closed session, so they didn't hear this." She stared at her fingers wrapped around a pencil. "A lot of them called the board members though, and Ian asked that I be considered for a possible first grade opening here. But Lewis gave his documented proof of complaints from unhappy parents, like it was a trial, and said I wasn't suitable for his building. I know not everybody likes my style, but he made it sound like a majority."

"That's outrageous. Unhappy parents? What, two or three? It was probably *their* fault, like mine, just a temporary lack of communication. I mean, your ability and your character are obviously—"

She touched his arm. "There's more."

He leaned across the corner of the desk. "What is it?"

She noticed how still he sat. The usual energetic bouncing of a leg or tapping of a foot was absent. "He said his son saw you leaving my tent, and he saw us alone early the next morning."

"And?"

"And nothing. Oh, Jade, the way he said it, he insinuated that it had to do with something immoral. I felt so absolutely filthy."

His mouth was a grim line. "Kendall, I stepped inside your tent for a split moment, to make sure you were all right after the climb. You were sleeping soundly. Scott must have seen me leaving." He shook his head. "Why would Lewis repeat something like that as if it meant . . . ?"

She took off her glasses and rubbed her eyes with her fingertips. She knew Lewis wouldn't let the past die; he would grasp at straws to remove her from his sight. "He wants me out of here."

"Why?"

"We don't get along. I told you he doesn't like my style."

"That's hardly grounds for dismissal when it's obvious

that your students' parents think the world of you. Can we come to the next meeting and tell the board that?"

"I guess so." A thought struck her. "Jade, did you say he's the chairman of the committee in charge of hiring the youth pastor?"

He nodded.

"Then you can't stick up for me. Don't even think about it."

"They're two separate issues. I'll talk to him and the others about those insinuations. That was just a misunderstanding on his son's part. There's no reason for it to affect my chances of getting the job."

She was amazed at his naiveté. "I told you how he feels about me. He'll hold it against you if you support me."

"Don't worry about that. We have to get out the truth that parents support you and that nothing wrong happened at the campout."

"Please don't. You can't make a difference, and I don't want you to jeopardize your work." She held up a hand. "Let me finish . . . He is *not* to be trusted."

"Kendall, he's a devoted Christian on a committee at my church. That doesn't mean he's perfect, but we can communicate, and we can certainly disagree about things not related to doctrine."

"Why do you say he's a devoted Christian?"

"First of all, to be on the church board he had to express faith in Jesus Christ. He takes care of his family, works hard, and is respected at the church."

"He's not like your father."

"Different people's personalities are different."

Kendall shook her head.

The first bell rang. She crossed her arms over her midsection. The knot that formed last night was still there.

"Do you have to go outside for recess?" he asked.

"No. Jennifer, the student teacher, is there. Jade, I've never *not* wanted to be here before. Maybe it's because I didn't sleep last night." She frowned. "Oh, why do I tell you these things?"

"Remember? I'm your knight in shining armor, and I'm an almost-certified counselor." He smiled softly. "What can I do for you?"

"Just go. It's an ugly situation, but I'll live through it. Don't try to save me this time. It's not like rock climbing. You'll hurt yourself for sure."

He reached out and gently brushed loose strands of hair from her cheek and tucked them behind her ear. "Well, I'll pray for you, for energy for this day and for wisdom about your job."

Maxine's prayers hadn't helped her sleep; she doubted Jade's would make a dent in the impossible.

"Kendall, will you please call me if you need anything? You could have called me last night, just to talk."

"At 1 A.M.?"

"Yeah. I mean it, okay?"

She nodded, unable to believe there was a knight in shining armor who could help her. Nothing could be worse than this uncertain mess, this feeling she was on trial for being herself. All she wanted was to just keep doing the job she'd always done.

Eight

Kendall studied Ian's profile as he studied the Friday evening freeway traffic. His smile and laid-back attitude were disarming, and disarming was exactly what she needed, a laying down of the defenses that she had tightly wound around herself since the board meeting earlier in the week.

He was an attractive man, with longish blond hair pulled back. He wore a soft, long-sleeved black shirt with silver tie and gray slacks. His slender hands were musician's hands that gracefully steered, now shifting into fifth gear. She noticed he drove the sporty red car conservatively by California standards, keeping it at seventy miles per hour.

He glanced at her. "Mind if I ask two business-related questions and then we'll forget about it for tonight?"

Kendall looked down at her hands and admired her nails. She was glad she'd had time after school to scrub off the tempera paint and apply a coat of clear polish. She smoothed her black, wool skirt, hoping it would keep her warm along with the white, silk sweater and long, light-weight coat. It was early in the season for an outdoor concert, something to do about a fund-raiser and special artist.

The evening would turn cool once the sun set.

"Earth to Kendall." Ian broke into her thoughts. "Hey, it can wait."

She folded her hands and looked at him. "No, let's get it over with. This is why I called you in the first place."

"All right. What happened on your camping adventure?"

And thus the doubts begin. "Ian, I called you right after that. Remember, we had lunch at that coffee shop and I told you about trying to climb and having a good time with my old students?"

"Yes. And you introduced me to that dad, the earthy, All-American-looking guy. Was he the one in your tent?"

"First of all, he wasn't in-my-tent in my tent! He had stopped by to see how I was after that silly climbing episode. I was sound asleep in the middle of the afternoon, and he was concerned and stepped inside to make sure I was all right. Scott Thornton must have happened to see him at that moment. The girls and mother who shared my tent can testify—that seems the word I need here!—that I slept for fifteen hours. Alone!"

Ian reached for her hand and gave it a quick squeeze. "I know it seems like you're on trial, but you're not. I just want to know everything so I'm not caught off guard again."

"I appreciated your response. It was the insinuation that bothered me."

"Anything else about the camping trip or your personal life I should know?"

She sighed. "No. I have not committed theft or murder. I do not spank the children or curse at them. I am not 'seeing' that dad or any other dad. Or any guy for that matter. Teaching is my life, and I do a good job of it. Not every parent or child likes me, but I think the majority don't mind me."

Ian laughed. "You certainly sound like a 'renegade influence.' "

"Don't laugh! Thornton was serious when he said that."

"I know he was. That's a disturbing thought." He glanced at her. "Did he ever make a pass at you?"

"You already used up your two questions."

"The first two were one and the same."

Kendall looked out the side window. They sped past high green hills that hid La Jolla and the sun from view. "No."

"You're a lousy liar."

"He's married, Ian."

"You're not that naive. Marriage wouldn't interfere. And in case no one has told you, you *are* a beautiful woman. Those sapphire eyes would stop any man dead in his tracks, not to mention those lips."

"Well, now I am thoroughly embarrassed."

He laughed long and hard. "No need to be. It's just a fact. So, what happened after he made the pass?"

"What do you think?"

"Nothing, which is why he's so ticked at you he wants you out. Did you file a complaint?"

"It wasn't obvious, and my job wasn't threatened. Some people would say it was just my imagination." She gave him a small smile. "Did you ever think of going into law?"

"Actually I did, but music kept getting in the way. Piano, guitar, saxophone, trumpet. Playing in a band. Wanting to teach kids how to play in a band. Tell me about that old piano in your apartment."

Grateful for the change of subject, Kendall talked about her mother teaching her to play the piano. The remainder of the ride was a pleasant time of getting to know each other.

Hospitality Point was a small peninsula that jutted out

into Mission Bay and was used for the most part by bicyclers and walkers. Only one road led to the isolated strip of land. Dusk settled in as Kendall and Ian made their way with the crowd around equipment trailers set up for the occasion. They stepped across thick electrical cables, the power source for the temporary stadium lights that brightened the large outdoor theater area.

They waited for an usher at the back near a set of bleachers, the least expensive seats in the "house." Ahead of these were rows of round, black wrought-iron tables and chairs set on the grass. Just beyond were rows of picnic benches. Up front was the band shell, large enough to hold an entire symphony orchestra. It looked beautiful, with its "shell" a cluster of bright lights and a backdrop of nighttime blue-black sky and dark bay water.

To Kendall's delight, an usher led them to a table. It was near the back, but in the center with a wonderful view of the stage.

"Oh, Ian." She grabbed his arm across the small table. "This is lovely! I've only sat on the bleachers."

He grinned, and his light blue eyes studied her face. "Do you know your nose crinkles up when you giggle? Right here, between your eyes." He touched the bridge of his own nose.

Quickly she covered hers, and he gently pulled her hand away. "Don't. It's another thing that stops us dead in our tracks. It kind of takes the edge off all that beauty."

He exaggerated, she knew, but still the attention was soothing. His soft hand caressing hers felt comfortable. She smiled. "Bet you say that to all the union members."

He returned her smile, then picked up a menu. "Not quite. Would you like something? They've got drinks and desserts."

"Tea sounds good."

"I was thinking champagne."

"We can't celebrate yet."

He frowned and lowered his voice in an exaggerated manner. "You doubt my ability?"

She giggled. "No, but it's not over yet. Ian?"

He looked up from the menu.

"Thank you. For the other night and for this."

He lifted her hand to his lips and kissed the back of it. "You're very welcome, my dear."

The waitress came then, and Ian ordered a bottle of chardonnay.

The sensation tingling from the back of her hand to her spine faded. "I'd like a cup of tea, please."

When the waitress left, he said, "Chardonnay goes so well with Bach." He scanned the program. "Oh, fantastic. They're doing *Toccata and Fugue in D Minor*. Do you see the organ?"

Kendall answered his small talk. He helped her into her coat, then slipped on a gray, V-necked sweater. The wine arrived with two goblets and her tea with a small pot of hot water. Busying herself with the tea bag, she declined Ian's offer to fill her glass.

The lights dimmed, and the concert began. The orchestra filled the stage, and Kendall was soon caught up in the magic of Bach's familiar concertos.

As the first half came to a close, the lights brightened again. Ian stood. His chair bumped into one close behind his. "Excuse me," he said over his shoulder. "Kendall, care to stroll around?"

"No. You go ahead."

"Be right back. Got to find the little boys' room."

She sat very still, her hands folded in her lap. The magic flowed away. She glanced at the wine bottle. It was more than half empty. His speech was . . . all right. His voice . . . not too noticeably thick. His eyes . . . glassy. The stumbling over the chair . . . well, the chairs were awfully close together.

Kendall glanced around at the milling crowd, searching. She needed something to hold on to. Half a bottle was too much for one man, wasn't it? And if he finished it . . . Was that too much to be in control of one's faculties, to drive on a freeway?

She had the solution. *She* would drive. She'd *insist* on driving. Friends don't let friends drive drunk, right? And she knew how to drive a four-speed. Her college roommate had had one. A five-speed was just one more gear, for going a little faster.

It was the sensible thing to do. Ian seemed a reasonable man. If he chose to not be reasonable, well, then she wouldn't ride with him. Simple as that. She glanced at her watch. Sara should be home soon, or Maxine's husband. She would call. She twisted around in her seat. Yes, there was a pay phone. She had her purse, money.

There. All right. She had something to hold on to.

She took a deep breath. A dull pounding echoed in her ears, and she knew that for her, the concert was over.

The phone ringing some time after 10 P.M. startled Jade. He set down his book and picked up the cordless at his elbow.

"Zukowskis'."

"Jade?"

He recognized the soft voice. "Hi, Kendall."

"Jade . . ."

Some internal alert clicked on in his mind. "What's wrong?"

"I need a ride." Jagged breaths underscored each word.

"I'm on my way. Where are you?" He stood.

163

"I'm sorry. Nobody's home, and there's no taxi—"

"Where are you?"

"Mission Bay. The outdoor concert place. I can't re-member . . . Take the 5 south, go past Sea World."

His dad walked into the room. "Hold on, Kendall. Dad, do you know where the outdoor concert place is in Mission Bay?"

Jeremiah nodded. "Hospitality Point. What's wrong?"

Jade shrugged a shoulder. "Is it Hospitality Point?"

"I think so."

"Kendall, are you all right?"

"Y-yes. I just need a ride home."

"Tell me exactly where to find you once I get there."

She didn't reply.

"Kendall?"

"There's a band shell. I'll go by the band shell."

"Okay. I'm on my way. I'll be there in—" He glanced at his father.

Jeremiah said, "Thirty minutes."

"Twenty minutes. Okay?"

"Okay," she whispered. "I'm sorry."

"Bye." He pushed the Off button and strode to the kitchen. "I don't know what's wrong. She sounds upset. Says she needs a ride home and she'll be at the band shell. Mind if I take your car?" His open Wrangler would be too cold for her.

"Of course not. However, I don't know if it'll make it in twenty minutes."

"You underestimate the power of prayer and a V-8 en-gine."

His dad followed him to the garage, giving him exit direc-tions. "Be careful, son."

Jade's prayers flew with him down the freeway.

Twenty-four minutes later he parked at a curb. In the distance he thought he saw the outline of a band shell. The area was in total darkness. The sky was its usual coastal misty overcast, obliterating any light from the stars. He walked near a trailer. Except for voices coming from inside, there was no evidence anyone was around. What in the world was Kendall doing here? Was he in the right place?

His foot bumped something hard, almost tripping him. He slowed down, carefully making his way toward the stage through a maze of tables, chairs, and benches.

"Kendall!" he called. He felt a movement in the dark before he saw any form. "Kendall!"

She rushed at him then, flinging herself against him, encircling his waist with her arms. "Oh, Jade!"

"Are you hurt?" He held her tightly, and despite her coat he could feel her small frame trembling.

"Oh, Jade, it's so scary. Everybody left, and they turned off all the lights. It's so dark. Sara wasn't home. And Maxine. And—oh, I'm sorry." Her voice was muffled against his sweatshirt, but he could hear the unsteadiness in it, the jagged breathing.

"Shh, shh. It's okay now. It's okay," he soothed until the trembling slowed. "Are you hurt?"

She loosened her death grip but clung to his arm with both hands and looked up at him, shaking her head. Her teeth chattered. In the darkness he could make out her small pearl earrings. Her braid seemed askew; loose strands of hair hung about her face. Her eyes were wide open, as if in fear. "No."

"Thank God. Let's go home." His other questions would have to wait.

She leaned heavily on his arm as they walked through the darkened grounds. He helped her into the car, then went around and climbed in the driver's side.

165

From the corner of his eye he watched her fasten the seat belt, slip off her shoes, and pull up her knees, wrapping the long coat around them, her chin resting on them. It was that position of self-protection she had sat in as they watched the sun set Easter night. She huddled against the door.

"What happened?" he asked.

The shudder that tore through her was so violent he could feel it across the car. "I couldn't ride with him." Her voice was softer than usual, almost inaudible. "Jade, you didn't see any accidents, did you?" She sounded anxious. "On the other side of the freeway?"

He thought about his drive down here. Would he have noticed backed-up traffic, flashing lights? Probably. "No. Why?"

She didn't reply. Jade gripped the steering wheel. Someone was responsible for putting Kendall in this situation, and he was determined to find out who it was. Whoever "he" was would answer to him.

"It's a left-hand turn," she prompted, "up there onto the freeway."

"Oh, thanks." He signaled and changed lanes. "Are you okay?"

"I'm cold."

He turned the heater on full blast and focused on traffic, letting her be quiet. He glimpsed her shuddering again. After a while her breathing sounded more regular. He thanked God that she was at least safe and fought back the anger that kept rising up inside him.

Twenty minutes later he coasted down the Solana Beach exit ramp toward a red stoplight. "Kendall, how do I get to your place?"

She looked at him, then out all of the windows as if unsure where she was.

166

There was no traffic behind him, so he braked in the middle of the lanes. "Right or left?"

She pointed to the right, stretched her legs to the floor and leaned toward the windshield. After a short distance she murmured, "Next left, then the first right, then an immediate left."

He thought she seemed almost in a state of shock. Wouldn't her usual Pollyanna mode be scared but getting over it by now, chattering about some impossibly bright side and thanking him profusely? But this was like the rock-climbing incident. She was lost somewhere deep inside herself, in some hidden, painful corner.

"There. Stop by those steps."

"Where do I park?" The small lot appeared full. He slowed for a speed bump.

No reply.

"I'm walking you to your door. Can I use this? It says Visitor's." It was next to a small building with a Manager's Office sign.

"At night."

"It is night." What was wrong with her? He pulled into the spot, jumped out, and hurried around to open the door for her.

He followed her down a sidewalk, around the corner of the manager's office, then down another sidewalk. From three sides three-story apartment buildings surrounded a courtyard of low bushes, palm trees, and benches. The area was well-lit. At the middle building she climbed an open stairway to the first landing, then stopped at the door on the left. A covered walkway led to the right and toward the back; more steps led up another flight.

She unbuttoned her coat and reached into her purse that hung underneath it, across her neck and shoulder. An outdoor lamp lit the door's keyhole, but her fingers fumbled. Jade took the keys from her, unlocked the door, and followed her through it.

Lights were on. Just inside was a closet door. To the right she walked through the kitchen area and dumped her coat and purse onto a dining table. He noticed a couch to the left, separating the kitchen from the living area. At the far end vertical blinds were pulled across what must be a sliding glass door. To the left of that, against the wall, was an old upright piano. This side of the piano, completing the full square, was what looked like a short hallway, probably leading to the bedroom. Kendall headed there now. He heard a door click shut.

He stood awkwardly in the kitchen. Well, she was home safe. He could leave, but it didn't feel right to leave her alone in the state she was in. And besides, he was still angry. He wanted to find out who had put her in such danger.

There was a phone on the counter near the table. He called his dad so he wouldn't be concerned. He agreed that Jade should stay if she were so upset.

He looked around the apartment. It was cozy like her classroom but with a definitely better smell. It felt feminine without being frilly. The lighting was soft. Pillows and afghans filled the couch and chairs. The walls were covered with handmade-looking crafts. Candles dotted tabletops and bookshelves.

He noticed a kettle on the stovetop and thought she'd probably like some tea. He filled it with water and while it heated opened a cupboard. It was the right one. Chamomile, Earl Grey, ginseng, lemon, green. Wasn't it chamomile that was supposed to be soothing?

Kendall entered and strode over to the small television on the bookshelf in the corner by the sliding door. She turned on the news and sat on the couch, clutching a pillow to her stomach.

Jade watched her, hoping he wouldn't startle her. She had changed into sweats and was pulling out her braid with agitated yanks. Noisily he found two mugs and made the tea, then carried it over to the couch.

"Kendall."

She glanced at him and accepted the cup. "The news might have accidents on it. I hope he got home all right."

Her fingers felt cold against his. "Who?" He sat beside her.

"Ian. Jade, I'm okay. You can go."

Ian? "That teacher, the union guy?" *The arty looking one at the coffee shop.*

"Maybe I should call him." She stared at the television. The sportscaster was talking about the Padres.

"Why couldn't you ride with him?"

"He's probably asleep. Or at dinner. We were supposed to go to dinner." She was trembling again, her breath coming in gasps. "You'd think he'd be asleep. If he didn't have the accident."

Jade took the cup from her and set it on a lamp table. "Kendall." He grasped her by the shoulders, turning her to face him. "Talk to me. What happened? Why couldn't you ride with him?"

She shook her head. "I'm okay."

She was obviously anything but okay. Jade breathed a quick prayer. *Lord, help me understand.* "Let me inside, sweetheart." He didn't know where the *sweetheart* came from.

Her face crumpled. "I'm okay." She pulled a handkerchief from her pocket.

Accident? Couldn't ride with him? "Was he drinking?"

She nodded, twisting the hankie between her fingers.

169

"They serve alcohol there? At the concert?"

"I couldn't ride with him then, could I?"

"No, it's good you didn't ride with him. He just left you there?" Jade's blood was boiling.

"I offered to drive, but he doesn't let anyone drive his car."

"Was he belligerent? Mean to you?"

"N-no. He laughed. We walked to the car, and when I refused to get in, he laughed. He said it could have been fun, and he called me something. Then he left."

That all sounded belligerent and mean to him. "He called you something? What?"

"It doesn't matter."

He hugged her then. If he didn't, he would at the very least tear apart the phone book in search of the man's address and then he would go there and ram his fist into his face. "It's all over now. Just forget about it, sweetheart." *Sweetheart again.*

The floodgates opened, and deep, heart-wrenching sobs flowed from her.

At that moment Kendall ceased to be Cait's teacher, or an acquaintance in need of counseling, or a distressed damsel in need of a defender. She was a woman whose heart unabashedly called to his on a deeper level, as if they were two halves of a whole, one incomplete without the other.

She had let him inside, and he knew no one else had been there. He sensed, too, that she cried from pain beyond tonight's ugliness.

It was not the time to speak. He held her close to himself, praying that Christ in him would absorb the unbearable hurt she carried. He caressed her loose hair, resting his cheek atop her head, resisting the urge to kiss it. That right was not his.

A long time passed before she relaxed. He thought she

slept against his chest and so did not move, wanting her to rest as long as possible. The television was still on and he watched an entire sitcom rerun before she stirred.

"Jade?"

"What?"

"I'm sorry."

"No, no. Don't be." He brushed her hair back. It felt so soft. Her face was small nestled alongside his hand. "Can you sleep now?"

She pushed herself to a sitting position and nodded, smoothing his rumpled sweatshirt. "You don't have to stay. I'll just lay down right here."

He stood. "Do you want the TV off?" Even puffy, red eyes and uncombed hair did not detract from her incredible beauty. His chest tightened.

She shook her head and pulled an afghan from the back of the couch to cover herself.

"I'll just lock the door then."

She gave him a small smile and settled down among the pillows. "Thank you, O knight in shining armor."

"Call me if you need anything, okay?"

"I just did."

As he pulled the door shut, her musical laughter reached his ears.

He called her this time.

It was late the next morning. She was cleaning, running back and forth to the laundry room, chatting with Sara when their laundry run coincided, adding layers and layers between herself and last night's horror. Her friend had pronounced Ian a cad, Jade a true hero.

"Hello?"

"Hi, Kendall."

He always said it like that. Familiar. A hint of anticipation.

A whispery tone lowering the strong, outdoorsy voice. "Hi, Jade."

"How are you?"

"Fine." She sensed the sincerity in his question and lowered her guard. "Really, I am. Thanks."

"Good. I was wondering if I might continue my knight in shining armor duties?"

A spontaneous giggle chased away the guard she was trying to push back up. "I hope this knight business isn't going to your head. You could get rather obnoxious." His knack for getting through to her even when she was on guard felt unsettling.

"You can tell me if I do. I just thought of something that seems an appropriate follow-up to last night."

"And what would that be?"

"I'd like to take you to tonight's concert. If you don't have plans?"

Emotionally, she scrambled, groping for bricks and mortar to patch up her defenses. "You know I'd just as soon forget last night ever happened. I appreciate what you did, but . . . but . . . well . . ."

"Mind if I sound like a counselor for a minute? I need the practice."

She hesitated, wary. "Okay."

"It would probably be best if you didn't forget it but rather worked through it. If you don't do it now, that outdoor theater and concert dates and even Bach will always carry a stigma. Every time you encounter one of them, you'll have to deal with it."

She knew he made sense. "Maybe, but it still seems easier that way. Anyway, I have this rule—I never date students' fathers."

"As a matter of fact, I don't date, period. Let's think of it as therapy or just some time out with a friend. We are friends, right?"

After last night? Absolutely. "Y-yes."

"Besides, I already have the tickets, and my dad's baby-sitting Cait, so I can't take him. Come with me?"

She took a deep breath. "Guess I'm out of arguments."

"Great. Should I pick you up about 7?"

"No. Let me take you to dinner first. Can you come at 5:30?"

"Sure. Is this a formal affair? I noticed you wore a skirt last night."

"Oh, I live in skirts. This is San Diego. You can wear whatever you're comfortable in. However, I am partial to tuxedos."

He laughed. "Mine's in storage."

"I suppose your armor is too?" She sighed dramatically.

"Sorry. See you at 5:30."

"Bye."

Kendall set the phone on the kitchen counter and put both hands to her head, clutching fistfuls of hair.

There was a quick rap at the door, and Sara popped in. "Do you want—Hey, what's wrong?"

Through gritted teeth, she squealed, "I think I just made a date with a dad!"

Kendall opened her apartment door and smiled at Jade. "Hi. Come on in. I'll get my coat."

He didn't respond.

She stepped to the kitchen table where she had draped her coat and a blanket. In a glance she had taken in his casual tan slacks and white cotton, crewneck sweater with sleeves pushed up. His jaw appeared freshly shaven, his short, soft waves damp. As always, he looked totally, solidly masculine.

She turned back around. "I'll bring this blanket to sit on if we have bleacher seats."

He still stood in the open doorway, his eyebrows raised as if in surprise. He cleared his throat and opened his mouth, but no words came out. He swallowed and tried again. "Where's Ms. O'Reilly?"

She had followed Sara's advice to lose her teacher-ish appearance for one night. Her naturally wavy hair hung loose on her shoulders, and she wore dangly gold earrings. Her favorite bluejay-blue knit dress with matching flats and white stockings were casual and comfortable. She shrugged. "I gave her the night off. Thought I'd just be a regular person."

"Regular's not the word." Jade shook his head. "You look sensational!"

"Thanks." She grinned. At Sara's insistence she had spent the afternoon pampering herself, a rare expenditure of time. It had served to help her relax and actually look forward to tonight.

"I'll carry those." He strode over to her and took the blanket and coat from her. "What's all that?"

She followed his gaze over her shoulder. He smelled nice, kind of woodsy. "Oh, it's my traditional gift for the kids when they're promoted from fifth grade. I make an album for everyone." She picked up a softcover, 4 x 6 photo album. "See, this one is for Tony. I fill it with all the pictures I've taken of him or of him with others."

He leafed through it. "This is great. You do have a talent for making all of them feel special. It must take a lot of work."

"I've got it down to a science. See these envelopes, one for each child? Each time I get a roll of film developed, I file the pictures. I try to get ten of everyone. Now I'll just sit down tomorrow and put them all together. There'll be enough time to take more pictures if someone is short." She pointed to a stack of photos. "I'll try to get more of Caitlin. Of course she's short because she hasn't been here all year."

He reached for his daughter's pile. "May I?"

"Sure."

Smiling, he studied the photos. "She'll enjoy these. Ha, this one's good!" He held out the picture the mime had taken of them at Sea World. "I wonder where that kid was from?"

"I thought Caitlin would like it. Wasn't that a fun day?" She smiled. The field trip had probably been the beginning of their friendship. "Do you like fish tacos?"

"My favorite." He grinned. "Rubio's?"

"Of course."

In the parking lot they walked toward a midsize white car. As he opened the door for her, she teased, "Well, at least it's white, but really, I expected a steed."

"He's at the vet's."

Kendall giggled.

Their banter continued during the drive and throughout dinner. It was only when they entered the outdoor theater that she sobered. They strolled onto the grounds with the crowd. Like last night, dusk was approaching, and the bright lights were on. Symphony members straggled onstage, plucking at strings and playing intermittent brass and wind notes. Her stomach knotted.

Jade seemed to sense her uneasiness. His hand slipped under her elbow. "I have to confess, I don't know the first thing about Johann. Other than," he looked down at her now, "when I heard you play, I felt something inside."

She studied his eyes, trying to detect a playfulness. There wasn't any. "Really?"

"Yeah."

"That's all you need to know then, about Johann or Ludwig."

An usher took their tickets and pointed them in the direction of the bleachers. They chose an empty center row. Jade spread the blanket, then held open her coat while she slipped it on. They sat down and quietly surveyed the scene before them.

"About last night," he said, "did you sit there at the tables?"

She nodded.

"Well, I'm here tonight." He scooted closer until their shoulders touched. "And I don't drink, and I don't leave my friends alone in the dark."

She smiled and murmured, "Slayer of dragons."

"Right." He chuckled. "Tell me about Bach."

"He was born in 1685 . . ."

During intermission they walked. It had been a long time for Jade to sit still, she knew. "You didn't fidget. Does that mean you like it?" she asked as they meandered about the area.

"Surprisingly, I do. It's like when I listened to you—something gets stirred up inside. There's no word for it except maybe worship. It makes me think of the vastness of creation, something so huge it can't be grasped."

"Much of what he wrote was church music. Sometimes when I listen, I feel this indescribable ache, like life is so absolutely wonderful it hurts. Does that make sense?"

"I know what you mean," he agreed. "Paul wrote in Romans that God's divine nature and eternal power are evident to everyone. All we have to do is look around us."

"Really?" She had never heard that before.

"I think that ache you describe is a deep, innate sense of knowing there's more to life than what we see. It's those invisible attributes of God, evident in creation, that call us to worship Him. And they promise that life is eternal and we can live with God forever if we choose to."

"My mother believed that. I remember her telling me that Jesus loved me, that I could always depend on Him, and that she thought she was going to live with Him after she died. Do you think so?"

"Definitely. That's what Jesus taught. I believe Deb is with Him now. You know, not believing it doesn't make it untrue—it just keeps people from truly enjoying life in its deepest sense, now and always."

"But why does He let mothers of little girls die? Why would I depend on a God who did that?"

"I don't know. All I know is that indescribable ache at the wonder of it all."

She pondered his words. Not knowing didn't seem to change his faith. "Is that why you don't date?"

"What?"

"You said you don't date, period. Is it because you think Deb is still alive?"

"Good question. No. I think we have to continue living this life the best we can. She was my past, and she will be in my unimaginable future, but that doesn't stop me from forming relationships now." He stopped talking.

"What does then?"

"I guess either no one has gotten my attention in that way, or it just hurts too much to notice again. Why don't you date students' dads?"

"Did it once. It hurt too much. Why does life hurt so much?"

As they climbed back up the bleachers, Jade chuckled. "My dad would love these questions. Come over anytime and ask away."

As the lights dimmed, she whispered, "I missed this part last night."

Wordlessly, he reached for her hand. After a gentle squeeze, he continued holding it.

The warmth of his hand around hers, their arms touching, brought to mind how he'd held her last night, how she'd slept to the rhythm of his heart beating against her ear. It would be all right. There was nothing to be afraid of with Jade Zukowski beside her.

"Chocolate," she announced.

"Definitely. How about that Del Mar coffee shop/bookstore?"

"Perfect. Have you ever had their quadruple decker, triple fudge torte?"

Jade laughed.

It seemed he wasn't in a hurry to end the evening, and to Kendall that was all right. She couldn't remember the last time she'd felt so relaxed, so completely at ease. She hadn't thought about school for hours.

Inside the shop, they eyed the desserts through the glass case.

"There it is." She pointed and groaned. "I can't eat a whole piece."

"Two forks?"

"I'll get them."

They put the plate in the middle of the small table between their cups of decaf vanilla nut.

"Ummm," he moaned. "I've never tasted anything like this."

"Isn't it marvelous?" She took another bite.

"If my sister-in-law Annette walked in right now, she'd swear we were on a date."

"No way. A date wouldn't be nearly this much fun."

He laughed. "Am I right to assume we've worked through

last night? Your nose has been crinkling a lot." He reached over and touched the bridge of her nose.

She rolled her eyes. *Not another one.* "I think so, thank you, Mr. Knight."

"You're welcome." A large piece of fudge torte filled his mouth.

"So, how many times have you rescued me?" She held up one finger at a time, counting. "The unbear-able-student-teacher day. The can't-get-down-from-here rock. The drippy-woe-is-me sunset. The need-a-ride-home concert. The work-through-last-night evening."

"The carried-your-picnic-basket weenie roast."

"Uh-unh. I could have done that."

"Yeah, right. Well, I got the wood."

"Okay, that counts. Six. Why do you do it?"

He set down his coffee cup and tipped his chair back, his eyes on her face.

She continued, "I mean, for me? You don't really know me. And you certainly don't owe me anything just because I do my job. Lots of children have a good, even significant year in my class, but their parents don't have concern for me. They don't get involved with my life." She took a breath.

"Kendall, before I knew Jesus Christ, my only concern was myself. When I understood that He died for me because He loves me so much, I wanted Him to be number one in my life. It's a day-by-day thing, but the more I learn to trust Him to take care of me, the more freed up I am to have concern for others. So when He puts someone in my path who needs en-couragement, I try to be available." He set the front of his chair back down and smiled. "That's why I do it."

It came then, without warning, like the sudden onslaught of an earthquake rumbling forth from unseen depths. "It was because of the accident. Last night."

"What?"

"I was in an accident. My dad died in it. He was an alcoholic." She looked toward the large blackened window. Their reflections blurred. She blinked rapidly.

"When, sweetheart?"

Sweetheart. He'd called her that last night. Her mother had called her that, such a long time ago. "Guess we didn't quite work through last night yet." She smiled briefly at Jade. "I was eighteen. Ian's drinking brought it back. I've been out with guys who've had a beer or two, a glass of wine, but something about Ian . . . I always figured out how not to ride with my dad. Except the last time. I was at a friend's graduation party. He came to pick me up."

"I'm sorry."

She looked down at her cup. "We went over a cliff. I woke up, my face against the rock. It took them a long time to get me . . . us up. I had some broken bones. And this." She pointed to her scar and met his eyes. "So, no drinking and no rock climbing. Either one undoes me." She inhaled sharply. "I'm tired. Can we go home?"

She sensed that he wanted to say more. When, instead, he stood and reached for her hand, she was grateful. The short ride home was a quiet one. Not an awkward quiet, just a peaceful one. He held her hand again as they walked to her apartment.

Jade glanced down at her. "Thanks for dinner, and for introducing me to Bach, and for sharing more of who you are."

"You're welcome. Thank you for taking me. And for finishing up last night."

"You're all right?"

They reached her door, and she dug in her purse for the keys. "There's something about you, Jade Zukowski. I always feel all right with you."

"You do?" He sounded surprised.

"Yes. Even when you're not wearing your armor."

He chuckled and pulled her into his arms.

It was an incredibly comfortable place. The place of discomfort came when he released her and for a moment he hesitated, his mouth so very close to her cheek, his warm breath at her temple, her lips a millimeter from his chin.

"Good night," he whispered.

She went inside and quickly shut the door before the giggle burst from her. The knots in her stomach were completely gone. There seemed to be butterflies winging about now.

Nine

Kendall sat at her desk in the empty classroom. It was Friday. The last of the children had just reached up for her traditional good-bye hug before scooting out the door. Jennifer, the student teacher, stepped out then, to "freshen up a bit" before Lewis returned to discuss her official review.

Kendall stared at the form before her. Except for the principal's signature, she had filled it out. She always filled these out; he normally did not become involved with the procedure. But it seemed Jennifer was a special case. Undoubtedly her long slender legs, most of which were revealed due to the shortness of the black skirt, and the clinging white cotton shirt that set off her thick, raven black hair had something to do with that fact.

What else is new in this school led by a spineless snake whose brain shuts down at the sight of a young woman? She sighed. *Well, young women who respond to his adolescent overtures anyway.* His brain didn't seem to be obsessed with her anymore. Currently it seemed to be in a serious state of cunning. *How can we get rid of this teacher who does not respond in a positive manner?* He still avoided her and not, she knew, because

182

of a conflict of interests as Ian had thought. There was something going on with that first grade opening, but she couldn't figure it out.

She sighed again. Few men were like Jade. Come to think of it, she didn't know *any*. His offering of friendship last weekend had given her a sense of rest that had lingered more or less until today when Lewis walked in to observe Jennifer's teaching. Now she felt like a Raggedy Ann doll with frayed seams. A little stuffing popped through here and there. Bits and pieces of Pollyanna were seeping away, the butterflies floating away with them.

She took a deep breath, as if that would hold the stuffing in place.

Maybe she would go to Jade's church on Sunday. It would be a way to see him. After all their talk of not dating, he couldn't call her again. Church had made her feel secure, too, the way he did. It would be an encouraging way to fill time before next Tuesday's board meeting.

Maybe Sara would go with her. She was in the midst of her own dilemma, trying to break things off with her married friend. Kendall had not stopped the subtle references to the dead-endedness of that road. It wasn't healthy for her friend to love a man whose wife could not trust him.

Another man so unlike Jade. As was her dad after her mother's death. True, he had faithfully taken care of her, seldom missing work, paying the bills, drinking only at night, at home. He was a quiet drunk, never abusing her but just embarrassing her. Emotionally he was never home though. Never. She grew up on her own.

And then there was Ian. He had called Sunday and tried to apologize in an offhanded way, still not taking responsibility for his actions, wanting another opportunity. Perhaps a movie? Her gracious attempts at brushing him off didn't connect, so she told him bluntly, "The last time I rode with a man who had been drinking, he died." Bottom line. He promised to see her at the board meeting and do his job.

It was Greg's news that kept her going at this moment, kept the fragile stitching from totally falling apart, kept her sitting in her seat, patiently waiting for the duo. She knew they would enter together, laughing, Dr. Thornton's arm around Miss Cunningham's waist.

Greg was a good friend and dedicated to his family and students. He was straightforward, thoughtful, conscientious. During today's short lunch period, he had invited her to ride to a nearby deli. She hadn't seen much of him this week and was glad for the chance to touch base.

They ate in his car in the parking lot. Well, *she* had eaten anyway. He seemed ill at ease and mentioned the rumored first grade opening. She, too, had noticed that it hadn't been posted yet. Whenever Kendall tried to track down the teacher, she was unavailable. Greg thought something smelled fishy about that situation.

He then confessed that he had interviewed for a job in another district. It would mean a move for his family. She gulped down a mouthful of pasta salad, not so much in surprise at his decision as in his not telling her and Maxine before he did it.

He had discussed it with Thornton. If the new contract came through, he planned to resign. "But," he said, "he doesn't want me talking about it. That's why we're eating in the car. Thornton's going to sit on it."

"Why?"

"As he put it, a vague possibility isn't worthy of his concern."

"Why?"

He shrugged. "You know how he seems incapable of handling more than one issue at a time. Ken, I did it now so my job would be available to you. It's not a done deal yet, but chances are good I'll be out of here. I'd quit on the spot, but I have to consider my family."

"I know." He was close to Jade. Real close. "Thanks, Greg. So, even if I don't supposedly know, it has to be posted when you resign and I can apply for it then, right?"

"That's my understanding. You should be able to stay at East Hills. Just what you want, Pollyanna. Thornton can't make my life any more miserable, so go ahead and tell what's-his-name, Edwards. It should help with the negotiating."

She knew Thornton could indeed make life more miserable for her friend and debated whether it was necessary to tell Ian just yet. She would try to protect Greg as long as possible.

Laughter interrupted her reverie. They entered her room now, Lewis's arm around Jennifer's waist. It was a distorted image. In age they had the appearance of father and daughter.

She saw the perturbed look cross his face when he spotted her.

"Oh, Ms. O'Reilly. Still here?"

The situation was so absolutely ludicrous, so obviously obvious, she almost burst out laughing at the absurdity. Not trusting her voice, she nodded in reply, propped her elbow on the desk, and rested her chin in her hand, scrunching back the smile that tried to form.

"Well, we have a prize student teacher here, don't you think, Ms. O'Reilly?" He stepped behind the young woman now, placing his fingers around her waist, and spoke into her ear. "You were fantastic, Jen."

Jennifer leaned back into him with a smile. "Thank you, Dr. Thornton. I just adore being here."

Lewis had held Kendall's waist like that once, in his office with the door shut. His mouth close to her ear, he talked about looking forward to a long working relationship. She had slipped from his grasp within two seconds. Not soon enough though. His breath and hands left a distinct imprint of slime.

He was a touchy-feely kind of person, a type she could usually warm up to because she herself was that way. Positive human touch was so important for the youngsters. On the occasions when she let down her guard and responded as she normally would, he zoomed in, trying to get close, physically and with the easygoing talk of a close friend. He always closed his office door when she was inside, giving the impression that they were on intimate terms. When others were around, he was overly friendly toward her as if they shared something no one else knew about. After a semester of her opening the doors he shut and pointedly ignoring much of what he said, he changed his demeanor to one of tolerance.

It was all subtle. Innuendo. Nothing *quid pro quo*. Nothing to even mention really, let alone take to court. Maybe it was just his way of being friendly. Maybe it was after all only her imagination.

He and Jennifer meandered over to her desk now and sat in the chairs she had placed for them, talking in a secretive way before he turned to her. "What have we got, Ms. O'Reilly?"

She slid the form toward him. "The usual. You just need to sign right there on the last page. Jennifer, you can go back and graduate now." Today was her final day. Kendall looked forward to having her class to herself for the two weeks remaining before summer break. "It's such an exciting time. Before you know it, you'll have your certificate in hand and be all set to teach your own class."

Jennifer smiled in Thornton's direction. "Oh, I plan to."

"Ms. O'Reilly, I think we can mark this higher here. And this. Jen's rapport with the students was excellent. I heard her speak Spanish to the little Mexican kids, and that trouble-maker Tony didn't give her any grief. Can you white this out?"

"With all due respect, Lewis, I feel after closely observing her that these are fair marks. In my comments here," she pointed to another page, "I give specific examples of what she did well and areas she could improve on." *Like what to do when Tony is his usual self and does act out, or how not to direct her trite Spanish phrases to the Vietnamese children.*

He sniffed, his way of announcing a forthcoming dictum. "You sometimes forget, Ms. O'Reilly, who the administrator is here." He took the paper from her hands and stood. "I'll have my secretary fix this. Oh, by the way, your friend Mr. Zukowski is being interviewed tomorrow. I hope you realize the conflict of interest he has placed himself in." He strutted toward the door and continued talking over his shoulder. "Getting involved with school board meetings doesn't flow with being youth pastor. Jen, about that other matter, make it five."

"Of course, Dr. Thornton."

He left, soon followed by Jennifer.

Kendall sighed in relief. She had her room back. Their flir-tation needn't concern her. She had done her best to instill in the young woman the importance of including tangible goals in her lessons and of listening to the children with her heart. And she had warned Jade. Thornton's none-too-veiled threat confirmed her suspicions. If Jade supported her, he wouldn't get the job at the church.

She felt like she was on overload, beyond weary. The thought of running or playing piano was too much. Going home and sleeping sounded appealing. And when she woke up, she could remember that Greg's position would more than likely become available.

Once again, Maxine drove Kendall to the board meeting. As before, the parking lot was rapidly filling up. The district boundary decision was to be voted upon first, right after the board came out from their closed executive meeting. Personnel matters would follow in another closed session.

Kendall spotted Jade parking his Wrangler. "Maxine, I need to talk to Jade."

"I'll go on in, hon, and get us a good seat."

She waved to him as he approached. On Sunday she had slept rather than attend church, so she hadn't seen him for over a week. Despite her anxiety, she noted how attractive he was in a pale yellow polo shirt tucked into his jeans.

"Hi, Kendall."

"Did you get my message?" She had called the night before and talked to his dad.

"Not to come?" He smiled, his hazel eyes crinkling. "Dad told me."

Her eyes widened. "You can't say anything. Promise? Lewis Thornton told me point-blank that your involvement here doesn't flow with being youth pastor."

He shook his head. "We'll see."

"Listen, Greg will probably resign in the next couple of weeks, so there could be a fifth grade opening, but Thornton told him he won't discuss it yet. You don't have to be here, because I can get that position."

"Kendall, I said we'll see." He wasn't smiling now. "Are you ready to go in?"

She glanced around the parking lot in the growing dusk and pressed a hand to her stomach. "You can't walk with me."

"I'm not one of your fifth graders."

She heard the edge in his voice and matched it, lifting her chin to meet his gaze. "I can't jeopardize your job."

"Thornton is in no position to hurt me. There is a higher authority involved in this. And my interview went fine."

"Jade, you can't trust him."

"You haven't said can't this many times in the three months I've known you!"

In frustration she turned and headed toward the building. A hug would have been helpful. The stitching was unraveling quickly now.

Maxine motioned to the seat next to her in the middle of a row. From the front, Ian caught her eye and gave a thumbs-up sign. She made her way to Maxine.

"You're all red, baby. Just calm down. Everything will be all right in the end. It looks like you've got quite a number of parents here."

From the corner of her eye she watched Jade enter and head toward the back of the gym behind them. His jaw was set like that first time he'd walked into her classroom, determined to take care of his hurting loved one. In spite of her determination to keep him out of this, she felt a twinge of hope. The knight was in attendance.

The administrators and board members entered. After the meeting opened, they voted on district changes. Someone explained them in detail, with maps. As far as Kendall could understand, the changes wouldn't be as drastic at East Hills as they had feared.

As the board left the gym for yet another executive session, the tediousness of the evening wore on her nerves. She stared at her clenched fists in her lap, only half aware of Maxine beside her making small talk with others.

"Kendall." She felt Jade beside her. He leaned down to

whisper in her ear. "Let's get some fresh air."

She shook her head. *What would people think?*

As if reading her mind, he said softly, "People are probably talking anyway. Might as well give them something to talk about." He touched her elbow, urging her to stand.

They made their way through groups gathered here and there. Outside they walked a short distance along the dimly lit sidewalk.

Jade stopped and enveloped her in his arms. "I'm sorry. I shouldn't have snapped at you earlier."

She leaned into his comfort. Her ear against his chest felt his heartbeat, heard his voice as a low rumble.

"Will you forgive me?"

She nodded.

"I mean for everything. That initial misunderstanding added weight you didn't need."

Kendall took a deep breath. For now, everything paled in comparison to the solid warmth surrounding her, diffusing all her fear and anger. Not trusting her voice yet, she nodded again. Of course she forgave him. If it hadn't been his complaint, it would have been someone else's. None of this was his fault.

He tightened his arms around her. "We should probably go back," he said, but he didn't release his hold.

She savored the moments of complete rest, a strange sensation for her. Was this what love was all about?

His chin was against the top of her head and when he asked "Ready?" she felt his lips move through her hair.

With monumental effort she ignored the tingling in her spine and stepped out of his arms. "Ready. Let's go slay some dragons, Mr. Z."

Back inside the gym they took their separate seats. The board was still out, and Ian made his way to her.

"Kendall, I got in on some of the East Hills discussion." His face was too sober to convey any encouraging news. "They'll be accepting that first grade teacher's resignation but are moving a kindergarten person to her spot and moving up a pre-K, leaving that as the opening. They want someone certified in that area."

She closed her eyes. Pre-kindergarten. Jennifer's minor.

He continued speaking quietly so just she and Maxine could hear. "And you'll be accepted for the eighth grade position. Nothing else is available in the district at this time that would work."

"Thanks, Ian."

He gave her shoulder a squeeze and returned to his seat. Maxine patted her hand, humming softly.

When the board reconvened, voices droned in Kendall's head. She thought of nothing, waiting numbly for East Hills to be introduced. Eventually it happened as Ian had said. A resignation was accepted, and teachers were promoted in the same way as students, in order to keep them together two years running. It was Thornton's pet project. A new position would be posted for pre-kindergarten. Required certification . . . not in her possession.

The other change was announced before the voting. Only two fifth grade classes left Kendall O'Reilly obsolete.

She stood. "Excuse me." Her voice was uneven, and she hardly heard it above Jade's from the back of the gym.

"Excuse me. There are some parents here who would like to speak in support of Ms. O'Reilly," her knight stated.

"Well," the president said, "it seems there isn't a position for her at East Hills."

Churning emotions raised her voice above the murmurs. "But there might be."

"Ms. O'Reilly?"

"Thank you. It's my understanding that Greg Jones will more than likely resign. Therefore, we may have a fifth grade opening at East Hills."

Thornton answered, "That is not official. It depends on if and when he gets the other job and submits his resignation. Until I post the job opening, there isn't one available."

"But can't this decision be postponed?"

The president replied, "It's not a good business practice to halt our proceedings based on another district's hiring schedule."

Thornton sighed loudly. "Ms. O'Reilly, you do realize there are extenuating circumstances?"

Jade's voice boomed again from the back. "Most of those were insinuations, not a true portrait of Ms. O'Reilly's work. I think it's imperative that the parents here be heard on her behalf, especially in light of the fact that there could be an opening for her at East Hills. We'd like to speak, just for the record at least."

The president called for order and then invited the parents to speak.

They did. Kendall sat in wonder as one after another from this year's class stood and gave a vote of confidence for her, describing changes in their children, everything from improved attitudes to reading scores. Seven of them and then Jade.

"My daughter started in the middle of the year. She lost her mother recently, and if it hadn't been for Ms. O'Reilly's love and special gift of teaching, not to mention saving her life by driving her to the hospital for an emergency appendectomy, I know we would be having difficulties that would reach even into her teen years." He made eye contact with her now. "I am deeply grateful to Ms. O'Reilly. It would be a tragedy for fifth graders not to know her." He sat down.

The president thanked the parents. A vote was taken to accept the East Hills personnel changes as proposed. Kendall O'Reilly was dropped from the list.

The meeting took on a surrealistic feeling then for her. It was as if people moved and spoke in slow motion. She kept thinking, *I didn't do anything wrong! I didn't do anything wrong!*

She turned to Maxine. "What did he say?" She saw tears in her friend's eyes.

"They've accepted you for the social studies position."

They stared at each other.

"Eighth grade?"

Maxine nodded.

Kendall shook her head. "I don't want it." She raised her hand and her voice, interrupting. "Excuse me. I would like to apply for Greg Jones's job."

The president stared at her with undisguised exasperation. "That's not an option at this time, but we have voted to hire you for the eighth grade—"

"I will not teach eighth grade social studies. I resign. Thank you." She folded her hands in her lap and sat very still. She sensed movement from the back and to her side, people murmuring and leaving.

Maxine's arm came around the back of her chair. "Want to go?" she whispered.

She shook her head, too stunned to move any more than that. They would wait until it was over. The truth settled in: even if Greg left, there would still be no place for her. Thornton would protest. He wanted her out. He had twisted the truth, and she had reacted like a silly fool. The board didn't want to be involved in such unnecessary proceedings. There were plenty of available teachers.

And she was tired of the conflict. Thornton had won.

193

Until this moment she had refused to recognize there was even a contest.

When the meeting was adjourned, she somehow found the strength to stand and walk outside, her friend close beside her. The surrealistic feeling remained. "I didn't do anything wrong," she stated quietly.

"Of course you didn't."

"Kendall." Ian came up behind them. "I did what I could. I'm sorry. Thornton ranted and raved in the closed session. He convinced them that your student teacher believed you acted incompetently with her, didn't give her responsibilities or train her."

Maxine exclaimed, "Now that one wasn't in her file!"

"I pursued that. He insisted it is and that she has received notice of it but hasn't responded."

"I didn't do anything wrong," she said.

"I know," Ian consoled. "He just wanted you out of his face. My guess is you really did a number on the guy's ego."

Maxine nodded. "You got that right. For good reason, but not good enough to sue him. Thanks, Ian, we know you tried."

"Kendall, I don't know what to say. You don't deserve this."

She shrugged.

He hesitated. "I'll keep my ear to the ground for any elementary openings."

She sensed it was her turn to speak, but she couldn't get past the devastating impact of losing her job. Her whole world had just evaporated. Her life! Maxine replied something, Ian walked on down the sidewalk, and the two women continued toward the parking lot.

"Kendall! Maxine!" It was Jade now. He caught up to them. "I'm so sorry."

They stopped under a street lamp near the car.

"I didn't do anything wrong." It was beginning to sound like a mantra, but no other words would take shape in her mind.

"I know you didn't. Is there anything I can do for you?" He touched her arm.

She shook her head. She just wanted to sleep and forget.

"Well, well." It was Lewis Thornton's voice. He stepped out of the darkness toward them. "I must say, Jade, I am surprised that you did it—that you put your job on the line for this woman. She must be really something, if you get my drift."

Jade's hand was immediately at Thornton's throat, the man's tie twisted in his fingers. "Wipe that smirk off your face and apologize to her."

The moments ticked by in slow motion again. She thought of his hand. Large, callused, with the strength to hold onto sheer rock and pull himself up. Yet with the touch of a feather it could tuck a stray piece of hair behind her ear.

"Right now!" Jade's left fist was raised. "I've got nothing to lose, bud."

"Sorry," he sputtered.

Jade let go but still glowered over the other man.

Thornton straightened his tie. "This'll look good on your youth pastor resumé." He spun on his heel and hurried away.

It was a bad dream. This had to be a bad dream. She opened the car door and climbed in.

Maxine was chuckling. "Well, Jade, care to come to our faculty meetings? We'd certainly get more accomplished. Thank you!"

He leaned inside the car before she could shut the door. "Kendall, I'll call you."

She nodded. *Whatever. Just get me out of here.*

Kendall wondered, what do you say to a man who has sacrificed his own life in an attempt to save yours?

She didn't know, so she didn't return Jade's messages. "Thank you" was so woefully inadequate, it seemed an affront to even mention it.

She sat outside on her balcony, legs drawn up onto the chair, arms hugging her knees. The damp coolness of evening played tag with the afternoon's warmth, chasing it at last over the horizon with the sun. One bright star twinkled above the eucalyptus trees.

The apartment complex was quiet. The majority of residents were career people who respected the nearness of neighbors and rarely held large open-house type parties, even on Saturday nights. She felt like she had the entire place to herself.

Sara had gone to visit her parents, to spend the night with them and attend church there tomorrow. It was easier to forget about her ex-boss that way, she said.

Kendall sipped tea now, grateful that the agitation of the week had calmed. It had been one of the worst weeks of her life. She vaguely remembered Maxine bringing her home Tuesday night, making her promise to stay home Wednesday, and saying she'd call in for a sub for her. Her friend knew she would sleep. It was her way of coping with difficulty and tension. She had slept soundly until noon that next day, then cried all afternoon.

I didn't do anything wrong.

Thursday and Friday were spent in a fog of going through the motions at school, at times lost in thought as she'd open a cabinet or drawer and become overwhelmed with the image of packing it all away. The more astute children had asked what was wrong. Caitlin hugged her extra tightly.

Jade had left two messages on her answering machine, saying both times, "I hope you're okay. I'm praying for you." Caitlin had given her a card from him, a just-for-fun, silly card that made her laugh. Inside he had scrawled, "I'm praying for you."

Praying for me for what, Jade? We all did what we could and I lost my job. It just didn't happen. And now you probably don't even have one either.

More stars twinkled now, and she remembered Jade's words about aching at the wonder of it all. She inhaled deeply, the thick coolness laden with pungent eucalyptus. Pollyanna knew it was magnificent, but . . . What did boundless stars and the vast ocean and trees that grew a hundred feet tall from a minuscule seed have to do with her everyday life? A good life she had worked so hard at. A life that in the blink of an eye disintegrated through no fault of her own.

What had Jeremiah said in his sermon? If you find it, you lose it; if you lose it, you find it? *Well, I found it in teaching, and it was good and right, and now it's gone, and I don't know if I can find it all over again. There's nothing left inside of me. It took everything I had to go on after Mom died, then live with my dad, go to college all alone, and then face Mark's leaving, and now this. Oh, God, help me find life again.*

Shivering, she went inside, slid shut the door, and sat at the piano. It was the place closest to comfort because it was her mother's.

Before I knew Jesus Christ . . . Jade's voice echoed her mother's. Kendall pulled an old book from the piano bench. She wasn't up for the intricacies of Bach and Beethoven. She yearned for the simplicity she suspected was in her mother's hymnal.

She played the notes, page after page after page. After a time she read some of the words. *At the cross . . . it was there by faith I received my sight . . . Christ the Lord is risen today . . . Dying once He all doth save . . . Amazing grace, how sweet the sound . . . I once was lost but now am found . . . What a friend we have in Jesus . . . what peace we often forfeit . . . all because we do not carry everything to God in prayer . . . I've got peace like a river . . . Turn your eyes upon Jesus, look full in His wonderful face, and the things of earth will grow strangely dim in the light of His glory and grace . . .*

She closed the piano and spoke out loud. "But, God, I didn't do anything wrong." Jeremiah's words came to her. "Human nature is still a sinful nature, imperfect, choosing its own way . . . We can't be in a right relationship with God until we accept the work of Jesus."

He is Lord, He is risen from the dead and He is Lord.

Before I knew Jesus Christ. A before and after. Before accepting the work, after accepting the work.

"Is that it, God? That I found my life without You, but it wasn't real life? I can't do it on my own—I don't want to do it on my own anymore. I want the real life. Take mine and make it Yours."

Kendall slipped to her knees. "Jesus, if You're anything like Jade, I want to know You." Jade hadn't let her down. He had shown her unconditional love.

"I accept the work You did on the cross. I did do something wrong—I didn't make You Lord of my life. Forgive me and be my Lord now."

She paused and let the thought come, the thought she had chosen daily for thirteen years to ignore. "Do You love me even though I was driving the car that night?"

He did. She knew He did, and she whispered, "Thank You."

Joy bubbled from deep inside of her, spilling out in uncontrollable giggles.

What do you do when a Man sacrifices His life in an attempt to save yours? You fall on your face at His feet, accept it, and say thank You.

With Jade, she would say thank you, bake him brownies, give him a hug . . . and tell him she was praying for him. Tomorrow. Right now she wanted to get to know Jesus better. Didn't she have her mother's Bible packed in a box somewhere?

Ten

Near the back of the church, Jade sat along the side aisle in one of the pews filled with teens, his leg bouncing to the mental rhythm of a song left over from last night's Christian rock concert. He stifled a yawn. He leaned around the boy next to him and squinted at two girls. Their whispering immediately stopped, and he gave them a thumbs-up sign. They were probably still discussing the fun outing that had continued past midnight at a local pizza place. He yawned again.

From the pulpit the pastor announced that the committee in charge of recommending the hiring of a youth pastor would meet that night. After that surprising tidbit, the man's voice faded to a background hum in Jade's mind.

This was two weeks sooner than expected. So be it.

He quickly reviewed the events that had undoubtedly already affected tonight's outcome. First and foremost was Kendall's priceless influence on Cait. Then came his phone call to Thornton to voice support for her that left him confused because the guy didn't seem in agreement. He remembered an exhausted Kendall sitting at her desk the morning after the initial board meeting, warning him not to trust Thornton.

Wanting to clear the misunderstanding about the camping incident, he had met with Thornton and again given his vote of confidence in the teacher. Any naive thoughts of the principal feeling the same dissipated at that point. He had said, "If you persist in poking your youth pastor nose into this school business that will not affect your child next fall, it is a conflict of interest that will jeopardize your position at this church."

But Jade had persisted. He knew even before grabbing Thornton by the necktie that when he chose to attend the school board meeting and defend Kendall, he chose to risk his being accepted for the job. So be it. It was the right thing to do, and he would do it again. *I answer to my heavenly Father, not the head of a committee.*

His brother Samuel had driven down from L.A. yesterday, probably at their concerned dad's prompting. Jade had told their father about the necktie, but not about Thornton's earlier threat. His dad would have to continue relating to the guy as part of the same church; he needn't know. Dad was diplomatic and conservative. Jade had always been his antithesis. Sam often intervened.

Their usual easy bantering the day before slipped into accusations. Sam pointed out Jade wasn't behaving responsibly in light of having a daughter; his angry reactions were reminiscent of a young Jade. Their playful shoving quickly escalated into a wrestling match that they had sense enough to carry out into the front yard before it turned serious. Thirty pounds and four inches on Jade, Sam, of course, pinned him without prolonged effort.

"Do you love her?" Sam asked, catching his breath.

Jade, the side of his face pressed into the grass, sputtered, "No."

"If you did, it'd make half sense anyway."

"Sorry to disappoint Annette!"

Sam had squeezed his knees around Jade's torso then and tightened the grip on his arm angled painfully across his back. "That's too low, J.D. Take it back."

Jade's face sank deeper into the grass, and he cursed.

"What did you say?"

He repeated it, louder this time.

Sam let go and rolled onto the ground, laughing. "The last time I heard you talk like that was the night you and Deb got engaged," he roared, stomping a foot and clapping his hands.

Jade sat up and brushed grass from his hair. "Ha, ha." When his brother had stopped laughing, he explained his thoughts about Kendall. "I just did what I could, Sam. I was put in this position. I mean, just think about the details. I happen to move in with Dad at this time in this particular school district and Cait gets her for a teacher. And by God's grace I offered the help Kendall needed. It didn't keep her job, but I'm praying she'll come to know God's grace through this. That's all that matters. The effect on my job wasn't an issue."

"You're something else. I do admire you, you know. I wish I were that focused on God. But Dad's concerned. We all are."

"I appreciate that."

"In spite of all your focus, though, you're not calm anymore. You seem edgy."

He shrugged. "I'll go climbing next week. I'm due."

"It's not just this week." Sam paused. "She *is* pretty. And intelligent."

Jade shook his head, pulling out blades of grass. "Yeah, but . . . I can't go through that again."

"Can't? You're the one who says can't is not in God's vocabulary."

"Won't then."

"Won't? That's even worse! What if you're choosing against what God has in mind for you?"

"It would mess up my focus."

Sam laughed. "Well, just don't get so focused you bury your head in the sand. Maybe Cait needs a mom."

He sprang on him then, and in the surprise of the moment he pinned his linebacker brother.

Sam laughed, his voice muffled in the ground. "Of course then Cait would have two unemployed parents! That's not so good."

The pastor's voice rose now, capturing Jade's attention momentarily before the memory of Sam's probing again pushed aside the present. How *did* he feel about Kendall? Concerned. He cared for her, probably deeply, as a close friend, one of the closest because of what she'd done for Cait. During last night's concert he couldn't stop thinking of her, had continually prayed for her as he had often during these four days since the board meeting. She hadn't returned his calls; he hoped she had friends around her. Perhaps she just needed some alone time, but the loss of her job had to be painful.

She wasn't Deb. Deborah with her tallness and earthiness, her ease of climbing, her solid build, both emotionally and physically, that so perfectly melded with his, filling his empty spaces, completing him, defining him. Where would Kendall fit?

Her wisps of hair, loosened from the braid, and those feminine pearls in the small earlobes and the long fingers that gestured musical notes to go with her always-gentle words, her love of Bach—all called to a softness he didn't possess. He was loud and rough and went to rock concerts with teens and still at the age of thirty-four threatened with ease by grabbing a necktie and doubling a fist. If he held her, would he crush the perfectly-shaped mouth and slenderness and refreshing beauty that stopped him cold in his tracks? *Dear God, where would she fit?*

Jade sensed movement about him now and stood with the others. Why did that thick braid the color of wheat intrigue him so? Why did he imagine her fingers weaving it? His fingers reversing the pattern? It looked like that woman's hair toward the front of the church, a number of rows ahead, bowed in the closing prayer.

He didn't close his eyes. Was it . . . ? Could it be . . . ? *Amen and amen.* The young woman turned then and caught his eye. Her smile lit up her face, and the small nose crinkled. His imagination heard the giggle. In an instant he knew exactly where she would fit.

The sensation of falling struck him with the force of a physical impact so real he grasped the pew in front of him. It was as if he were climbing and the anchor gave way. He shut his eyes until he felt the kids push at him, trying to get to the aisle. They talked at him, but he couldn't decipher their words over the pounding in his head. He let them surround him, moving him along in the middle of their group, out of the sanctuary, away from those eyes that danced like sunlight on the ocean, a beauty of wrenching dimensions.

Once outside he took a deep breath, easing the tightness in his chest, then hastened around the building toward another entrance. He would go to his office. He should check his calendar. Maybe he had an appointment with some parent. Anything.

Some time later his breathing returned to normal, and Jade went home. He found his father and Cait in the kitchen fixing lunch.

"Daddy! Ms. O'Reilly was at church! She gave us a bunch of her special brownies."

"Yeah, I saw her."

"Well, son, I spoke with her." Dad was beaming. "She was sorry not to be able to thank you in person for speaking up at that board meeting. She said she'd call." He winked at Cait.

"What else?" Jade asked.

"Oh, that's all."

As if on cue, the telephone rang. Cait had it answered and handed to him before he could duck out.

"Hello?" He sank into a chair at the kitchen table.

"Jade. Oh, Jade," she giggled, "I don't know where to begin. Thank you for the board meeting."

"You're welcome, but it didn't work."

"Oh, but that's not the point. You showed me who Christ is."

"What?"

"You gave up everything to help me. Last night I told Jesus that if He's anything like you, I want to know Him."

Jade jumped up, whooped, then yelled, "Yes! Thank You, Lord! Kendall, this is fantastic."

"Oh, I know. I just lost my most precious thing, my job, but I have this peace that it'll be okay. It will be, right?"

"It won't be easy, and that peaceful feeling might disappear, but yeah, the bottom line is, God is taking care of you now. Just do what you can to get another job and don't worry about it. He has things in store for you that you can't imagine."

"Then He does for you too. Should I pray for you, that you won't worry?" she asked. "I mean, Thornton won't let you be hired. I'm so sorry, Jade."

He was silent for a moment. "It's part of the adventure of saying yes to Jesus. I did what I thought was right. If I have to move on, then that's right too."

"I have so much to learn. What can I do for you?"

205

"Well, I heard you made brownies for us. That helps."

"Seriously. Can I go to the meeting?"

"No, it's closed. Somebody will call me when it's over. Just pray, sweetheart. It's the only thing at this point, and it's always the best thing to do. Thanks."

"Okay. Thank you, Jade. You did it again, O knight in shining armor! Big-time. Good-bye."

"Bye." *Sweetheart.* He hung up the phone and stared out the window. *She believes. There goes that roadblock . . . but . . . no way, José.*

Dad put his arm around his shoulders. "Hallelujah, huh?"

He hugged his father. "Hallelujah!"

The next morning Kendall arrived early at school, eager to begin the dismantling of her old world. She knew she'd grieve over it, but she also knew she had to go through it before continuing down a new path. Summer break would start a week from tomorrow. She didn't want to linger in this room after the children were gone.

She sat on the floor in front of an open cabinet, digging through files in a large cardboard box, pulling out bulletin board materials that she had not personally created and purchased. What remained in the box would be hers and invaluable in beginning a new position elsewhere. She had already begun the search, perusing yesterday's newspapers.

"You certainly look chipper."

"Maxine! Good morning. Do you want this?" She held up a laminated U.S. map. "It belongs to the school."

She took it from her. "Looks like a nice one. How are you doing?"

Kendall stood and straightened her skirt. "Great."

"My, my! Your Pollyanna streak is stronger than I would have imagined."

She grinned and shook her head. "Not Pollyanna, Max. I decided Jesus knows better than she does."

Maxine laughed. "I've been telling you that for years, baby."

"But I wasn't listening." She gave her friend a hug.

"And now you are. Guess it's time for you to go then." She gave her an extra squeeze before letting go, then wiped a tear from her eye. "Well, I'm trying to help God along here. I called Lois yesterday."

Lois was their former principal, now at another school just a bit north in Orange County. Kendall caught her breath. "And?"

"She's fairly certain she'll need a fourth grade teacher."

She threw her arms around her again, and they laughed. "Thank you, thank you, thank you!"

"Well, it might not work out, but I figured it's some encouragement. There will be a place for you somewhere, I'm sure of it. See you at recess."

A short time later Jeremiah entered. "Hello, Kendall."

"Jeremiah." She rushed to take his hand. "Did he get it?"

He shook his head. "I wanted you to hear it from us."

"Oh, it's all my fault. I am so sorry."

"No, no. You mustn't blame yourself."

"Why did he have to do it? He didn't owe me anything."

"He felt he did, for Caitlin."

"I was just doing my job, just being myself."

He smiled. "So was he, Kendall. He'll be all right. He may have to teach or do something else for a while, pull back on his studies."

"When will he be finished at the church?"

"A week from next Sunday the youth group has an outing planned. That will be it. As you can probably guess, he left at the crack of dawn for the mountains. His friend Jerry plans to join him for a few days. It will help."

"I hope you don't hold it against me?"

Briefly he touched her cheek. "Of course not, dear child. You didn't ask him to do what he did." He sighed. "But I need to know something."

"Here, have a seat." They sat at her desk. "What is it?"

He studied the desktop for a moment. "As Jade said, I'm getting slow, and not just on the soccer field. What does Lewis Thornton have against you?"

"It doesn't matter now, Jeremiah."

"It does. You don't have to protect him."

She looked at the strong face of the white-haired gentleman. In his gentle, slow way he still exuded power. He could bring down the man who had ended her career at East Hills Elementary and brought Jade's plans to a crashing halt. She bit her lip.

"Kendall, I won't use it against him, but I will watch him very closely."

"He made subtle . . . overtures, and I didn't respond."

"And your student teacher did?"

His question startled her.

"I see the answer on your face. That's all I need. How are you doing?"

She took a slow, deep breath, then smiled. "I should be moping, but I'm dancing."

He chuckled in reply and stood as the bell rang, then started singing in his clear baritone, "I've got peace like a river . . ."

Kendall joined in, "Peace like a river in my soul . . ."

They sang their way across the room. He chuckled again. "Maybe we can sing that on Sunday. I hope you'll come back?"

"To tell you the truth, I feel a little strange because Lewis is there."

"That's understandable. But he usually goes to second service, and it is a large congregation."

"You've talked me into it. Thanks for coming in, Jeremiah."

"You're welcome. Good-bye."

Kendall hummed the song through much of the week, organizing and packing early in the mornings and after school cherishing moments with her students, completing the photo albums and wrapping them, thanking God for that river of peace now flowing through her soul. Jade was often in her thoughts, too, accompanied always with the butterflies that chased away her appetite.

"But, Kendall, you're just such a *good* person." Sara carefully painted the candy-apple red polish over her thumbnail. "You're kind and honest—"

"You look so pretty in red," she interrupted her friend. Having finished stacking their dinner dishes in the sink, she slid into the chair across the kitchen table and studied her friend's tan-complexioned face, the lowered dark lashes, the deep chestnut curls pulled back in a bouncy ponytail.

Sara dipped the brush into the bottle. "I bet you won't even keep those San Diego historical maps we used on your bulletin board."

Kendall's eyes widened. "Why would I?"

"See? The school paid a few bucks for them, but *we* found them in some obscure used bookstore and designed the display years ago. And then there's that rat Thornton—he deserves to be tarred and feathered, and you haven't so much as said one ugly thing against him."

She shrugged. "I have thoughts, but it wouldn't help to tell anybody."

"There you have it, folks. I rest my case." Sara tightened

the lid on the nail polish bottle and examined her fingers. "So, I don't get this Jesus business."

"It's simple." Kendall pointed to the Bible lying open on the table between them. "Jesus said, 'I am the way and the truth and the life. No one comes to the Father except through me.' If we don't accept that, we can't be right with God."

"You weren't right before?" Her friend's tone was incredulous.

She shook her head. "The fact is that now, no matter what, I'm okay with God, and because of that there's a point and an order to life that wasn't there before."

"It's easy for you."

"It's *true* for everybody."

Sara lowered her eyes. "Terry never spent the night, but . . ."

"I know. Sara, that's why Jesus died. He forgives everything except not accepting that."

"He's not calling me for dates anymore."

"That's good, huh?"

Sara nodded.

The phone rang, and Kendall answered it.

"Ms. O'Reilly?"

She couldn't recognize the voice of the crying child. "Yes?"

"Ms. O'Reilly, Daddy's not coming tomorrow."

"Caitlin?"

"He's leaving!"

"Leaving? Is he home now, honey?"

Caitlin hiccuped. "Yeah."

"Can I talk to him?"

"He's real mad. I don't want to talk to him."

A flash of instant anger flooded through her. "Is your grandfather there?"

"No."

"I'll come and talk to him. I'll be there in ten minutes, okay?"

"Okay."

"Bye." Kendall punched the Off button and clenched her fists. "Oh!"

"What's wrong?" Sara asked.

"That was Caitlin, in tears. Jade's leaving; he's not coming tomorrow."

"Not coming tomorrow? He can't do that!"

"I know." She glanced down at her sandals, faded blue jeans, and oversized denim work shirt. It would have to do. "You know it, and Caitlin knows it. Why doesn't her father know it? He's not that stupid!" She grabbed her purse and keys from their hook by the door, then paused, her hand on the doorknob. "Sara, he's not. He probably just doesn't realize how important fifth grade culmination is."

"Well, nobody can explain it better than you. Go!"

She shut the door, ran halfway down the steps, then turned around and hurried back to push the door open. "Sara . . ."

Her friend looked up as she poked her head in the door. "What?"

"Uh, don't clean the kitchen." She had wanted to tell her to try reading the Bible, but she was already doing just that. "It'll mess up your nails."

"Okay, thanks." Sara winked with a smile. "Let me know what happens."

He opened the door and stared down at her, not saying a word.

This was going to be more difficult than she thought. "Jade, I need to talk with you."

"Shoot." He looked like he did that night at the hospital.

Square jaw clenched, eyes narrowed, fingers combing rest-lessly through the wavy hair. Fighting unseen demons. What were they this time?

You're just her teacher. She took a deep breath. "May I come in?"

He stepped aside. After she passed, he shoved the door, and it slammed shut. "Can you make it quick? I'm busy." He turned on his heel and strode to a desk in a corner by the bookshelves.

Kendall followed, talking to his back. "Jade, Caitlin called me and said you won't be at tomorrow's ceremony. It is *such* a special event for the fifth graders. Could you possibly change your schedule?" *The rocks will always be there for climbing,* she thought.

Not looking at her, he leaned over an open drawer and yanked out a handful of manila folders. "No way, José."

"It's like this major emotional moment," she persisted, directing her words between his shoulder blades, hoping they'd hit his heart. "Everybody is there with cameras—all the relatives come. All the students get special awards, and we sing songs we've been working on for weeks and weeks."

He shuffled through the files, not looking up.

"We wanted it to be a surprise, but . . . well, Caitlin is reading a poem she wrote. The class voted hers the best—"

"She told me," he cut in, his tone curt.

"Well then . . ." She lifted her palms as if offering the per-fect, ready-made, father-daughter memory.

He glanced at her. "Well what?"

"Well . . . well, this is bigger than chaperoning at Sea World! She'll remember the details of this day for the rest of her life. It won't even take ninety minutes out of your day, and there's no bus ride involved."

No response. He brushed past her and headed into the kitchen.

"Jade!" She followed. "She needs you to be proud of her. What could be more important than participating in a ceremony that recognizes your daughter's accomplishments?"

"Oh, I don't know." Thick sarcasm laced each word as he reached into a cupboard. Several plastic bottles tumbled out, clattering on the countertop. "Maybe getting a job so I can support her."

"A job?"

"You haven't heard?" Sorting through the disarray of what looked like vitamin containers, he found one labeled ibuprofen and snapped off the lid. "I lost mine. I have some interviews, out of town, tomorrow. When a potential boss says come, you come. Do you understand that?" He poured tablets onto his palm, then threw them at the back of his mouth and swallowed.

He may as well have slapped her and saved his breath. Her face burned. Anger and shame clambered for expression, leaving her speechless, her legs watery.

Jade shut his eyes and hooked his hands behind his neck. "That wasn't fair. I'm sorry. It's not your fault. Look, just butt out. This doesn't concern you anymore." He turned his back to her.

She was struck then with his vulnerability. He was out on a limb, and he'd probably spent most of the last few years out there, first watching his wife die, then being solely responsible for their camp and Caitlin. Now this recent move that could have lasted for years had collapsed in less than five months, forcing them to venture into the unknown again. She wanted to put her arms around him, hold him as he had her, but staring now at the back of those broad shoulders, she knew he wasn't letting her in. And that made her mad. "I thought it was for free, Jade."

He expelled a breath, as if he'd been holding it. "What?"

"The gift that you gave me. Your life, so to speak, so that I would know Christ. His was free, no strings attached, unconditional love."

"It was. It is." He still didn't turn around.

"It's not free if you take it out on Caitlin, if you exact this payment from her. It's as if she pays for what you did for me."

"The two aren't related, and it doesn't concern you."

"When one of my children is hurting, it *does* concern me."

"She's not your daughter."

Kendall wiped at the tears welling in her eyes. "Well, I've spent more time with her these past few months than you have." She rushed from his presence, through the living room and out the front door. It was obvious his mind had been made up long before she arrived, and nothing she said was going to budge it.

The peaceful feeling may disappear . . . The bottom line is, God is taking care of you now. Kendall clung to Jade's earlier words. There was no peace in these final hours at East Hills Elementary. Since rising early this morning, she had been on the verge of tears, an emotional state totally foreign to her even on fifth grade culmination day. Oh, she would choke up during the last good-bye hugs, but nothing like this time, this continuous dabbing of tears and pausing in mid-sentence to stave off the sob that threatened to erupt.

Well, it was over. The shared pre-ceremony jitters that sobered even Tony. The presentation itself, outside on the blacktop, folding chairs accommodating seventy-four students and at least twice as many relatives and friends, under a typically gray June morning sky. The young voices, less in tune than enthusiastic, singing about friendship as she played the piano and Maxine directed. The release afterwards . . . laughter, smiles, hugs, high fives. Ninety minutes. An eternity.

It was over. She sat now at her desk, surrounded by emptiness except for a box of tissues at her elbow. Never again would she say good-bye from this classroom.

She took a deep breath.

And on top of that, her knight's shining armor had rusted before her very eyes last night. Today it lay somewhere in a crumpled heap, empty.

Elbows propped on the desk, Kendall covered her eyes with her hands and slipped into an internal conversation she'd started a little over a week ago. It meandered through all kinds of topics and never seemed to have an ending point. *Father, please take care of Jade right now. Help him find a job. Please protect Caitlin; don't let her be so hurt by today that it will interfere with their relationship. Oh, I miss him so much. I wanted him here for her, but I really wanted him here for me too. He's my knight, Lord. I need him right next to me, right now. I want him to hold me.*

She bit her lip, remaining still for a few moments. Waiting.

Grace. Sufficient. The tune came now, a song. What were the words? *His grace is sufficient for me.*

Jesus was all she needed! She longed for Jade's strong shoulder to lean against, his laughing, green-flecked eyes, his personality as big and energetic as all outdoors, but . . . God's grace and His alone was enough.

Jesus, are You my true knight? Was it sacrilegious to call Jesus a knight? She'd have to ask . . . Jade.

A knock on the open door caught her attention.

"Jeremiah . . . I thought you'd gone."

He smiled. "Caity and I were headed to lunch and she said, 'Ms. O'Reilly looks so lonesome, can't she come with us?' Would you? Quite truthfully, for our sake? This is probably an imposition—"

The sob that had been waiting since last night now burst forth, but she smiled through it and nodded. There was nothing she'd like better than to be with them. She grabbed her purse and a handful of tissues and pushed him through the door, pulling it shut behind herself. For a moment she stared at the silver knob, sniffling.

"Kendall, are you all right? No, of course you're not."

Between the sobs she moaned, "I can't lock it. They took my keys!"

Jeremiah's arm came around her shoulders and nudged her away, down the sidewalk. It was a father's touch. Just what she needed.

Later that afternoon Kendall clutched the steering wheel, maneuvering her car along the tight curves up into the hills of Rancho Santa Fe, still hearing Jeremiah's voice from lunch.

He had kept her and Caitlin laughing, bolstering them through that first tender hour after leaving East Hills Elementary. As they ate, they made plans for turning Sunday's youth outing into a surprise going-away event for Jade. And when she talked about next week's run, a fund-raising event for breast cancer research, they decided it would be a good experience for Caitlin to join her. The good-bye wouldn't be final yet.

And Jeremiah talked with her about forgiveness. "I don't think you're one to hold grudges, Kendall, but Lewis certainly deserves one."

Surprised at his words, she confessed, "I've never felt such dislike or disdain for anyone."

"That's natural. It's hard to feel pity for one who has deliberately treated us so wretchedly. It's nigh unto impossible to forgive such a person."

"Does God want me to?"

"It's an ethereal kind of thing. It's not letting Lewis off the hook—it's letting yourself off a hook that's got hold of your heart. That hook opens a slow leak. Love and energy drip from it, draining away your best. It hurts to pull it out, and it leaves a wound for a while, and then scar tissue. That seems to be the nature of forgiveness though—it requires something of ourselves."

"It required God to give His Son, and we didn't deserve that, right?"

Jeremiah smiled at his granddaughter. "Caity-did, this teacher of yours is a smart one."

Lunch churned in her stomach now as Kendall drove into a spacious, circular drive and parked behind a long line of cars. She walked toward the low, rambling house with at-tached three-car garage. Tall eucalyptus trees shaded the area on this hot afternoon. Neighbors were strategically tucked from sight behind great distances of hills and foliage.

The teachers were gathering for an end-of-the-year party at the home of a fourth grade teacher whose husband owned an enormous software company. The woman obviously didn't have to work; she taught for the love of it.

Kendall's chin quivered. For the most part it was a good group of dedicated teachers, and she would miss them. She had planned on skipping this in hopes of skipping the hurt and anger it would produce, but Jeremiah's words had changed her thinking.

The doorbell echoed from within. A uniformed maid opened the door, then led her through a labyrinth of rooms and out a back patio door that led to an unhindered, breath-taking view of a valley. Laughing, her coworkers stood around a large pool.

The sight of a table laden with hors d'oeurves and drinks tumbled lunch around in her stomach again. She walked to the nearest group, moving on a short time later. There didn't seem to be much to say except "It's been nice knowing you." After a few more good-byes, she decided to quit stalling, took a deep breath, and walked to the far end of the pool. *Father, help me.*

"Lewis." She glanced at Jennifer by his side. "May I talk with you for just a moment, alone?"

"Well, certainly. Excuse us, Jen?"

With a smile, the young woman glided away.

She looked him square in the eye. "I just want you to know that I forgive you."

"For . . . ?" he prompted.

She blinked. "For taking away my job."

"Young lady, that was your doing."

"Then I forgive you for putting me in such a position that I was forced to lose it."

He threw back his head and laughed. "That's rich. I'll never understand women's convoluted thinking."

"I just wanted you to know I don't hold it against you." She held out her hand.

"Well," he took her hand between both of his, "good luck."

Firmly, she withdrew her hand and smiled. "I don't need luck. God will work it out for my best. Good-bye."

Before he could reply, she turned and walked quickly away, waved to a few people, and found her way back through the house and out the front door. Striding down the long drive, she felt a wave of embarrassment wash over her. She should have pushed him backwards into the pool, soaking his snazzy little Greg Norman outfit, wiping that smirk off his face—

I'm sorry, Lord!

As the embarrassment crested, a wave of refreshment took its place, a soothing balm to the fresh wound. She stretched her neck, gazed at the dazzling blue sky above the slender eucalyptus, and laughed out loud.

Eleven

Kendall watched Caitlin across the dining room at Tony's Jacal, a cozy restaurant tucked away in a Solana Beach residential area. The girl sat in a corner booth with a few other children, all siblings of the youth group teens, munching tortilla chips and salsa. Parents mingled, some standing, some sitting, chatting comfortably. Dusk settled outside. Through large windows soft spotlights illuminated a patio and fountain; the faint trickling of water could be heard. Wrapped gifts were piled on a nearby table. All awaited the arrival of the guest of honor.

Jeremiah walked over to her with a smile. "Jade will appreciate this, Kendall."

"I hope so." She glanced at the *Thank You* banner she had draped across the windows. "Making a few phone calls and reserving this room was the least I could do. He doesn't exactly seem the frilly type, so I skipped the crepe streamers and balloons."

He chuckled. "You're right. He wouldn't like a fuss."

"Do you think he'll be surprised?"

"He didn't have a clue when he left this afternoon. The kids were prepared to blindfold him, though, if he insisted on eating down at the bay, so the surprise may have already started."

The group had spent their last outing this Sunday at Mission Beach, rollerblading, riding the roller coaster, playing volleyball. Some of the girls had invited her to join them when they discussed this going-away party, but she had declined. Under different circumstances it would have been fun. If Jade weren't leaving because of her . . . if Jade hadn't seemed angry with her when she'd tried to persuade him to attend the school ceremony . . . if she could wield some sort of butterfly net to squish those flapping wings every time she thought of him—

"Jeremiah, does everyone know it's my fault?"

"Kendall," he remonstrated.

"I can't help it."

He gave her a brief hug. "I'm sure you're wondering what people think. The relationship between your job and Jade's is not common knowledge. He announced that his leaving was a mutual decision, that he did not wish to remain at the church and so someone else was hired. I'm sure there's gossip. Lewis had to do some arm-twisting to get the others to see things his way."

"There's probably somebody here who knew somebody at the school board meeting too."

"Probably. At any rate, you're not to blame yourself, understood? The other youth pastor seems a good choice. And my son is confident God has a position for him. It will work out for the best."

"How did his interview go last week?"

"Well, it didn't seem promising. It was for a part-time school counselor job, far from Westminster Seminary. He'll find something. Meanwhile, he's taking a summer course and promised Caity a climbing trip."

There was a commotion at the doorway, and they looked over to see Jade, a white scarf tied around his eyes, being led inside by some of the boys. The others were close on their heels, laughing and talking.

"Surprise!" everyone shouted as one teen pulled away the blindfold.

Jade laughed, and the teens shoved him into a booth. Everyone else found seats and ordered dinner. Kendall sat with some parents and watched from the periphery. She wondered why she was there. The young people and some parents took turns giving little speeches, some humorous, some tearjerkers. Over his protests, they gave him gifts, small mementos. Dinner was served. She shoved a chimichanga around her plate with a fork and tried to make small talk.

"So you're the one to blame for this!"

Startled, she jerked up her head to see Jade standing behind her, grinning. His choice of words left her dumbfounded. The others at the table laughed. She smoothed her already-smooth hair.

"Hey, I'm just teasing. It's great." Resting a hand on the back of her chair, he leaned close to her ear and whispered, "Really. I would never blame you." Breaking the brief moment of eye contact, he glanced at the table. "Are you going to eat that?"

"No. Do you want it?" She passed her untouched plate to him, wondering how the man could eat at a time like this.

"Umm. Thanks. Is that an extra fork?" He reached for it, then meandered off to another table.

Soon after, Kendall slipped out through the door, avoiding all good-byes. Despite her hand in organizing the party, it just didn't seem like hers. School was over, and the lives of her students and their families—even Caitlin, Jade, and Jeremiah—truly didn't concern her anymore. It was time to move on, in spite of that tingling where his fingers had brushed her shoulder.

It might be time to move on, away from the Zukowskis, Kendall thought the following Saturday morning, but it would have to wait until after the cancer research fund-raising event. Caitlin had already been promised, arrangements already made. Her grandpa was bringing her this morning. She would walk the 5K with Kendall and Maxine, along with their acquaintances, a small group of mothers and daughters who had made this an annual outing. What brought them together was the shared pain of watching a loved one suffer from breast cancer.

Seagulls squawked overhead, and harbor water lapped at the pilings a few feet below the sidewalk where she stood. She waited alone near Anthony's Restaurant while her friends roamed through booths set up for the occasion, full of freebies. The largeness of the city always amazed her. Surrounded by thousands of people, she noticed there was still plenty of breathing space along the Navy Pier, the sidewalks, and the blocked-off section of Harbor Drive. A ferry was docked nearby; beyond that an aircraft carrier glided silently through the bay.

She crossed her arms against the cool, early-morning mist, thankful that a distant patch of blue in the eastern sky promised a burning away of the coastal gloom before long. Soon she could tie the sweatshirt around her waist and be glad she had worn shorts. Some women nearby slathered suntan lotion on their arms. Kendall inhaled the scent of coconut oil mingled with that of fish and seawater.

She and Maxine had arrived extra early because in all of the confusion at school this year, they'd forgotten to register in advance. She searched the crowd, hoping to spot a tall, white-haired gentleman. Instead there came into view short-cropped curls the color of a shiny new penny.

Jade made his way toward her, his daughter at his side, large Styrofoam coffee cup in hand, eyes at half-mast, early-morning stubble outlining his jaw. He mumbled a greeting.

"Good morning to you too," she replied, then smiled down at Caitlin. "All set? You look bright and peppy."

"Yep. Daddy doesn't though." She laughed.

She glanced at him again. Dark half-moons underlined his eyes that now scanned the surroundings. "Not your time of day, huh? I would have picked her up, but I left at 6, and your dad said he wanted to see what this was all about. You're welcome to stay. Men participate too. Oh, here, Cait." Not pausing for a breath or a reply, she pulled out a fuchsia T-shirt that had been tucked under her arm. It matched the one she wore beneath her sweatshirt. "Let's just pull it over your other one."

She helped the girl into the official shirt that named the event and date on the front, company sponsors on the back. "I got you a big one. You can use it for a nightshirt. Now we'll pin this number on the front." From one pocket she pulled out two thick papers, from the other, a handful of safety pins.

"What's that?" Jade asked, his tone as gruff as the expression on his face.

"What? Oh, this is the 'in memory of' sign. Mine's underneath my sweatshirt; it's got my mom's name on it. See, Caitlin?" She held it up. "I wrote in your mom's name. Turn around, and I'll pin it on your back. Did I spell Deborah right? I was hoping it was like the Deborah in the Bible."

Caitlin answered, "That's the one." She stood still while Kendall pinned the tag to her shirt.

"What's that one?" He nodded toward a passerby. " 'In

celebration of' so-and-so?"

"Those are for the ones who beat it." She swallowed. "This side of heaven anyway. Okay, we need to go over that way. The 10K runners are starting, and we can do some aerobics to warm up. There's music to make it fun." She took Caitlin's hand. "Jade, are you staying?"

He was still looking around, the forgotten coffee cup held loosely at his side. He appeared uncomfortable.

She suspected he was reading name tags. In memory of . . . in celebration of . . . Just reading the name tags was an intensely emotional experience. For the women, by far the majority in attendance, it was a releasing time that comforted, encouraged, and healed. For men it often seemed a different story. "Jade?"

"There aren't many little girls here."

"Maxine and I will keep her close."

"Aren't you running?"

"No. I walk in this one. If you want to leave, we'll bring Caitlin home."

"Okay." He turned and walked toward the street.

"Bye, Daddy!"

Kendall called, "We're stopping for pancakes!"

Caitlin squeezed her hand. "That's okay, Ms. O'Reilly. He'll be home all day. He's packing again."

Packing again. She wondered if Jade could ever travel far enough to get away from the pain he'd so obviously displayed this morning.

After dropping Maxine off at home, Kendall drove toward Caitlin's. The girl was dozing in the backseat. It had been a morning full of exercise and laughter and pancakes and good conversation.

She thought about the talk she'd had with Caitlin. What a

distance they'd traveled together these past few months! From Caitlin's despair and refusal to come to class to this, a sharing of her innermost thoughts and feelings, a position of total vulnerability, complete trust.

Thank You, Father, for that. Is this more than trust? It's as if she has entrusted me with something. Maybe with her care? Oh, I do care for her. I do love her. Should I talk to Jade? It seems that something should be said. But I tried that once, and he wouldn't even listen! Anyway, he didn't do anything about it, like come to the culmination. She sighed. *I guess the doing part is between him and You though. Maybe I should say something. Lord, please give me the words. For Caitlin's sake.*

In their conversation the girl had drawn a picture of an emotionally distant father, one that unearthed haunting memories for Kendall.

"It's like he's in the room, Ms. O'Reilly, but he's not. He doesn't laugh. Sometimes I talk to him, and he doesn't answer. He didn't talk the whole way here this morning. And he didn't come to my culmination." Her lip had trembled on that one. "Most the time he's not even home. He's always going to the mountains or to a new job place. Was your dad like that because your mom died too?"

Kendall had caught her breath. "Sort of. Caitlin, your dad's probably just worried right now because he's looking for a new job. He hasn't been like this the whole time since your mom died, has he?"

She thought for a moment. "No, not all the time, but it makes me kinda mad."

"You could tell him."

"I don't think he hears me, and it doesn't feel good to be mad at him. Ms. O'Reilly, did you have to forgive your dad?"

From the mouths of babes . . . She had never considered that one. Burying the thought of him, even when he was alive, had been the solution, the key to her sanity. A child shouldn't have to forgive a parent, should she? After all, the parent was the adult.

Then again, Jade definitely needed a reminder.

Kendall parked the car now and twisted around in the seat. "Caitlin? We're home, honey."

The girl rubbed her eyes.

"I want to talk to your dad. Is that all right with you?"

A worried look crossed her face. "Are you gonna tell him I'm mad at him?"

"Only if you give me permission. Remember when he came to visit me, to tell me that you were upset with me? He didn't tell me everything you said, but he let me know that you were upset and that I could probably do something about it because I was your teacher. That's kind of what I want to do. Does that make sense to you?"

Slowly, she nodded. "I think so."

They climbed out of the car. Kendall hugged the girl. "He loves you, you know. Can I tell him what I think he needs to hear?"

Caitlin returned the squeeze. "Okay."

Inside the condominium, Jeremiah greeted them with his usual enthusiasm. His granddaughter plopped beside him on the couch and immediately launched into a detailed account of their morning. Kendall spotted Jade through the open patio door. He sat reading at the picnic table in the shade, book and notepad before him, tapping a pencil to some silent beat. A royal blue baseball cap sat backwards on his head. He hadn't shaved yet.

"Jade?"

"Yo."

"I want to talk to you."

"Shoot." His eyes were still on the book.

She sat across from him. "Can we talk?"

"Sure." He was chewing a piece of gum.

It occurred to her then that he really hadn't looked at her for quite some time. Not since the disastrous board meeting. There was a quick glance this morning, and the other night at the restaurant. The last time she came here he'd kept his back to her. Now he was— "Jade Zukowski, look at me."

He lifted narrowed eyes at her. "You sound like a teacher."

"You know very well that's because I am one."

"But you're not mine."

She took a deep breath. "I need to talk to you about Caitlin."

"Thought we covered that."

"She said some things this morning that concern me. Good grief, give me ten minutes. I wouldn't bother you if I didn't care about her."

"I have a lot on my mind." He looked back down at the book. "I've got studying to do."

Where was the Jade she knew? Maybe it would help to get away from the condo. "Take a short break. Walk with me at the beach."

"She'll outgrow whatever's bugging her, just like she did when she didn't like you."

She stared at the top of his head for a moment. "If you mean that, you are more despicable than my dad ever was, and he was ill and didn't have the answer you have."

He closed his eyes briefly, then flipped shut the book and stood. "I'll meet you at the beach. That place by the steps. I have errands to do in that direction." He walked into the condo and headed through the kitchen.

Jeremiah and Caitlin weren't in sight, so Kendall let herself out the front door. Round 1 was over. She wondered why this felt like such a battle. What was his problem? Well, to start with, there was the obvious—he didn't have a job, and he had a daughter to support. And she, Kendall O'Reilly, if not directly responsible for that situation, was at least irrevocably entwined with it.

The beach by the steps.

With a sense of dread, Kendall walked along the sidewalk. Lined with lush semitropical plants and trees, this public access was tucked between two two-story, oceanfront, cliff-hanging apartment buildings. The moist air promised sea, but she didn't hear or glimpse it until she reached the steps, a steep staircase that hugged the side of the hundred-foot bluff. There the view and breeze took her breath away.

She usually avoided this area. For her it was too breathtaking in another sense. She clutched the damp, rusty railing and scanned the small beach area far below. It was deserted except for Jade walking—no, it appeared more like pacing. Hadn't he mentioned that he ran here? Of course. He would prefer the steps; running them would enhance the leg muscles.

She took a deep breath and looked at her feet clad in tennis shoes. She had to talk to him for Caitlin's sake. She had to. After another deep breath, eyes lowered, she slid her right foot down a step, pulling the left one after it while leaning heavily against the railing. The steps were damp, sand-covered, narrow in width and height. One more breath, one more step.

It took awhile and all of her concentration, but at last she planted her feet in the soft sand. She looked up. To her right was a pile of boulders. With the tide in, the north route was blocked. She spotted Jade, striding the other direction along the ocean's edge. Smiling to herself, she realized he was probably a bit frustrated. She ran to his side.

"Well, anyway," she began, as if there had been no interruption in their conversation. She slowed, matching two of her steps to one of his. "Remember when you had to tell me Caitlin was having a problem with me?"

"Yeah." He wore silver-framed sunglasses and the backwards baseball cap. His thumbs were hooked in the back pockets of his jeans.

"I listened. I tried to figure out a better way to communicate with her. And I thought you were probably a crummy dad who didn't pay attention to her."

He turned his head toward the surf.

"But then I got to know you and saw the two of you together, and I knew you weren't like that. And you aren't, Jade, but nevertheless she's feeling left out. I wanted to be sure you're aware of that."

They neared an area where the cliff jutted out. The incoming tide lapped close at its base, blocking their path. He stopped and looked down at her. "What do you want me to do? Of course she feels left out. My mind is elsewhere. She's got Grandpa filling in. She'll be fine."

"But she needs her *dad*." She couldn't see his eyes, only her own reflection in silvery lenses. As if his hearing were obstructed too, she raised her voice. "She needs—oh, what's that song? 'Butterfly Kisses.' She needs to feel from her dad that sense of total, unconditional love. She needs to feel that you cherish her as your most precious treasure. That you're in awe of the fact that she is your child. Right now she feels you're shutting her out. Jade, you know what to do. Just give her some of yourself, like you do to everybody else." She bit her lip.

He faced the ocean again, took off the cap, and combed his fingers through his hair, then replaced the hat. "There's nothing left right now."

"Then the two *are* related, aren't they?"

"What?"

"You giving yourself for me and now not having any left for her."

He shook his head and let out an exasperated breath. "It's the job thing, the man's loss of identity, all that junk. It's not you."

"Oh, Jade, you know where your identity comes from, and your resources. And you know they're unlimited. You haven't stopped giving to the kids in your youth group, have you? I heard you're even taking some of the guys climbing. You'll keep giving there until you move on to another situation. Why is it you can give to us strangers and not to your own daughter?"

His jaw muscles tensed. "You haven't lost a wife." He shook his head again. "These distant relationships work because when you lose them, it's not that big a deal. It's easier to give at the office than at home. You can choose exactly what parts you give, exactly how much, exactly where and when."

"You still have control then, is that it?"

"Yeah. When you give up control like with Deb, it becomes . . . risky, unbearable."

She studied his profile. "Please don't shut Cait out. That makes her whole life just too . . . unbearable."

"I know. I won't. I hadn't realized . . ." He turned toward her. "Thank you, Ms. O'Reilly, once again."

You're just her teacher. "You're welcome."

"I'd better go." He backed away. "I have some packing to do. I promise I'll work on it with Cait." He lifted a hand, then turned and began jogging toward the steps.

Still no smile, no eye contact with those silvery lenses between them. Tears filled Kendall's eyes. What was unbearable was giving God control and then getting in return a love for this man and watching him run away because she meant nothing to him aside from the fact that she was just his daughter's teacher. *Former* teacher.

She pulled a tissue from her pocket and slowly trudged through the sand toward the steps, the tears falling now. Jade was long gone, easily running up the stairway like a ram across the mountaintops. *Dear God, I don't understand this. I love him, but it hurts too much. I didn't sign up for this. I know I didn't. Just take it away.*

She was halfway up the steep flight when it struck, an unseen fist pounding a blow to her stomach. Nausea instantly swept through her. Letting go of the railing, she clutched her arms across her midsection and sank to her knees against the step's sharp edge. The gentle surf far below became a raging windstorm in her head.

No!

Eyes shut, she inched her way around until she sat huddled on the narrow step. Laying her forehead on her knees, she covered her head with her arms, warding off the images that bombarded her mind.

Insisting on driving.

The wet windshield, the wet pavement. Was it only tears?

Sliding. Flying. Falling. Impact. Again. Again.

A splintering, then silence.

"Daddy!"

Deathly silence.

Rock everywhere. Pain. Searing, excruciating, unrelenting.

Let me die!

Sirens. Voices, voices, voices.

Hands touching. Her screaming.

At last, blackness.

"Kendall!"

God, I can't, I can't. You know I can't.

"Kendall!"

I can't go up. Eyes still tightly shut, she pictured the tide. It was in now, closing off both directions. She had done this once, but the tide was low, and she had walked south into Del Mar all the way beyond where the cliffs ended, then finally out to the highway, backtracking to her car. *But the beach is gone! I can't go down.*

"Kendall! Look at me!"

Jade?

Slowly she peered over her shoulder. High above there was a figure, a shining, silver figure, sunlight glaring off of it.

"Listen to me, sweetheart," he called. "I want you to walk up to me. Just walk up."

Her knight. Of course, her knight would come. God would send him.

"I can't," she whimpered.

"You can do this. Take hold of the railing."

Come and get me!

"Just stand up. Hold on. That's it. Think of the sonata, Kendall. Play it. Just move your hands, slide them on the railing. It's as easy as playing the sonata. Think of the music. The notes you play. Now walk to me. You can do it."

His hand was stretched toward her, but the rest of him was hidden in that silver glare. His voice soothed. She listened. Step by step she listened to his voice, to the music in her mind.

"Jade!" She fell into his arms.

"You did it! Don't cry, sweetheart. You're okay now. I wanted you to do it. I knew you could."

"You were all in silver, like armor."

"What?"

"There was shining armor all over you—"

"It was probably the sun's reflection—on these." He took

233

off his sunglasses. "Or those windows." He waved his arm toward the wall of windows on the apartment building at his left. "My belt buckle. Whatever. Kendall, don't make me into something I'm not."

"You're my knight. You always save me."

"I'm not a knight, and I'm not Jesus. Nowhere near either." His arms tightened. "Please don't cry."

But she did. She couldn't help it. There were so many tears to catch up on. Tears for her sad childhood, for conquering those steep steps, for joy that his arms held her. "Jade, I was driving that night my dad died, and I was crying, and I couldn't see the road. I never really cried after that, not until that night when you held me."

"Shh." Gently, he brushed at the tears with his fingertips. "Shh. Everything is okay now," he whispered. "Don't cry. I can't stand seeing you cry." He lowered his face then and started kissing away the tears. "Please don't cry."

Her words stopped. Her crying stopped. He kissed the trail of tears until his mouth found hers. The surf stopped rolling, the seagulls quieted, the earth held its breath.

After a time Jade groaned and looked at her, his eyes drinking in every detail of her face, his hand tracing the outline of her ear. "Oh, Pollyanna, I'm sorry. I can't be your knight. I won't be your knight." He touched her cheek. "I didn't even shave." Turning then, he hurried down the sidewalk.

She stood still, watching him jog around the distant corner, out of sight.

Stunned, she sat down on the top step, at the top of that cliff that had lost the power to cast its fearful spell. She had just sensed all of nature come to a standstill. What could be more frightening after that? Nothing . . . except maybe the knowledge that it would never happen again.

Not that big a deal?

"Daddy, you look a mess!"

"Mind if I come in?" Jade walked into his daughter's room and plopped onto the stuffed chair. He *felt* a mess. That one moment of being unable to ignore the love growing in his heart had left him a total wreck. His stomach churned. "I think I need one of your neck massages. Got one for me?"

"Sure." Cait set down the book she was reading and jumped from the bed to stand behind him. Her small fingers kneaded at the tight muscles.

"Umm, that helps."

"Where did you go?"

"Oh, for a walk with Ms. O'Reilly. She told me you've been feeling left out."

"Are you mad at me?"

"No, of course not, sweetie. Are you mad at me?"

"Kinda."

"I'm sorry. I haven't been paying much attention to you."

"That's okay, Daddy. Ms. O'Reilly says it's just for now cuz you're worried about getting a job."

"She's right, but I'm sorry I've ignored you so much lately. And I'm real sorry I missed your culmination. Will you forgive me, Cait?"

"Sure."

He had to get away as quickly as possible. He had to just go and hike and climb and push himself to the physical limit and forget. He'd bury these emotions because he couldn't live with them. Better now than later, when she realized he wasn't a knight . . . or when she died—

"Cait, I have a big favor to ask. Will you forgive me if I leave tonight instead of tomorrow?"

She sighed a grown-up sigh. "Well, all right. You look like you need it really bad."

He turned to face her. "What does that mean?"

Cait giggled and rubbed his cheek. "You got whiskers, and your hair's sticking out by your ears, and that hat looks silly."

"You think I'll look better after camping?"

"You always do." She shrugged.

He pulled her onto his lap and gave her a bear hug. "I love you, Caity."

"I love you too, Daddy. When can we see Ms. O'Reilly?"

After a long moment he answered in a hoarse whisper, "I don't know."

"I think she likes us a lot." She slid from his lap, stepped over to her desk, and pulled something from a drawer. "Here." She handed him a pile of torn pieces of construction paper.

"It looks like a valentine."

"Yeah. Ms. O'Reilly made it for me."

"What happened to it?"

"I tore it. It made me think of Mom. She always made them like that and wrote poems too. I showed it to Ms. O'Reilly, and she said it was okay. You know what she told me today?"

"What?" His daughter was chattering, eagerly making up for lost time.

"When her mom died, somebody else tried to teach her piano, and she ripped the music book apart and never took a lesson again."

"Really?"

Cait's curls bounced as she nodded. "She said it's hard to let somebody else love you when your mom dies, and she was real glad I let her love me. She said I was a smarter little girl than she ever was. Do you think I could be a teacher too? Like Mom and Ms. O'Reilly?"

"You'd be a great teacher." Should he tell her now that

Ms. O'Reilly, like Mom, was part of their past? That they couldn't let her love them anymore? He'd wait. Right now facing another tearful female was beyond his capabilities. The situation would change soon, and then it would be a natural separation.

His breath caught. It was as if he felt a groaning in the depths of his soul, as if something within him protested. There would be nothing natural in that separation—

"Maybe Ms. O'Reilly could get pizza with me and Grandpa tonight?"

"Uhh, I need to finish packing."

"Want some help, Dad?"

He smiled. "Yeah, I'd really appreciate that. Hey, Cait, are you too old for a butterfly kiss?"

She thought a moment, then leaned toward him and brushed her eyelashes against his cheek. "Nope."

"Did you have to forgive your dad?"

Brushing her hair, Kendall replayed Caitlin's words in her mind. She hadn't given the girl an answer. In the twenty years or so since the ugliness began, she had never asked herself the question. She studied the white jagged scar on her forehead. Daily she chose to ignore this reminder that something had to be forgiven.

An afternoon of busywork and avoiding thoughts was long enough. In the past she would have slept until they went away, but that route was closed to her now, just as surely as the beach had been earlier. *Lord, help me get this all straightened out.*

She sat at her kitchen table and devised a plan. What was it the teens had done at the campout, that night she missed? Something about writing down difficulties and decisions, then throwing the pieces of paper into the fire, symbolic of giving it to Jesus. Just letting it go.

She reached for the pad by the telephone, then decided this required nice stationery. After getting the box of yellow linen paper from a drawer, she sat down, pen in hand.

Okay.

On one piece of paper she wrote *Jade.*

Lord, I love him, but he doesn't want it. So . . . She took a deep breath. *I give him to You. Caitlin and the teenagers need him more than I do. Help me to trust You for the strength to let him go.* She sighed. *Every day, probably.*

She pulled out another piece of paper. *Job.*

I need one.

And another. *Thornton.*

He still comes to mind with a bunch of bitterness.

Dad.

Lord, this is a tough one, but here goes.

Dad, I'm angry that you didn't take better care of me. But I have a good life. The past is over and done with, and I'm choosing to let it go. And I'm choosing to forgive you, which I can do because Jesus forgave me. You didn't know what you were doing.

She continued writing, filling both sides of the paper with regrets and questions and hurts. At the end she signed her name and wiped her sleeve across her face. Goodness, she was tired of crying.

"Okay, Jesus, now what do we do? No campfire, not even a fireplace. Aha, matches." She spoke aloud as she found matches in a cupboard and carried the papers to the sink. "This is it, Lord. You can have all of it. I can't handle these on my own. My dad, a job, Thornton. And Jade. Dear Jade." She struck a match, held the pages over the sink, and watched them burn. "Even Jeremiah David Zukowski the Third."

She rinsed the ashes down the drain. "Okay. Done. Time to move on with life. I need Your help on this one, Lord, big-time. I just lost *my* life. I guess I need the one You've got for me now. Well, let's play some music."

At the piano, she played from her mother's old hymnal. After a time she pulled out the Beethoven music. Jade had been so impressed with the sonata when he overheard her playing it in her classroom. He didn't seem to mind that she couldn't finish it correctly. *He thought life was like climbing or playing the notes, just following what's put before us, trusting God to get us to the top or put the melody to the notes.* Jade was so fun, so full of life, so good-looking . . .

In earnest she began the *Moonlight Sonata.*

And she finished it. Correctly. As it should be played. And then she did it again. No do-overs. No breaks. No fumbling fingers.

Well, hallelujah.

Twelve

"You're losing your grip, Zukowski," Jerry admonished.

"That's obvious." Jade stared into the flames, avoiding his friend's eyes that bore into him from across the campfire. "It was a rough climb."

"Rough is a mild term for a climb that includes a thirty-foot fall. Besides, I was referring to your grip on reality. It's not just your hesitant movements up the rock and missing a toehold. It's on your face, in the way you unroll your sleeping bag, in your not eating, in your silence. What's up, bud?"

He lifted a shoulder. "Did I say thanks, by the way?"

Jerry grunted. "It wasn't our first time, huh?" He reached behind the stone he was sitting on, picked up a log, and tossed it onto the fire. "Remember in the beginning? What's it been, seventeen years? They almost banned you from the camp. Nobody else would go up with you."

"Yeah." Jade thought back to when they had met. He was a teen, Jerry an older college student who taught him how to climb, taught him how to harness his wild energies into the vertical dance. There had been plenty of falls back then.

"Jade, we've been belaying each other for a long time, securing each other on the wall. Of course you've taken more dives than I have."

He snorted. "One or two." His shorter, wiry friend was by far the most intensely focused man he'd ever known.

"You trust me, right?"

"With my life, Jer."

"Listen up then. I feel like you need another line secured for you here, figuratively speaking. You're not talking to me, so I think I'll take off early in the A.M. and you can do your talking to Someone else who's got better answers. Why don't I take the food too? My guess is this would be a good time for fasting. Clear your head and your gut. Got a Bible?"

He nodded.

"Okay." Jerry crawled into his sleeping bag. "Good night."

Jade added logs to the fire, then lay awake gazing up through the pines at the stars until they faded in the coming dawn. When he awoke, the fire was smoldering, the sun shining. His friend and the food were gone. He found a note under a stone.

"Z—Read Isaiah 43:18–19. P.S. Most of them like diamonds."

Puzzled with the postscript, he ignored it and dug into his backpack for the Bible and a water bottle. This was always the toughest part of the adventure for him. It was like that first backwards plunge into midair at the beginning of a rappel. It was letting go of his natural instinct to keep his feet on the ground and follow the direction they pointed. It was pushing aside his control and trusting an unseen hand to secure the line that held him to this life.

He hadn't let go for some time. Probably not since Deb's illness, but that had been a no-brainer. What other choice was there right then?

Now he had a choice. *Father.* He opened the Bible.

"Do not call to mind the former things, or ponder things of the past. Behold, I will do something new, now it will spring forth; will you not be aware of it? I will even make a roadway in the wilderness, rivers in the desert."

"Knock, knock."

"Come on in, Sara." Kendall glanced up from the large cardboard box she was taping shut. "I'm just about ready. Where do you want to eat?"

"Some all-you-care-to-stuff-yourself-with buffet." She stood in the open doorway, facing the hot, late-afternoon sun. "All this packing is making me hungry. Hey, a Fed Ex guy is headed this way. Hi!" she called out to the man. She disappeared from view for a moment, then returned with an overnight-type square envelope. "For you."

"Maybe it's my contract. It should be coming soon." She had accepted an offer for a fourth-grade teaching position in Escondido.

Sara beamed. "I'm so excited for you. For us!"

"Me too." Kendall washed her hands at the sink. "Two new jobs, one new Escondido apartment." The inland community wasn't far, but she preferred spending her time with students rather than commuting. They had decided to move together.

"New friends," Sara added.

"New church."

"And Bible study with *single* guys."

"Oh, Sara, isn't it amazing the way life changes? We never would have decided on our own to move. Just think, four weeks ago I was moping about having no job."

"And I was moping about my oppressive job with that certain man across the hall."

Kendall sat down at the table and picked up the envelope.

"And I was trying to find a church without old acquaintances like a principal in it." She didn't mention Jade. It was easier to ignore that memory as much as possible. She didn't mean to pull a Pollyanna, but at times it was the only way to get through a moment. Jeremiah had called a couple of times. The first time he said Jade had been in the mountains for almost a week. She figured he'd gone right after the last time she saw him. Another time she learned that they were all spending a few weeks out of town, Jade interviewing, Jeremiah and Caitlin visiting relatives. He told her to keep in touch, but they were gone when she got the new job and besides . . . She probably wouldn't keep in touch.

"And," Sara continued, "I wasn't even interested in church. Or God. Then I start praying and before I say amen I've quit my job, found a new one, and agreed to be your roommate—even if you do talk to yourself and the city is miles and miles from the ocean."

"Only thirty minutes, if the traffic—Oh, my goodness!" She pulled a rectangular ticket from the envelope.

"What is it?"

"Mozart."

"That's it?" Sara examined the empty envelope. "Fed Ex for one ticket to a concert?"

"Sara, it's the *Festival,* and it's outside in Balboa Park Sunday afternoon, and it costs *sixty* dollars! I've never ever gone. Oh, you are so sweet! But you really shouldn't have done this."

Her friend laughed. "Me? Sorry, Kendall, I'm not that creative, and I happen to be unemployed for a few weeks. Where did it come from? There's no return address."

"You really didn't? Well, who would . . . ? Ian! Ian Edwards, I bet. How thoughtful! He's still trying to make up for things."

"Wonder if he's going too?"

Kendall shrugged. The phone rang, and she answered, "Hello?"

"Is this Miss Kendall O'Reilly?" a pleasant female voice inquired.

"Yes."

"This is Red Carpet Limousine Service. We're scheduled to pick you up on Sunday to drive you to and from Balboa Park. Will two o'clock be all right with you?"

"Uh, well . . . yes."

"Thank you. Good-bye."

Sara asked, "Who was that? You look absolutely flabbergasted."

She giggled. "A limo service. They're picking me up for the concert. Do you believe it?"

"Well, if Ian does go, at least you won't have to ride with him!"

With one hand Kendall clutched the program; with the other she smoothed the folds of her dress across her lap. A matinee concert had seemed too early in the day for her more formal black, so she had worn a simple, ankle-length peach rayon dress with capped sleeves. It was comfortable in the afternoon's warmth, but she wasn't. The longer the seat next to her remained vacant, the more wrinkled became the program, and the more often she smoothed the dress folds. She glanced again to her right.

Ian must be coming. After all this—expensive ticket, luxurious white stretch limousine ride—she probably should take him to dinner. That would be all right. He could be pleasant company, and she certainly did appreciate this gift. She had brought a shawl with that thought half formed. July evenings could be cool. The cordial but tight-lipped chauffeur named

Julius had assured her the shawl was safe with him and yes, the vehicle was available to her for the entire evening.

The minutes ticked by. Still no Ian. Maybe it was Sara after all. She had hung around until Kendall climbed into the limo; she would have had to get ready after that. Despite her protests, she was this creative and yes, she would splurge this outrageously on her friend.

The theater was almost full. It was a fairly small area with high, dark-colored walls and no roof, open to the sky. Tops of eucalyptus trees were visible, swaying gently, shading the mid-afternoon sun and helping mask the occasional scent that wafted from the nearby zoo. It was an outdoor theater, but the concrete steps and auditorium-style seats made it seem more civilized, not the picnic-on-the-lawn type. Formally dressed orchestra members were taking their places.

She heard a rustling to her right. People down the row were standing to let—

Jade?

"Excuse me. Excuse me. Sorry."

She blinked. He was wearing a tuxedo. A silver gray tuxedo. Matching vest and plain, starchy white, mandarin-collar shirt, buttoned to the top, no tie. He carried a single white rose.

He smiled and gestured at the empty seat. "May I?"

Trying to assimilate this new information, she frowned.

He sat down, leaned over, and whispered in her ear, "You look especially lovely, Ms. O'Reilly."

She accepted the rose he held before her. Her face felt warm. From the corner of her eye she could see people turning, watching them. Those butterflies so painstakingly banished in the four weeks since she had last seen him converged now in full force, thumping wildly inside her.

245

"I hope you like Mozart?"

She looked at him. The broad shoulders draped elegantly in the jacket. The solid neck accented with satiny gray lapels. The clean-shaven square jaw and the deepened laugh lines. The hazel eyes dancing with that tangible energy that always permeated the air around him. The crown of coppery waves. She opened her mouth to speak, but no words formed.

He raised his eyebrows. "Is that a yes?"

She nodded.

"I thought you might." He smiled. "You look surprised. I figured you'd recognize my white steed."

The butterfly wings merged now, uniting into one giant pounding in her chest. Butterflies turned condor. She didn't want this. She had accepted his leaving, realized it was for the best, it was easier. Why was he doing this? Why? "Why—?"

"Shh." He held a finger to his lips and nodded toward the stage.

The music began. Pressing an arm against her midsection, she quietly took several deep breaths, fighting down the confusion, the panic. By the end of the first concerto, the beauty took hold, and she calmed down—to a certain extent . . . As long as she kept her eyes forward . . . As long as Jade sat still and his arm didn't brush against hers.

At intermission, he turned to her. "I liked that. Care to go for a walk?"

It couldn't wait. "Why—*why* are you doing this?"

His smile spread slowly until his eyes crinkled. "Because I'm courting you, Kendall O'Reilly."

She flew to her feet, the rose and program tumbling to the floor. "Excuse me for a moment."

Jade leaned over, retrieved them, and then stood aside. As she passed, his low voice breathed, "I'll be here, sweetheart."

She glanced over her shoulder at him, then hurried

through the crowd. She had approximately twenty minutes to decide whether this was a dream or a nightmare.

Outside she walked swiftly, past the nearby round Old Globe Theater, out under the alcove past the Museum of Man entrance, on down the sidewalk along Laurel Street. When she reached the Cabrillo Bridge, freeway traffic roaring far below, she was finally able to pray.

Father . . . help! I thought You took him away. I thought . . . I thought . . . Oh, help me think right.

The breeze blew her skirt, her hair. She strode two more blocks to the lawn bowling courts. So green, so peaceful, the players wearing all white. Her eyes burned. *Help me feel what's right.*

Answers didn't come. She turned and hurried back, a new anxious thought forming. What if he left?

At the sight of him standing near their seats, unmistakable relief flowed through her. Her knight in his semi-shining armor waited.

He smiled as she approached. "Just in time."

"Jade, I have to know." The words were barely audible to her own ears, overwhelmed by the chattering crowd. Her teacher voice had vanished.

He leaned toward her.

"Will you—" She pressed her lips together, then tried again. "Will you leave me like you did at the beach, at those stairs?"

Immediately he sobered and held her eyes with his. "No."

"No?"

"No. Never. Never ever, sweetheart."

They sat then, and the music began again. Kendall was thankful for the quiet time, letting the knowledge of Jade's intentions weave itself through her, like the notes floating from the violins and flutes, until at last everything settled into her heart. When it was over, she smiled.

"Ah," he said, "at last a smile. I was getting concerned." As they headed out with the crowd, he reached for her hand.

With fingers nestled against his large, callused ones, she also at last found her voice as they strolled down a sidewalk toward the parking lot. "Thank you, Jade. The concert was absolutely marvelous."

"You're welcome. There's the steed."

It was impossible not to see the long white limousine blocking several other cars parked in the lot. Julius greeted them with a smile and opened the back door. "I hope you enjoyed your concert, Miss O'Reilly, Mr. Zukowski."

"We did," Jade replied. "Thank you, Julius."

Kendall's feet sank into the thick burgundy carpet, and she slid onto the matching, luxurious leather seat. "Do you know him?" she asked as the door closed behind Jade.

"Being part of a large congregation means plenty of contacts. Limo service owners. People with discounts at formal wear rental places. People who don't want their concert tickets after they hear a desperate tale of woe." He rested his arm along the back of the seat behind her and grinned. "With my non-salary these days, I couldn't exactly afford some things that I thought were extremely crucial to the situation."

"The situation?"

"The courting situation."

"I see. And exactly what makes you think I'm interested in that *situation?*"

He placed his hand along the side of her face, gently tilting it, locking his eyes with hers. "Nothing," he whispered. "It's just that I can't *not* court you any longer."

That condor was flapping its gigantic wings again. "Was that your tale of woe?"

248

In reply, he kissed her. "I hope you don't have other plans for this evening."

"I was going to take Ian out for dinner."

His eyebrows shot up.

She shrugged. "I thought he sent the ticket."

"Really? I hope you're not disappointed?"

"Oh, not too."

He narrowed his eyes for a moment and then kissed her again . . . for a very long time. "Not too?"

She giggled. "Umm . . . Not at all."

"Good. I'm glad we've got that settled." He straightened. "I've missed you. Tell me what you've been doing. Did you find a new job? How is Sara?"

She quickly brought him up to date. It was such a satisfying pleasure talking with him again.

He seemed delighted with Sara's questions about faith, and he laughed aloud when she explained about her new fourth-grade teaching job. "You say it's in Escondido?"

"Yes. What about you?" she asked.

"In time." He hugged her and laughed again. "Escondido."

She noticed they were heading into La Jolla. "Oh, Jade, are we having dinner here?"

"You have to wait."

Julius parked the limo in the middle of the street near the Cove where she had joined the Zukowskis for Easter dinner. He opened the door for them, and Jade led her across the grass between groups of picnickers, toward the ocean, toward two high-backed lawn chairs. A small white table and picnic basket were arranged between them.

"I thought we'd have hors d'oeurves here first."

"Before dinner?" she asked as she sat down.

"I'm not telling." He settled into the other chair. "It's a

day of surprises for you. Do you like surprises?"

"I don't know how many more I can handle." She giggled. "You look really good in a tux—I mean, shining armor. I have this condor beating its wings in here." She touched her chest. "It used to be a bunch of butterflies. Oh, I shouldn't tell you that."

He was staring at her across the low table.

"Definite disadvantage," she mumbled.

"I'd say that puts us on equal footing," he countered, then opened the picnic basket and pulled out linen napkins and a plate of vegetables and cheese and crackers, all intricately shaped. Next came crystal goblets and a bottle of sparkling apple juice.

"Oh, how lovely, Jade! Let me guess. Caterer friend?"

"Right." He poured the juice.

"How is Caitlin?" The small talk continued while he nibbled and she broke apart crackers. "Your father told me you went to the mountains."

He nodded. "Right after I left you at the top of the steps. Kendall, I'm extremely sorry for that."

"Why did you do it?"

He rested his elbows on his knees and gazed out at the ocean. "I was afraid of losing you. It was just easier to run than to become open again to the devastation if you . . . if you died."

He was silent for a moment. "While I was climbing, I kept hearing your voice, reminding me that my identity is in Christ, my resources are unlimited in Him." He took a deep breath. "Then Jerry left, and I fasted and prayed. And argued. A long time. And I read that I was not to ponder things of the past, that God would do something new, like make rivers in the desert."

He turned toward her with a smile. "By the way, I got a

new job. High school history teacher, not far from the seminary. I can still take classes. And Cait and I found a house to
rent."

"Not far from the seminary?" Her eyes widened.
"Escondido? You'll be in Escondido?"

Jade smiled. "I know. Your news was like a confirmation
to me. Kind of fun when you see these things happen, isn't
it?"

"Wow!" They were both moving to the same town.
"There's your river in the desert. What about pondering the
past? Or fearing losing me?"

"Well . . ." He stood, stepped in front of her, then knelt on
a knee and took her hands in his.

She shivered when his eyes met hers.

"Kendall, I love you. Ever since I quit arguing that I
wasn't going to, all that pondering and fearing have been
fading away." He reached into his pocket, pulled out a piece
of pink construction paper the shape of a folded heart, and
laid it on her lap.

"Caitlin's valentine! You taped it all together!"

"Cait helped me see that when we met you, our hearts
were broken, but you taped them back together again. They
still hurt, but they're healing, and now you're an integral part
of them."

"Oh, Jade, I love you. And your daughter." She fingered
the rough, patched-up heart, then opened it. Taped inside,
just below the poem, was a diamond ring. She gasped.

"I leave socks on the floor, and teenagers are always stopping by unannounced because I tell them to. And I'll climb
rocks more often than go to concerts. And I want enough kids
of my own to field a soccer team. Will you marry me?"

"Yes." She kissed his cheek. "Oh, yes. But I can't go to
sleep until socks are picked up and papers are graded. If I

don't go to a concert every so often, I get real grouchy. Will you marry me?"

Jade laughed and took the valentine from her. "Yes. We'll take it one toehold and one music note at a time." He pulled the ring away from the tape, reached for her hand, and slid it onto her third finger.

Applause and whistles startled them. Nearby picnickers were watching. Grinning, Jade stood and bowed.

"Nice private moment, Mr. Zukowski. Oh, my." She was looking at the gold ring with the large heart-shaped diamond reflecting the low sunlight. "It's absolutely beautiful."

He knelt before her again. "And no, I don't have a jeweler friend. That's from Cait's shopping with me. She thought the bigger the better. Do you like it?"

She nodded. "I agree with Cait. I want people across the room to be able to see it. I want the world to know I have this absolutely marvelous knight." She wrapped her arms around his neck. "Even when his armor gets rusty."

"How about grass-stained?"

Their laughter ended in a kiss.